Praise for the novels of
JOHN ALTMAN

THE WATCHMEN

"Altman excels at taut psychological confrontations, engrossing procedural and nerve-wracking action set pieces, replete with the theory and practice of mind control, interrogation techniques, cryptanalysis, and murder. But the intrigue and mayhem spring from recognizable human beings."   —*Publishers Weekly*

DECEPTION

"An exciting and moving adventure."
                                        —*Publishers Weekly*

"The chase isn't simple, but at every turn the consequences are deadly."   —*New York Daily News*

continued on next page . . .

A GAME OF SPIES

"A book full of stunning action set pieces that also manages to maintain a distinctly believable human presence."
—*Chicago Tribune*

"Altman creates driven, morally conflicted characters."
—*New York Daily News*

"A gritty World War II thriller . . . Altman is an elegant, spare writer who doesn't romance war, but rather fills his novels with a grim reality. Ranks with the best espionage thrillers."
—*The Orlando Sentinel*

"The excitement in Altman's story comes only in part from Eva and Hobbs's flight. It is also in waiting to see what effect their escape might make on the war. In his second novel, Altman has shown the truth in the adage that it is always best to begin at the beginning. Grade: A."
—*Rocky Mountain News*

"It's spy versus spy, agent and double agent, double cross and triple cross. It's taut and lean and filled with action, yet author Altman still finds room for insightful reflections on the motives, morals, and misgivings of all the primary characters. A first-rate military thriller."
—*Booklist*

"Tightly plotted, briskly paced . . . what thrillers ought to be and seldom are."
—*Kirkus Reviews*

"A powerful historical spy tale that never slows down . . . a deadly game of trump. Fans of the genre will want to read this superb World War II novel that brings the era alive."
—*Midwest Book Review*

A GATHERING OF SPIES

"A major new talent. If there are thriller writers better than this, I'd like to know who they are." —Jack Higgins

"Gripping and faster than lightning." *—Boston Herald*

"A sizzling zinger of a classic spy story, full of action, suspense, and wheels within wheels. With his lean, taut style, Altman doesn't waste a word. Wow!"
—Stephen Coonts

"A pulse-pounding debut thriller." *—Glamour*

"A thrilling read with a fine ending. Extremely assured."
—New Orleans Times-Picayune

"Just when you thought the World War II spy thriller might have breathed its last, along comes a U.S. author of barely thirty years to prove there's life in the genre yet. This is a ripping read, a book to devour at one sitting."
—Daily Telegraph (London)

"Old-fashioned fun with the feel of one of those great old movies about World War II." *—Denver Post*

"John Altman has spun a spellbinding tale that is at once terrifying, amusing, and enchanting. His cinematic prose is so vivid you can smell the cigarette smoke."
—Ronald Kessler, author of *Moscow Station* and *FBI*

"This atmospheric debut smells deliciously of Hitchcock and 1940s British spy films. It is an irresistible page-turner from a welcome new voice." *—Publishers Weekly*

JOHN ALTMAN

THE WATCHMEN

JOVE BOOKS, NEW YORK

THE BERKLEY PUBLISHING GROUP
Published by the Penguin Group
Penguin Group (USA) Inc.
375 Hudson Street, New York, New York 10014, USA
Penguin Group (Canada), 10 Alcorn Avenue, Toronto, Ontario M4V 3B2, Canada
(a division of Pearson Penguin Canada Inc.)
Penguin Books Ltd., 80 Strand, London WC2R 0RL, England
Penguin Group Ireland, 25 St. Stephen's Green, Dublin 2, Ireland
(a division of Penguin Books Ltd.)
Penguin Group (Australia), 250 Camberwell Road, Camberwell, Victoria 3124, Australia
(a division of Pearson Australia Group Pty. Ltd.)
Penguin Books India Pvt. Ltd., 11 Community Centre, Panchsheel Park, New Delhi — 110 017,
India
Penguin Books (NZ) Cnr. Airborne and Rosedale Roads, Albany, Auckland 1310, New
Zealand (a division of Pearson New Zealand Ltd.)
Penguin Books (South Africa) (Pty.) Ltd., 24 Sturdee Avenue, Rosebank, Johannesburg
2196, South Africa

Penguin Books Ltd., Registered Offices: 80 Strand, London WC2R 0RL, England

This is a work of fiction. Names, characters, places, and incidents either are the product of
the author's imagination or are used fictitiously, and any resemblance to actual persons, living or dead, business establishments, events, or locales is entirely coincidental.

THE WATCHMEN

A Jove Book / published by arrangement with the author

PRINTING HISTORY
G. P. Putnam's Sons hardcover edition / August 2004
Jove mass-market edition / April 2005

ISBN 0-515-13931-9

JOVE®
Jove Books are published by The Berkley Publishing Group,
a division of Penguin Group (USA) Inc.,
375 Hudson Street, New York, New York 10014.
JOVE is a registered trademark of Penguin Group (USA) Inc.
The "J" design is a trademark belonging to Penguin Group (USA) Inc.

PRINTED IN THE UNITED STATES OF AMERICA

10   9   8   7   6   5   4   3   2   1

FOR SARAH

PROLOGUE

AL GUHRAIR SAW THE MAN—sitting alone in a sidewalk café, nursing a cup of coffee as he watched the pedestrians shuffle through the marketplace.

He was surprised at the man's smallness, as he had been during their first meeting. The little assassin was slight of build; his dark clothes hung loosely off a slender frame. There was something nervous in his eyes as they swept back and forth across the crowded marketplace. Something of the hunted, Al Guhrair thought in that first moment, instead of the hunter.

As he had during their first meeting, Al Guhrair felt a pang of skepticism. Could this little man possibly live up to his reputation? It was hard to believe. Yet they had already set the wheels in motion—so they would move ahead with their decision, doubts or no.

After a moment, he moved to keep the rendezvous.

Around him, the ancient Marché Rue Mouffetard bustled with chattering shoppers and well-stocked market stalls. Shellfish and octopus and sugarcane were sold alongside garlic-stuffed snails, fragrant wheels of cheese, and traditional French kitchenware. As Al Guhrair approached the café, the man's dark eyes moved up and fell on his face. They glinted with recognition.

Al Guhrair sat, squeezing his bulk into the chair. A pretty waitress caught his eye. He pointed at the man's coffee; she nodded.

For a few seconds the two men sat in something not unlike comfortable silence, as if they were old friends. The late afternoon light was turning pale. The waitress brought a cup of coffee. Al Guhrair gave her time to move away. Then he reached down, lifted his briefcase, and set it on the table.

He hit the latches, opened the case, and passed over the first item. He watched as the assassin opened the passport and considered the bundle of papers rubber-banded inside: driver's license, social security card, and several hundred dollars of American currency. The expression on the man's face remained blank, impossible to read.

Again, Al Guhrair felt a stirring of doubt. In most cases, when one created a false identity, one chose a nationality different from the sphere in which one would be operating. Yet the assassin had insisted that he would be able to pass for American, to blend in more completely than any foreigner ever could. Al Guhrair wondered. The man's ethnicity was indeterminate—his complexion was European, yet his features hinted at some other ancestry. He was a combination of breeds, Al Guhrair thought. America was filled with such combinations. Perhaps the man had been right in his insistence that the identity be American; yet Al Guhrair still had his doubts.

Then the passport with the accompanying papers disappeared into a fold of the man's black shirt—so loose that it might better have been called a tunic.

Al Guhrair reached into the briefcase again, and passed over a slim folder.

There were two maps in the folder. One represented the compound surrounding the safe house, the other the layout of the house itself. The assassin leaned forward, peering at the maps in the pallid light. Then he leaned back and closed the file. He left it on the table as Al Guhrair reached once more into the briefcase.

The final item was another folder, containing a photograph of the target. He handed it forward. The assassin took it, lifted a corner, looked inside flatly, and then closed the folder.

Al Guhrair cleared his throat. "I'll be back in New York next week," he said in English. "If you need to get in touch with us, for any reason . . ."

He produced a calfskin wallet and removed an embossed business card. When the assassin accepted it, their eyes met. Al Guhrair saw something there that surprised him: a flash of intensity, completely unexpected considering the man's quiet demeanor.

The assassin stood.

He picked up the folders, spun a coin onto the table beside his untouched cup of coffee, and then moved away, melting into the crowd.

Al Guhrair watched him go. He reached for his own coffee and sipped. The meeting had been shorter than he had expected. And the assassin, he was realizing, had not spoken a single word.

He sipped the coffee and then looked for the man again. But already he was gone.

Could he do it? He was small and slight, almost meek. Yet there had been that unexpected flash in his eyes. . . .

Al Guhrair raised his coffee again, and wondered.

PART ONE

PART ONE

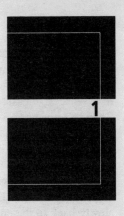

1

FINNEY'S BREATH caught in his throat.

He took a moment to steady his hands, then swept the binoculars back across the path they just had followed—over the dilapidated fence, past the stables, to a tangled thicket near the edge of the forest. There.

The Bachman's warbler.

He found it perched on a low branch, seeming to look directly back at him. The Bachman's warbler was the rarest songbird in North America. From the black cowl, Finney knew that it was a male.

As he watched, the bird gave its distinctive call: a low, grating *bzz-bzz-bzz*.

Then it took wing and vanished from his field of vision.

He lowered the 804 Swift Audubon binoculars. His heart was pounding. He hadn't yet remembered to start breathing again. That brief glimpse, he knew, was all he would get. But he was not complaining. In seven years of combing these woods behind his farm, he never before had seen a Bachman's warbler.

For another few moments he stood, trying to hold on to a sense of pleasure that already was slipping away. Then he remembered to take a breath. He consulted his watch. It was ten minutes before noon. His visitor would be arriving shortly.

He spent one last minute looking in the direction of the thicket, hoping against hope that the warbler would reappear. Then Dr. Louis Finney turned and headed slowly back to the converted farmhouse that he called home.

HE KNEW upon opening the door that Arthur Noble was not well.

The last of his hair had gone; the sides of his head gleamed smoothly beneath the brim of a felt hat. He was supporting himself with a cane, using both hands. His face, which always had been somewhat suggestive of a basset hound, had hollowed, the folds drooping lower than ever. Yet he had managed to drive himself, Finney noted; and now he managed a crinkle-eyed smile.

"Louis," Noble said.

"Arthur," Finney answered stiffly.

After a moment he turned and led Noble through the foyer, to his study.

The study was furnished with two Windsor cherry sack-back armchairs, a burnished Queensleg desk, and much evidence of Finney's interest in ornithology: calendars, posters, and photographs representing flickers, bluebirds, pheasant, and shrike. The window was open, letting in the sluggish drone of bumblebees from the garden. A gray-cheeked thrush was perched on the rim of the copper birdbath, looking off grandly into the distance.

Finney gestured at one of the armchairs. Noble sat gingerly, without removing his hat. The man seemed ten years older than his age, Finney thought. He wondered, with sudden self-consciousness, if he was making a similarly decrepit impression on Noble. His gray-threaded beard was likely windswept after his morning spent in the pasture; his posture was no doubt as stooped as ever. He tried to stand up straighter as he moved around the desk, and then to slip with some grace into his own leather-upholstered chair.

For a few moments, the men considered each other in silence. Then Noble gave another smile.

"It's good to see you," he said.

Finney only nodded.

"Is Lila here?" Noble looked around as if she might have been hidden somewhere in the room. "It's been too long. It would do these old eyes good to see . . ."

Finney shook his head.

Another moment passed.

"Louis—I'm sorry."

"It was a blessing," Finney said gruffly. "By the end."

Silence, except for the distant, plaintive call of an oriole.

Finney's eyes were drawn to a spot on Noble's throat. A mole, or something like it. In the next instant, Noble had produced a dark handkerchief and pressed it against the spot.

Then he coughed, and the handkerchief moved reflexively to cover his mouth. Finney saw that the mole on his throat was bleeding. Except it wasn't a mole, he understood suddenly.

Noble coughed again; his color rose. He looked up and saw the expression on Finney's face. He smiled darkly, lowering the handkerchief into his lap.

He nodded.

"Kaposi's sarcoma," he said.

"Good Christ," Finney said.

"They give me a month."

"Good Christ."

"I'm glad you agreed to see me today, Louis. I'd like to . . . not have enemies, when I leave this world. Especially not enemies who once were counted as friends."

Finney paused.

From the hallway, the grandfather clock ticked solemnly.

Noble was talking again—but Finney was no longer listening.

Instead, he was remembering.

HE REMEMBERED a young woman who refused to meet his eyes.

She was looking at her own hands, clasped tightly in her lap. The room was furnished only with the plain wooden chairs in which they sat. Except for the one-way mirror through which they were being observed, the lemon-colored walls were bare.

Finney watched, waiting.

At last, the woman stirred. When her eyes raised, they were not the eyes of Susan Franklin—the young woman's primary identity. They were the eyes of Robin, her strongest alternate identity.

Those eyes locked onto Finney's, and glimmered.

Then she was covering her mouth. *Nauseated,* Finney understood. In Susan/Robin's mind, her personalities lived in her belly. When one came to the forefront, the other submerged. It was understandable that the transference might involve some upsetting of the stomach.

She gagged for a moment, then swallowed. Her eyes found his again. Those eyes were bright, intelligent, accusatory.

The face around the eyes was drawn and cadaverous. To access the personalities, they had subjected Susan Franklin to a harsh treatment that had lasted six months. The treatment involved sleep deprivation, sodium Amytal, electric shocks, Thorazine, and hypnosis—one reinforcing another. They were ruining her, Finney understood. The Hippocratic Oath had been thrown cheerfully over the side by the doctors involved in this project. Yet they had done it, wrapping themselves in the exalted cloak of *national security* as an excuse. . . .

"WOULD YOU EXCUSE ME?" Finney muttered.

He moved out from behind the desk without waiting for an answer, stepped into the hallway, and then came to an abrupt stop.

There was no point in holding grudges. Particularly not against the dead, or the soon-to-be-dead. And particularly, as Noble had said, when one's enemies once had been counted as friends.

Yet he couldn't bring himself to say the words that would confer forgiveness. Saying the words might imply that Noble had not fully been responsible for the things they had done together. And if Noble had not fully been responsible, then the burden of responsibility would have to shift somewhere else.

Onto Finney's own shoulders, perhaps.

But he had been so young, when they had started working together. He had trusted Noble as a student trusts an accomplished teacher. Perhaps he had been . . . complicit . . . in the things they had done. Of course he had been. But he had been too young to know better. The fault was Noble's. Not his, not theirs; just Noble's.

But what was the point of this meeting, if he wasn't prepared to offer forgiveness?

He stood for another moment, his brow furrowed. Then he threw back his shoulders and returned to the office. Noble's eyes followed him as he moved around the desk. There was something implacable in the man's gaze, and something vaguely pitying.

Finney took his seat again. He opened his mouth; and again he paused.

The things he wanted to say were not things that two grown men said to each other. Or p⬤ they simply were not things that these particular two grown men could say to each other: both flinty, both proud, neither given to suffer fools gladly.

I trusted you, he might begin.

I followed your lead—and as a result I've had nightmares that only recently have begun to leave me in peace.

Or something less accusatory, and perhaps more honest. *If I accept your apology, Arthur, I'm also accepting responsibility. And I'm not convinced that's right.*

But had Noble offered an apology? Not in so many words.

The handkerchief pressed back against the throat. Now Noble was looking at him with the thinly disguised impatience of a man who hasn't a moment to waste.

"I shouldn't feel the need to make excuses to you," he said suddenly.

Finney blinked.

"I shouldn't," Noble repeated. "But I do. I haven't accepted a government contract in fifteen years, Louis. But the nightmares still come."

"I trusted you," Finney heard himself saying.

"And I led you down some difficult roads. For that, I apologize. Whether or not you accept my apology is up to you."

The oriole gave another call: *tee-dee-dee, tee-dee-dee*.

Two moments passed. Finney was on the verge of answering when Noble continued:

"In any case. I've got another reason for being here today. I haven't accepted a government contract in fifteen years, I said. But that's not strictly true. Last week I received a call. And I've decided, despite everything, that the call is too important to ignore."

Finney couldn't conceal his surprise. "Are you in any shape to . . . ?"

"Hardly. This may take a few weeks, or a few months. Possibly even a year."

His eyes twinkled, almost mischievously.

"I'm in no shape," he agreed. "But you . . ."

* * *

THE DRIVER PULLED UP to the freight elevator and then found Al Guhrair's eyes in the rearview mirror.

Al Guhrair licked his lips. Around the car, the echoes of engines off concrete reverberated through the underground garage.

"Five minutes," Al Guhrair said, and reached for the door.

Two steps brought him into the elevator. He punched the penthouse suite button and then hit the door close button. Nothing happened. He kept pressing. At last the doors began to drift shut. In the next moment, the elevator was carrying him up.

He reached into his coat and withdrew the Heckler & Koch P7 pistol from the inside pocket. This was the first time the gun had left the drawer of his office desk for nearly three years. Al Guhrair had never fired the gun. He wondered if he would be able to fire it now, if the need arose. The mechanisms seemed simple enough— a clip was already loaded, and the safety could be switched off with one thumb. Yet he was hardly a gunslinger. He was a sixty-four-year-old man with a bad heart and a fairly serious case of arthritis, and gunslinging was not for him.

But he would manage—if the need arose.

The doors opened.

Before stepping into his apartment, Al Guhrair paused to listen. The place was quiet and dark, smelling faintly of Lemon Pledge. For the past twelve years, ever since his second divorce, he had lived here alone.

Yet if the assassin was here, he would not be making a sound. Had he made a sound when he had killed the others in the cell? Those men had been years younger than Al Guhrair—decades younger, in some cases—and some had had military experience. Yet the man had dispatched them with no apparent difficulty. He was not the type to make unnecessary sound.

Or perhaps the apartment truly was empty.

Al Guhrair licked his lips again, and stepped forward.

Through the vast polished windows on his right lay Central Park at night. Beyond the park was the scintillating East Side, bejeweled with lights. To his left, a hallway led past the kitchen, past the foyer—where the front elevator was located, the elevator he had avoided—to the bedroom.

He moved down the corridor slowly, holding the gun with both hands.

The bedroom was deserted.

He stood in the doorway for two full minutes before reaching for the light switch. Then he flipped it, moved to the closet, and looked inside. He crouched, with some effort, to look under the bed. He pushed open the door to the bathroom and ran his eyes over the marble and brass. No sign of an intruder.

He set the gun on the bed, tore a suitcase from the closet, and hastily began to pack.

When he had finished, he closed the suitcase, zipped it, and picked up the gun again.

Now the safe.

He returned to the darkened living room. If the man was here, how would he attack? Two of his other victims had been knifed; the third evidently had died of a heart attack. Poisoned. All of the deaths had been camouflaged to appear explicable—one stabbing, a mugging, the other a failed burglary.

But Al Guhrair knew the truth: The ghost wind was eliminating the very men who had hired him. During the twelve days since the meeting at the Marché Rue Mouffetard, every member of the cell besides Al Guhrair had met his fate.

He clutched the gun a bit tighter, and sent his eyes across the room.

The long, low, L-shaped sofa. The dusty bookshelves, the baby grand piano. He looked at these objects every single day, yet felt as if he were seeing them for the first time. He remembered the marketplace in Paris, the assassin's striking smallness. The ghost wind might be hidden behind any of these objects, or none of them.

Al Guhrair crossed the room. He put the gun into his pocket, then took a painting off the wall—a lesser-known Hopper, but one of his personal favorites. He set it on the floor and spun the combination on the safe.

Inside were four fat envelopes. He pocketed them, closed the safe, and turned.

Would he ever return to this apartment? It was a question for the future. For now, all that mattered was getting away—far, far away.

After fetching his suitcase, he returned to the freight elevator. There had been a time when servants would have used this elevator to take away trash and bring up deliveries, so that the resident of the penthouse never was forced to witness the realities of his consumption. Now, however, times had changed. Now the deliverymen and the maids used the front elevator. Only especially cumbersome or embarrassing items were delivered by this back door; the freight elevator almost never was used.

And yet it wasn't waiting. Someone had called it away.

Al Guhrair frowned.

His thumb moved to the safety of the gun and clicked it off.

A minute passed. He could hear the gears grinding as the elevator rose. He was beginning to perspire, although the penthouse was carefully climate-controlled.

The doors opened.

The elevator was empty.

He heaved a sigh, picked up the suitcase, and stepped inside.

THE ASSASSIN repositioned himself atop the elevator.

Now gears were ratcheting; they were beginning to descend. Through the cracked-open hatch, he watched his quarry. The man had not yet looked up. He was not as capable as the assassin had assumed. A strike inside the apartment would have sufficed. Yet he had erred on the side of caution, as he had been taught.

The target was holding a gun—but even so, it would be almost too easy.

The assassin slipped his fingertips farther beneath the edge of the hatch in the elevator's ceiling. Then he lifted it, slipping his legs down in the same, fluid motion.

As he fell, he sharpened his knees, making his body into a dagger. He caught his target on the left side, riding the body down to cushion his own impact.

He whipped his left forearm around the man's throat. He pressed his right palm against the man's skull, just below the left ear, pushing forward. A careful application of pressure separated the skull from the spinal column.

Death was instantaneous.

The assassin straightened. His hands moved over the corpse, exploring the pockets. He found the four envelopes and transferred them into his own tunic. Then he stopped the elevator on the third floor, opened the doors, and listened.

A kitchen: quiet and deserted. To his left, a television was playing. To his right, a polished hallway led to a front door.

He moved silently, back against the wall, using a cross step. Once he was outside the apartment, he raised a hand and drew back his hood. He tucked it into his collar, then straightened his tunic and headed for the front stairwell.

When he walked out through the main lobby, he nodded at the doorman. The doorman nodded back and returned his attention to the newspaper in his lap.

THEY WERE ENTERING a small town.

The main street looked like a slightly updated version of an old-fashioned *Saturday Evening Post* cover. Finney saw a red-bricked school, a church, a bait-and-tackle shop, a pizzeria, and a store selling glass. None of the buildings was more than two stories tall; the little town evidently enforced strict zoning laws.

Despite himself, he felt a flicker of disappointment. This bucolic little town was a far cry from the game he remembered—the game he had played with Noble, so many years before. Back then, it had been exotic and exciting: flying overseas on the government's dime to conduct secret experiments, flashing covert signals at foreign airports to indicate that coasts were clear. Now he wondered if Noble might have made a mistake. Had he driven them to the right place? Perhaps the man's illness had confused his judgment. . . .

"By the way," Noble said.

Finney looked over. Noble wore the same felt hat as the day before; his face looked even more pale. A Band-Aid on his throat was spotted with blood.

"You may notice that the house is wired—one-way mirror, hidden microphones."

Finney stiffened.

"It's standard procedure for a safe house, of course. There will be no experiments, Louis. You have my word on that."

After a moment, Finney relaxed. He turned his head to look out the window again.

They left the main street in favor of a gravel road that climbed a wooded hill. Modest houses lined the road, as rural and postcard-perfect as the town itself. Noble's old Mercedes groaned, laboring up the incline. Soon the houses thinned; the land opened. The safe house, Finney thought, was as remote as it could possibly be.

This was no surprise. According to Noble, the interrogation being conducted in the safe house was of vital importance.

The subject of the interrogation was a man named Ali Zattout. Two weeks before he had been transferred from Pakistan—where he had been captured in a joint raid by the CIA and Inter-Services Intelligence, the Pakistani equivalent of the agency—to this isolated stretch of farmland in the American Northeast. Zattout merited special treatment, Noble had explained, because he occupied a key position in al Qaeda: a member of the inner circle since the earliest days of al Qaeda's existence.

Furthermore, Zattout had proved cooperative. Until now the interrogation had been polite, and the CIA was eager to keep it that way. They had not yet learned anything of special value from Zattout, but hopes still were running high.

Yet the ease of the interrogation worried them.

At various times Zattout had lived in England, Germany, Pakistan, Afghanistan, and the United States. He was thoroughly Westernized, and exhibited a fine understanding of various cultures. This made him a perfect candidate for interrogation; no time was wasted on making obvious things understood, and no translators were necessary. Zattout had proven himself a dream candidate in other ways as well. The possible breadth of his information, and his willingness to share it—according to Noble, Zattout regretted what he had done in the name of al Qaeda, and was anxious to make amends—made the man potentially invaluable.

Which led to suspicions, of course, that Zattout was a double agent, here to lead them down the wrong roads, to waste their time and attention with disinformation.

Noble's job—and now Finney's—would be to play the role of watchman, observing the man during the interrogation and judging his veracity. He would assemble a psychological portrait of Zattout, noting in what direction his eyes pointed when he gave his answers, and whether or not that corresponded with his dominant hand. In general, a man looked away from his strong hand when he was retrieving information—telling the truth. When he was creating information—coming up with a lie—he looked in his direction of strength.

The watchman would compile a complete behavioral profile, which would be used by the interrogator as the process went on. Should questions be asked at morning or at night? Should they be put aggressively or gently? Would polygraphs be of value, or was Zattout capable of willing himself to believe he told the truth, even as he lied? (Already he had passed two polygraph tests, according to Noble; yet the value of the results was debatable.) Should he be isolated, drugged, threatened? If so, how? If not, what other options might be productive?

Noble had promised Finney that he would be engaged only with the profiling. He would not be directly involved in interrogation, nor in implementation of his recommended methods. And Finney had agreed. But not witnessing the implementation of his methods, of course, did not remove the burden of responsibility for recommending that implementation.

Yet they were at war. He had tried to conjure what Lila might have given him, in terms of advice, and those were the words that had occurred to him: *We're at war, Louis.*

He kept looking out the window, even as the frown in his brow deepened. One hand moved to his breast pocket, fishing for his good luck charm—his security blanket, Lila had called it teasingly.

He found it, brought it out, and turned it over in his hand. The charm was a doubloon: 8 escudos, 128 reales.

The date was 1641. The monarch, name printed along the bottom, was Philip IV. The coin felt grimy, coated with a granular layer of dust. It had been a gift from Lila; and despite her teasing, Finney knew she had been pleased by the way he'd taken to it.

They were turning onto a smaller road. Gravel was replaced by dirt. He caught a glimpse of a black-billed magpie perched on a fallen tree. The black-billed magpie rarely found its way farther east than the Great Lakes. Every once in a while, however, one lost its bearings and ended up in this part of the country. Finney felt a sudden pang of sympathy for the lost little bird. Or was it empathy?

He saw a log gate crossing the dirt road, a small cabin set on the left. As the car slowed, a uniformed man came from the cabin. He had a pistol in a waist holster, prominently displayed.

"Seems like old times," Noble said dryly, as they stopped before the gate. He opened his door and stepped carefully out of the car to be searched.

Finney returned the doubloon to his pocket, and did the same.

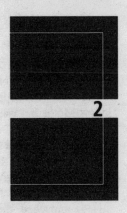

2

AT FIVE MINUTES PAST ten o'clock on the morning of April 14, a dark blue coupe merged onto Interstate 95 just north of the George Washington Bridge.

For over an hour the coupe held to 95, heading north. Then it turned west. Rambling farms dotted the countryside; every so often a turquoise river wound down from the Catskills. The coupe moved at precisely the speed limit, although the roads were nearly deserted on this late weekday morning.

The sun climbed, crested, and began to sink. Presently the car passed a small town of low buildings and old-fashioned charm, with a main road featuring a church, a pizzeria, a school with a red brick facade, a bait-and-tackle shop.

After passing the town, the coupe continued west for nearly half an hour. The countryside opened again, rolling.

As afternoon shaded toward evening a sign arose: EXIT 24, with icons indicating gas, food, and lodging.

* * *

THE DOOR CHIMED; Sonya Jacobs looked up from the miniature television set on her desk.

The man who stepped into the lobby of the Sleepy Hollow Motor Inn was very short—five-foot-six at the most, Sonya thought, and that would be generous. He had dark hair cropped short over wide-set black eyes, an aquiline nose, and a heavy, expressionless mouth. An American, she thought, but with a hint of something underneath—perhaps Middle Eastern, or Spanish.

He approached the desk, and his expressionless mouth twitched into something resembling a smile. Sonya reached out and turned down the volume on the television. The players of the soap opera began to go through their dramas in pantomime. "Can I help you?" she asked.

His voice was flat and unaccented, giving no clues as to his origins. "I'd like a room," he said pleasantly.

"For how long?"

"One night, and I may extend it?"

She nodded, and passed a registration form across the desk.

As the man studied it, she stole more impressions of him. She was struck again by the sublimely exotic cast to his features. His English had been proper but stiff. He began to write in small, precise letters. He wasn't good-looking in any conventional sense—not at five-foot-six. And yet . . .

Sonya cleared her throat.

"That's sixty-two dollars for the night. If you decide to register for a week, the rates go down. A week costs three hundred and five."

He didn't look up.

"Complimentary coffee is served in the lobby each morning from six until ten. Would you like some information about local sights? I've got brochures . . ."

"I'll be busy with work," he said. "But thank you."

"I'll need to see your license. How will you be paying?"

He produced a Connecticut driver's license and passed it over, along with the registration form. "Cash," he said, as she read the name off the license: SIMON CHRISTOPHER.

Sonya turned to the computer, entered the man's information, then spun in her chair to face the wall of keys. "Smoking or non-?"

"Non-smoking. Thank you."

"You're going to drive around to the right and park close to the stairwell. It's room twenty-two, on the second floor. Local calls are free. . . ."

His bill was printing. She tore it loose, then slid it across the desk with his license and key. "That'll be sixty-seven twelve, with tax."

He handed her three twenties and a ten. She made change, then smiled. "Have a good stay."

His mouth twitched again, and he went out through the front door.

She listened to the jangle. She watched, waiting for his car to pass in front of the door. Soon enough she saw it: a small, dark blue coupe.

She leaned back in her chair, toying with a strand of blond hair.

A mysterious stranger, she thought. *A dark, mysterious stranger.*

And a handsome one, too—in that odd way on which she couldn't quite put her finger.

What type of work might it be that would keep him too busy to visit local sights? Perhaps the man was a poet. He seemed intense enough, dark enough. Out here, in the middle of nowhere, she imagined a poet could get a lot of work done.

Or perhaps he was something else. These days, one couldn't take anything for granted. A man with indeterminate ancestry, whose English was smooth but stiff—and had there been a current of apprehension beneath his stiffness, even of fear?—why, that man could have been anything at all.

A terrorist, for example.

Or perhaps she was simply bored.

A few moments passed. She stopped twirling her hair around her finger and reached again for the television set. She turned up the volume, and for the time being forgot about the dark, mysterious stranger who had checked into her parents' motel for a night, at least.

BEYOND THE LOG GATE, past a quarter-mile of winding, wooded road, was a second gate: polished metal, with barbed wire curling across the top. The gate interrupted a tall stone wall. Atop the wall were dormant searchlights, flashing like semaphores as they caught the afternoon sun.

Past the wall was another stretch of road. Finney saw poplar, oak, ash, locust, and hickory. Bridle paths curled off into the forest. They passed occasional cabins, set deep in the heavy shadows. In several of the cabins were hints of motion. They were all guardhouses, Finney realized. Evidently Noble had not overstated the importance of the case.

Then the Mercedes came out into open land. Here was another guardhouse, winding paths of gravel, occasional patches of brush. There were no longer any trees—nothing that could possibly provide cover for an intruder, except the small scraps of brush. A lone figure caught Finney's eye. It took him a moment to realize the figure was a scarecrow, propped lopsidedly against a cross, looking sightlessly out across the field.

The safe house itself was two stories: a large converted farmhouse not unlike Finney's own. A half dozen cars were parked out front. Noble eased up alongside them, then killed the engine. They left the car and entered a foyer furnished with a windowed Pennsylvania cupboard, a tiger maple hall table, and an antique sideboard. Understated oil paintings on the walls pictured benign nature scenes: lakesides, seashores, hilltops, and valleys. The foyer, Finney noted, could use a dusting.

"First," Noble said, "the grand tour."

He led Finney through a living room done in maple, a kitchen with stone floors and a huge, aromatic pantry. They passed through a genteel dining room, a small and mostly unfurnished study, a breakfast nook. Noble pointed out a second porch, facing west. Then they were back in the foyer.

Finney scowled. Something about the layout was not right. They had covered the entire first floor—yet the house seemed smaller, from the inside, than it had from the outside.

His mind made a sudden and unexpected cross-connection: a memory of standing with his father, looking through a book in the public library. The book had been the big kind, bulky and glossy, too heavy for Finney to lift by himself. His father had carried it from shelf to table with his huge hands. Then he had opened it, and they had explored the contents together. On the pages were images that played with the eye—fish blending into birds and then back into fish; staircases marching up and down at the same time. In this artist's world, one could not trust what one thought one saw. In that moment, Finney could almost smell the pipe tobacco on his father's clothing, could almost hear the sibilant whisper of rain outside. A bucket was set in one corner of the library, catching a slow steady drip from a leak in the ceiling. . . .

Noble was climbing a wide staircase, moving slowly and laboriously. Finney followed behind, trying not to rush him.

The second floor, unlike the first, corresponded with the impression he had gathered from outside. There were a half dozen bedrooms, none quite as clean as they might have been.

"You'll be here," Noble told him, as they stepped into the last and smallest of the bedrooms. "I'll have your luggage brought up. I hope you find it satisfactory."

Finney grunted. The room was small but comfortable, with a canopied bed, a bookshelf, a writing desk, and a private bathroom. The curtained window had a fine view of the sprawling land outside the house. He could see the scarecrow, staring eternally forward.

"Now," Noble said. His eyes glinted mischievously, as they had in Finney's study. He coughed. "The rest of it."

THEY MOVED into the kitchen's pantry, into the smell of fruit and vinegar. Noble touched something on the wall and twisted it. The something was a doorknob; and the wall was a door.

Behind the door was a room. Equipment was piled haphazardly: a polygraph, a Reiter electroshock machine, an assortment of microphones and transformers and tape recorders, sterile syringes in plastic bags. Closed-circuit monitors displayed views of the countryside from each side of the house. Blue-tinted windows were set into the walls at eye level. As he looked at the windows, Finney realized that he was seeing the benign landscapes in transparent reverse. Through the landscapes he could see the study, the living room, the dining room, and the foyer.

A staircase led down. Noble took it carefully, leaving the hidden door ajar—Finney noted a formidable-looking dead bolt on the inside of that door—and holding tightly onto a banister.

"Zattout's been here for twelve days," Noble said over his shoulder. "All of them in his little basement cell. As far as he knows, there isn't any house at all. All he sees is his cell. Four times a day he's interrogated, for two hours at a stretch. We've been treating him well. No drugs, three square meals. As the interrogation goes on, he may find his comfort level diminishing; but for now, he's got nothing to complain about."

The space into which they descended was lit by a

wire-caged bulb in the ceiling, furnished with one table—a tape recorder sat on it, spools unrolling—three empty chairs, and a one-way mirror. Through the mirror was Zattout's cell.

The man was sitting on a cot: tall and gaunt, with a full black beard and long, attenuated fingers that moved deftly to describe his words. Another man sat facing him on a bare-backed wooden chair. Except for the cot, the chair, a bare bulb, and a toilet and a sink, the cell was empty.

The words themselves were inaudible. Noble moved to the table and flicked a red switch on a small box. A speaker mounted in one ceiling corner came to life:

"—no more than one at any given time. The brother has been instructed to memorize all information that may possibly be pertinent—"

"Pertinent?" the interrogator interrupted.

"Name, profession, place of residence . . . place and date of birth, local dialects, local sights . . ."

"I see."

"As I said—to be entrusted with this responsibility, the brother must be fifteen years old. But often the younger ones are overly eager. They elaborate too much—"

Noble flicked the switch again; the voice cut off. "First impressions?"

Finney moved closer to the one-way mirror and watched for a few moments as the man gestured.

"He certainly talks with his hands," he said then.

"Mm."

"He's an externalizer. He needs attention. That

doesn't necessarily reflect, of course, on whether or not he lies to get the attention."

"Mm."

Finney kept watching. His hand moved to his pocket and began to toy with the doubloon.

"A role adaptive individual. A flexible personality, and a charismatic one."

"I'd agree."

"Have you given him the Wechsler?"

"Yes. But I haven't yet found a chance—"

The words were lost in a sudden coughing fit. Finney looked over. Noble was pressing one hand over his mouth, trying to stifle himself. The pose made Finney think of Susan Franklin. Suddenly he felt very weary.

Noble held his hand over his mouth for several seconds, removed it, and found Finney's eyes.

Finney said nothing.

Noble straightened. "Let's have some lunch," he said formally. "Then we can introduce you to Tom Warren, the case officer in charge. He must be around here somewhere."

He turned to move back up the staircase, shuffling slower than ever. For a moment, Finney thought the man would be unable to climb the stairs without help. He held a hand ready. But Noble found it within himself to make the ascent, moving painstakingly but doggedly. Finney gave him time to gain some distance, then slowly followed.

They found Thomas Warren II in the kitchen, sitting at the table with a cell phone to his ear. He was an agency man of the type Finney remembered from the old days: Ivy League, Waspish, with a square-jawed face, bright blue eyes, and carefully groomed blond hair. When Noble and Finney emerged from the pantry, he looked up. "Good," he said into the phone. "Let me get back to you."

He stood, then gave Finney's hand two energetic pumps. "Doctor. Your reputation precedes you. I'm very much looking forward to working together."

Finney bowed his head.

"If there's anything you need," Warren said with a plastic smile, "I'm the man to see. You'll never mistake this place for a four-star hotel—but there's no reason to be more uncomfortable than necessary. And don't believe a thing Dr. Noble might have said about me. Lies, all lies."

A secret joke passed right before Finney's face. Noble smirked narrowly. "I'm afraid I hadn't gotten around to it yet."

"So I've got a clean slate?" Warren turned his smile up a notch, then abruptly let it fall away. "Well," he said, checking his watch. "Have you gentlemen had lunch?"

THE SCHOOL BUS pulled away with a hydraulic hiss.

The stranger's car, Sonya Jacobs noticed, was gone. Had he checked out already?

She frowned. After a moment she shouldered her backpack and moved toward the front office.

Her mother was behind the desk. "Maria called in sick," she said without looking up. "You'll need to take care of housekeeping today."

Sonya pulled a face.

"And get that look off your face," her mother said.

Sonya stuck out her tongue, then moved through the office, into the apartment she shared with her family. She set down the backpack on her lower bunk, went into the bathroom, and washed. She considered her reflection in the mirror, fingering her latest earring—the fourth in her right ear. The earring couldn't seem to decide whether or not to become infected. After a moment, she decided it was okay for now. She left the apartment and went to find the linen cart.

The low hills surrounding Sleepy Hollow were rustling with spring: insects and squirrels and chirruping birds, leaves flicking in a slow wind. If she could get the housekeeping done quickly enough, perhaps she could manage to get into the hills for a few minutes before the sun went down. Her favorite secret spot, by a creek that cascaded down from Devil's Peak, would be in full bloom on a day like today. And she had more than half a pack of cigarettes, hidden between her mattress and box spring, just waiting for her to get to them.

Only three rooms on the first floor were occupied. She handled them quickly, changing the sheets and towels, restocking the miniature shampoos and soaps in the bathrooms. Then she wheeled the cart to the elevator and rode it up to the second floor. Here were only two more rooms that required attention. Then she would be done, and out into the hills.

Room twenty-two belonged to the man who had arrived the day before. She rapped twice on the door. "Housekeeping," she called.

But his car was gone, of course. Checked out or not, the man wasn't here. She let herself in with the passkey.

The bed hardly seemed to have been used. When

Sonya woke up, each morning, she found her blanket kicked into a tangle on the floor. Her sister, who slept in the top bunk, often complained about the tossing and turning. But this man seemed to sleep soundly, or not to have used the bed at all.

She changed the sheets and moved into the bathroom. He had limited himself to a single towel, which hung neatly folded from the rack. She replaced it, then made a quick circuit of the main room with a feather duster.

A bag was tucked into a corner near the desk: small, made of black leather. So he had decided to stay for another day, at least. She looked at the bag, then looked away. She went on with her dusting.

Just as she was preparing to leave, she looked at the bag again.

A poet? Or a terrorist?

Her mouth quirked.

She looked around as if someone might be watching. Then she moved, quickly and stealthily, to the bag. She knelt beside it and reached for the zipper.

You shouldn't do this, she thought.

It was what she always thought when going through a guest's luggage. Not that she did it that often. But she had done it before, and she had done it with guests about whom she was far less curious.

Before reaching into the bag she took careful note of how the items were arranged, so she would be able to hide the evidence of her snooping. On top was a folder and a passport. Below them were clothes: a few items, mostly black. A pair of corduroys, a T-shirt, and a curious dark tunic. As her hands touched the tunic, she felt something unexpected—a strange hardness, as if something had been sewn into the material.

She lifted it out. In one sleeve of the loose garment was a handful of small metal bars. Yet they were not decorative, for they were on the inside. She frowned. What was the point of sewing something *into* the sleeve of the tunic?

Below the tunic was something else. She saw a glint of metal. She reached into the bag again—

—and then she realized that someone was standing behind her.

The man had come into the room without making a sound. He was looking at her with cold black eyes.

Sonya stood. Suddenly her knees felt weak; but when she spoke, her voice was steady.

"There you are," she said. "We've got a little bit of a mouse problem. I wanted to make sure your bag, um . . ."

He kept looking at her.

"Everything looks okay," she finished lamely. "Well. I'll just get out of your way."

She moved forward, toward the door.

As she drew closer, she found her arms coming up to hug her torso. She had the feeling this man might hurt her, as she stepped past him. Then she was slipping out, buttonhooking hastily to the right before she remembered the cart.

She stopped and turned. The cart was parked outside the room. The man was still there, still looking at her.

She moved back, smiling sheepishly. "Forgot my cart," she said.

He said nothing.

Sonya put her hands on the cart, turned again, and

began to wheel it away. She resisted the urge to look over her shoulder. There was no need. She could feel the eyes burning into her back.

When she reached the elevator, she pushed the button. The doors seemed to take forever to open.

HE WATCHED the girl move into the elevator, and watched the doors close. Then he stepped into his room, pulling the door shut behind him.

It was nothing. Just a teenaged girl, no doubt bored out of her skull, stuck out here in the middle of nowhere. She snooped around as a matter of course, no doubt, thanks to her boredom.

She suspected nothing.

Calm.

He twisted the lock, took a moment, and then sat on the floor. He relaxed his shoulders, straightening his back. Closed his eyes and tried to empty his mind. Meditation would calm him.

He clicked his teeth together gently, thirty-six times, feeling the tension drain away. *No cause for alarm,* he thought.

He knew his target's whereabouts. Thanks to a mole in the enemy's own ranks, he knew the design of the safe house, the security measures, the lay of the surrounding land. Soon enough, it would be finished.

Soon.

Calm.

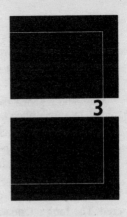

3

"LAST NIGHT," Thomas Warren said soberly.

He hesitated, letting the news sink in. "Pneumonia," he said, and then let that sink in as well.

Finney propped himself up on one elbow. It was a hell of a way to wake up, he thought—somewhat ungraciously, he realized in the next moment.

"The hospital's about twenty miles away," Warren continued after a suitable pause. "We should find time to pay a visit tonight, I think. If not tonight, tomorrow. He'll be there for several days, at least."

Finney nodded remotely.

"In the meantime, there's work to be done here. I'll give you a few minutes to wake up. When you feel ready, please join me downstairs." He paused again. "I feel certain Dr. Noble would want us to press ahead," he added.

For another moment he sat, feigning deep thoughts. Then he brightened, clapped a hand onto Finney's leg, and left the room.

Finney remained in bed, looking out the window. He

wanted to lie back down, pull the covers above his head, and stay in bed for a day—a week—until the end of time.

Instead, he took five minutes. The day seemed determined to move ahead, with or without Arthur Noble here to see it. A bird chattered outside the window—a piping plover, calling *peep-lo, peep-lo.*

At last, Finney put his legs over the side of the bed.

BEFORE ANSWERING the question, Zattout considered. The long attenuated fingers of his right hand slid around the rim of a drinking glass, thoughtfully.

When he began to speak, Finney had trouble focusing. He was thinking of Noble, of the brief telephone conversation they'd had following breakfast. Noble had sounded disoriented, perhaps drugged, his voice a deep and rumbling bass. When Finney had promised an imminent visit, he hadn't seemed to understand the offer, let alone provide encouragement.

Finney's hand moved for the doubloon in his pocket. But there was little solace to be taken there.

". . . you and Dr. Noble worked in the field of disassociative disorders," Warren was saying. "Is that correct?"

Finney blinked. He nodded.

"A separate personality may be created," Warren continued, "and then submerged, to be activated later by post-hypnotic suggestion. Is that the idea?"

"In a nutshell, yes."

"And the primary personality would have no knowledge of the secondary one. A devoted patriot might suddenly be turned off, like a light switch being hit; and the

secondary personality who emerged might be a sabo-
teur, or an assassin."

"That's correct. In theory."

"So perhaps Zattout doesn't even know that he's lying. That's why he passed the polygraph."

Finney didn't answer. He turned back to the window.

Breakfast was sitting in his stomach like a rock. At
first, he hadn't thought he'd be able to eat at all. How
could one consume breakfast with one's mentor in the
hospital, with time to offer forgiveness quickly running
out? The answer had turned out to be simple. One put
food in one's mouth, chewed, and swallowed.

One could do a great many things, he had discovered,
when put to the test. As his presence here, now, confirmed. . . .

He thought of Lila. *We're at war, Louis.*

And they had been at war during the Susan Franklin
experiments, he supposed. It had been a cold war, but a
war nevertheless. At the time, the specter of mind control had seemed not only real but terrifying.

The fears had started in the early 1950s—more precisely, in 1949. That was the year that the Hungarian
government had publicly tried a man named Josef Mindszenty for treason. As Mindszenty (Finney had taken
some ironic pleasure from the name) had confessed, he
had exhibited peculiar, disassociated traits. The lack of
intonation in his voice and the glassy look in his eyes had
brought to mind the comportment of other "criminals"
who had given similarly unconvincing confessions, during postwar trials across Eastern Europe.

Then there were the U.S. prisoners of war who had escaped from North Korea and passed through the Soviet

Union, on their way home, who had exhibited amnesia about a certain portion of their journey—in Manchuria. This had led to speculation that the men may have been conditioned, during that mysterious blank period, by the communists. And if the communists had mastered mind control, then Americans needed to do the same.

The initial project had been code-named BLUE-BIRD. As the years wore on, BLUEBIRD had become ARTICHOKE. By the time Finney and Noble had come aboard, in the 1960s, ARTICHOKE had been absorbed into MKULTRA. Tests had been conducted on prisoners, soldiers, and mental patients around the world. The Hippocratic Oath had been thrown cheerfully over the side by the doctors who had participated, yes; but they had done what they thought was best, for the sake of their country and the world.

Yet even at the time, Finney had known they were doing wrong. Susan Franklin had not been an enemy.

Warren was making a note on a pad. Finney brought himself back to the present, making himself concentrate.

For now, he was only observing. That he could live with. If it went further . . .

. . . but he would cross that bridge when he came to it.

He returned his attention to the man on the other side of the glass.

THE WORLD SLEEPS most deeply between three and five A.M.

At twenty minutes past two, the assassin let himself out of his motel room. The night was drizzly, moonless—perfect for his needs.

He wore a black tunic, but left the small black bag behind, along with his identification. If he were caught driving without a license, it might present a problem. Yet he would rather risk that than risk having his cover identity compromised.

Simon Christopher was as good a name as any. At the temple, his name had been *little mouse*—a title he always had resented. In a way, he already had begun to think of himself as Simon Christopher. It was a solid name, a man's name, with no implication of *little*.

He moved silently down the concrete walkway outside his room; the motel slumbered around him. He took the stairwell lightly, a shadow among shadows.

In the parking lot, he approached the coupe. He slipped behind the wheel and then waited for the rain to pick up, covering sound. When it did, he keyed the ignition. He waited until he was on the road to switch on the headlights.

He drove.

SONYA JACOBS crept into the drizzle, shivering.

She pulled the sweater more tightly around her body, pressing herself into the recessed doorway by the front office. Then she took out her pack of cigarettes and put one into her mouth. She had needed the cigarette—her body had woken her up with the need.

Being addicted to nicotine made Sonya feel very grown-up. Of course, she was not yet doing it exactly right. She smoked only three or four cigarettes a day, whenever she could find the time and the privacy. But she was working on it. Soon she would be smoking half a pack a day, even a pack. She could imagine the look on her mother's face when she realized that her daughter had become a smoker.

If her mother caught her smoking now, however, there would be hell to pay. So she ducked farther back into the shadows as she struck a match, and tried to be as quiet as possible.

In a few months she would graduate. A few months after that, she would be at college. Then she would be able to give her burgeoning habit the attention it deserved. When her parents came to visit her, at college, they would find a sophisticated young woman who smoked long, elegant cigarettes—not Marlboros, the brand she had now, which she had stolen from Jimmy Batterberry at a party the weekend before. Virginia Slims, she thought. That was what she would smoke. Did Virginia Slims come in menthol? It would be something so grown-up she couldn't even picture it now.

Something moved in the night.

She exhaled, hiding the ember of the cigarette behind her body reflexively.

For a moment, she thought it had been a trick of her eyes. The rain was falling, swirling patterns in the wind. And she was tired. Who could have been moving, here in the dead of night, in the parking lot in front of the Sleepy Hollow Motor Inn?

She saw it again: a person, slipping into a car. The small, dark blue coupe that belonged to the mysterious stranger.

After she saw the movement, nothing happened.

Sonya dropped the cigarette and stepped on it. Then she stood, hugging herself, still watching.

Minutes passed. She had imagined it, she decided at

last. The whole thing was a dream. What was she doing out here, smoking cigarettes? This was not like her. A year before, the thought of a cigarette would have been anathema. A year before, she had been a good girl; she had behaved herself; she never would have smoked. The entire past year, she decided, had been a dream. The parties, the pot, Jimmy Batterberry clawing at her sweater in some strange parents' bedroom . . .

The rain picked up, and the car turned on.

She watched as it drifted backward, out of its space, and then gained the access road running in front of the motel. The headlights blazed to life. The car pulled away.

She kept watching, shivering in the drizzly night. She took out her pack of cigarettes and carefully, quietly, lit another.

WAR LOVES to seek its victims in the young.

The words are Sophocles'—written before his death in the year 406 B.C. They are as true today as they were then. And Sonya Jacobs was not the only youth who would pay a price in the latest war to absorb the world.

In lower Manhattan, a young man entered a post office.

He wore an oversized basketball jersey and baggy DKNY blue jeans, with a black scarf tied around his forehead. On his right, a line of glum customers waited before a row of windows. On his left were machines selling stamps. Overhead were signs reading HELP STAMP OUT BREAST CANCER and KEEP OUR MAIL SAFE and YOUR PATIENCE IS APPRECIATED.

Covering the rear wall were rows of post office

boxes. He walked calmly forward, removing a key from his pocket. He slipped it into the lock and checked the box.

An envelope was waiting.

He withdrew the envelope and locked the box again. He turned, his soft eyes focusing on the grimy floor, and left the post office.

THE YOUNG MAN'S NAME was Muhammad Nassif.

Only recently had he begun to use this name—his given name. As a child, he had been known as Mickey. His mother had wanted to deny her origins, and had Americanized her youngest son to the best of her ability.

The process that led to Nassif's reclaiming his true name had begun, oddly enough, during a fight with his girlfriend Lisa. He had been sitting alone on his bedroom floor, arguing over the phone about the upcoming prom. Lisa had wanted him to rent a limousine for the occasion. She was a strong-willed girl, who favored body piercings and belly shirts that exposed her skin to the eyes of the world. One time—and only once—he had dared to criticize her choice of dress. *What do you want me to wear,* she had snapped back, *a burka?*

As a matter of fact, he'd thought—why not? A burka would have been better than the clothing of a whore. Yet he hadn't dared to say this to Lisa. He had become such a part of the society in which he had been raised that he hadn't even been conscious of his own rights as a man.

While Lisa's voice had fed into his ear, Al Pacino's dull eyes looked down from the wall. Pacino was brandishing a machine gun over a balcony railing, a sneer etched on his face. The poster's caption read: "Say Hello to My Little Friend." All at once, everything about the scene struck Nassif as wrong—the girl on the other end of the phone, the poster on the wall, the squalor of the building, and the smell of Chinese cooking lingering in corners. Didn't he deserve more? Wasn't he *meant* for more?

Hadn't that been the lesson he should have taken from his brother—that he was meant for more?

Nassif's elder brother had always been more in touch with his roots than had Nassif. Even as a teenager he had spent time at a local mosque, meeting people who then had taken him deeper into the fold. At the urging of the brothers he had encountered, he had signed up for religious classes; he had undertaken a pilgrimage to Mecca. Then, at last, he had turned his back on America completely. He had returned to the land from which his family came, to do work that would further the cause.

Predictably, their mother had been horrified. Years before, she had lost her husband to the fundamentalists. Now she had lost her eldest son. So she had focused all her efforts on keeping Nassif by her side, on playing up his sense of Americanism and modernism and secularism. And this was his reward—a whorish girlfriend, a cheap apartment, the insistent smell of old noodles.

But he knew what could be done, if he decided he was better than this. His brother had given him a name. Iqbal Ajami was the man who had given his brother direction in life, who had convinced him to return to the homeland and devote himself to furtherance of the cause.

At that moment, the instant of enlightenment, Nassif knew that he *was* better than this.

So he had gone to the mosque, that very day, and taken the first step on the path that had brought him to the place he was now.

THE MOSQUE featured separate entrances for men and women.

Nassif picked up what to do by watching others. He removed his shoes, washed his hands and face at the *hammam.* Then he went to hear the Friday sermon, the *khutbah*—although at the time he didn't know what he was hearing.

Nearly half of the mosque's attendees were black. They listened to the Arabic sermon with the same polite, blank expression as Nassif; the words, of course, made no sense to them. Yet they prayed as if they meant it, arranged in neat rows but undulating like a human ocean, heads touching the floor and then rising again. When the service was finished, Nassif approached a woman wearing a long white *hijab*—but no nail polish or makeup, he noted with approval—and asked if she knew the man named Ajami.

She indicated a bright-eyed, well-dressed man in his forties, with a heavy black mustache and an unmistakable sense of purpose, surrounded by a group that hung on his every word.

When the group dispersed, Nassif approached. He introduced himself as his brother's brother, and genuine pleasure crossed Ajami's face. Then Nassif received his first lecture: about the unity of the Muslim people, and about every young brother's duty to devote himself to increasing that unity. Clearly, Ajami was a man who knew about bigger things than Al Pacino and proms.

On that day, Ajami had gone no further than this introductory lecture. He had not spoken of the ideology underlying their cause—of the history of the Middle East, or the threat posed by the crusading Americans and Zionists. He had not extended any invitation to Nassif except one to return the following Friday, to listen again to the *khutbah*.

Nassif had returned. Again, following the sermon, Ajami had been surrounded by sycophants and eager followers. Again, Nassif approached him after the group dispersed. Then he volunteered his services. Ajami looked him over, bright eyes twinkling. "If you mean it," he said at last, "come again next week."

Nassif had expected that to be his last week spent living in America. After Friday, he doubtless would be sent to a training camp in Afghanistan. There he would learn to take up weapons, to fight for the cause.

Yet the job for which Ajami recruited him proved undramatic. Nassif was given the number of a post office box and the key that would fit its lock. Once a week, he was to check the box. If something was waiting, he was to take it home, put it in a new envelope, and mail it to Ajami. Along with the man's name and address came instructions to destroy the paper on which they were written. But Nassif did not trust his own memory; so he tucked the scrap into the bottom of a dresser drawer, beside the key. Until recently, the paraphernalia in the drawer had been of a decidedly different nature: pipes and plastic bags and scales, rolling papers and screens.

Now he had replaced the drug paraphernalia with something that truly mattered.

* * *

THIS WAS HIS SECOND TIME visiting the post office—and the second time he had found an envelope waiting.

After retrieving it, he rode the subway home.

He climbed the four flights to the apartment. He let himself in, wrinkling his nose at the fishy odor in the hallway, and moved to his own room. He returned the key to its drawer, then consulted the scrap of paper, placed the envelope in a second, larger envelope, and wrote Ajami's address on the outside.

He found a snack in the refrigerator, ate it standing by the counter. Not so long ago he would have spent the afternoon smoking dope, listening to hip-hop, and talking to Lisa on the telephone. Wasting time.

Now, he returned to his room, crouched, and removed the prayer mat from beneath the bed. Using the prayer mat made him feel awkwardly self-conscious. He was still new to this. He still wore his old clothes, ate his same diet, and lived much the way he always had. With time, he would improve. For now he was doing the best he could. And perhaps it would not do to show in public too much of his newfound piety. Better to walk among the enemy as one of them. Hadn't he been warned away from too many visits to the mosque by Ajami himself? Hadn't he been told not to grow his facial hair, not to attract attention?

He unrolled the prayer mat, vaguely aware of Al Pacino's eyes boring into his back. Eventually, he would take down the poster. It was part of his old life. But for now, it was important to keep up appearances. The poster stayed.

He knelt. Praying was foreign to him; he never knew

in which direction to face. But he did his best, kneeling and touching his head to the floor. Allah would guide him, if only he opened his mind.

In the next apartment, someone tossed a new piece of fish into a frying pan; the sizzle filled the tenement's narrow hallways.

4

SONYA WAITED for the man to sense her presence. After a moment, he did.

He looked up from the combination washer/dryer tucked into a concrete atrium behind the motel's front office. He had been transferring his laundry from one to the other, and stood holding a soggy bundle. Sonya sidled closer, trying to steal a peek at those clothes. Was the black tunic there, the one that for some unknowable reason had jewelry sewn *into* the sleeve, instead of on the outside?

Before she could see, he had stuffed the clothes into the dryer. Then he reached into a pocket of his jeans, took out a handful of coins, and began to sift through them.

She closed the distance between them, careful to keep her chin held high. She had spent hours practicing this walk: a swanlike motion, cool and willowy and unflappable. "Hi," she said.

He began to feed quarters into the machine, and didn't answer.

Sonya let a few moments pass. Despite her cool and willowy demeanor, he seemed determined to ignore her. Probably because she was half his age. But didn't older men have a soft spot for younger women? If she could overlook *his* age, surely he could do the same for her.

"I saw you last night," she blurted out suddenly.

He didn't react. He finished with the quarters, chose a cycle, and started the dryer. It had been a stupid thing to say, Sonya thought. But now she had said it, and she had no choice but to continue:

"It was, like, three in the morning. I was smoking a cigarette. You didn't see me. But I saw you."

He turned from the machine to face her.

"You looked like a criminal or something," she said, and smiled nervously. "You didn't turn on your head-lights until you were on the road."

"I didn't?"

"I was standing by the office, out front. Smoking a cigarette. And I saw you—"

She was beginning to tingle inside, the way she did when she was going through someone's luggage, when she knew she was doing something wrong.

"It's just weird," she continued. "You creep out to your car, then get in and drive away before you turn on the headlights. In the middle of the night. I mean, it's just weird."

For a few moments, he considered her. "How old are you?" he asked then.

"Eighteen." She drew herself up straighter. "Almost."

"In a few more years," he said, "you might learn to mind your own business."

He began to move back toward the stairwell. Sonya followed.

"See my earrings?" she asked. "They're on the outside. It wouldn't do a lot of good to have them on the inside, would it? That would be *jejune*. That means stupid. But oh, what's my point? I don't know. I'm sorry if you think I'm, you know, snooping. But I do that. It's because I'm a curious person. I don't think there's anything wrong with being curious. But—"

They had reached the stairs. He stopped abruptly.

"I don't know," she said again. She offered a hand, limp-wristed, ladylike. "I'm Sonya."

He looked at the hand.

"Sonya," he said after a moment. "Do your parents know that you spy on the guests?"

She felt the same dark, excited thrill. She took the hand back. "They suspect," she said seriously.

Then she lost her composure, and laughed.

"Simon. What are you doing, sneaking out in the middle of the night?"

The man's brow darkened. For a few seconds, she thought she may have gone too far. She entwined her hands behind her back, biting her lip, and bounced on her toes.

He turned and ascended the stairs.

"Simon," she called.

He didn't turn back.

"There's a liquor store about five miles down the highway. I like Stoli."

He ignored her.

"You can buy it, and I'll pay you back. And then I won't tell anyone about what I saw."

He reached the top of the stairs and disappeared from view.

She stood looking up after him for a few seconds, still biting her lip.

His clothes were in the dryer. She could go have a look, and see for herself if the curious tunic was there.

But all at once the thought didn't hold much appeal. It was impolite to snoop. And she was not an impolite girl. Or hadn't been, once.

Besides, *General Hospital* would be starting soon. Then *TRL*.

She looked up the stairs for another moment. Then she turned and headed back to the office.

THE PHOTOGRAPH showed Lila as she had looked on a Saturday morning during their honeymoon: smiling into the sun, her green eyes sparkling even more brightly than the aquamarine water over her shoulder.

Louis Finney held the photograph for a moment. He sniffled—coming down with a cold, he thought—and set the framed photograph on the edge of his desk.

He resumed unpacking. There was not much to be done with the little bedroom, but the place was beginning to feel a little less strange to him. Lila's face was on the desk now, beside a copy of the latest bulletin from the American Ornithologists' Union. His clothes were folded neatly in the dresser, his favorite bathrobe hanging in the closet. His good luck charm sat on the nightstand near the bed, beside a paperback novel and a softly glowing lamp. On the sill below the curtained window were his 804 Swift Audubon binoculars, in a corduroy case.

A knock came at the door. He sniffled again, and went to answer it.

Thomas Warren II looked freshly showered, with his blond hair standing on end from a quick towel-drying. He wore a clean blue Oxford shirt and cream-colored slacks. "I hope I'm not interrupting," he said.

"Not at all."

"I've spoken with the hospital. Dr. Noble was awake for a few minutes tonight. We may want to try a visit to-morrow, if we find a chance."

Finney nodded.

"In the meantime," Warren said, "I was thinking of having a nightcap. Join me?"

"I think I may be coming down with a cold. Probably best just to turn in early."

Finney started to close the door, but something was in the way—Warren's foot.

THEY SAT on the screened-in porch on the west side of the house, drinks in hand.

Warren had fixed himself a scotch and soda. Finney had limited himself to plain soda. Anything stronger would knock him out. His eyes already were tired as they ticked across the scene before him: the sunset, the scare-crow, the guardhouses, the parking lot with its half dozen cars glimmering, and in the distance, over the treetops, the searchlights atop the high stone wall.

Warren produced a pack of Camel Lights. "I don't think you remember," he said. "But you knew my father.

He supervised an experiment in Frankfurt in seventy-two. You and Dr. Noble were participants."

"An agency experiment?"

" 'Quantitative electroencephalographic analysis of naturally occurring and drug-induced psychotic states in human females.' Do you remember?"

"The experiment? Yes."

"My father?"

"It was a long time ago," Finney said evasively.

Now that it was mentioned, however, he thought he did recall the elder Warren. He had been cut from the same Ivy League cloth as the younger—part of a breed known within the agency as "royalists." Recruiting from the ivory tower had been standard operating procedure for the CIA since the agency's founding, following the model of the OSS. Under the leadership of Wild Bill Donovan, the OSS had culled its agents from the tony Eastern establishment; the initials had been said to stand for "Oh So Social."

Warren blew smoke from one corner of his mouth. "It must feel a bit strange, to be back in the game after so long away."

"A bit," Finney allowed.

"I get the impression, Doctor, that you have some reservations about what we're doing here."

So this was why the man had dragged him down for a nightcap. Finney shrugged neutrally.

"You've retired from private practice," Warren said after a moment. "Is that right?"

"That's right."

"How do you fill your time? If you don't mind my asking."

"Filling my time doesn't seem to be a problem."

"Do you have a family?"

Finney glanced at the man, who surely would have read his file and known about Lila. "No," he answered shortly.

Warren drank more scotch and soda, and smoked his cigarette. He French-inhaled the smoke, rolling it from his mouth into his nose.

"I'll tell you the truth," he said presently. "I'm curious about why you've agreed to take part in this. I trust Noble's judgment, of course. But you, Doctor, are something of an unknown."

"I'm here as a favor to an old friend."

"You mean Dr. Noble."

"Of course."

"I read a piece you published about ten years ago. It seemed to indicate a certain lack of warmth between you and the good doctor."

Finney raised an eyebrow.

"In a psychiatric journal. You made a comment about funding . . ."

"Ah."

"You implied that he had manufactured his results, over the years."

"Not manufactured," Finney corrected. "Perhaps he massaged them a bit."

"So you consider him an old friend, although you've had some differences?"

"Show me old friends who haven't had differences," Finney said with a slight smile, "and I'll wonder how old the friendship really is."

Warren did not return the smile. "Does he share your . . . mixed feelings . . . about government work?"

Finney remembered Noble's visit to his study, at the farm in Pennsylvania. *I haven't accepted a government contract in fifteen years, Louis. But the nightmares still come.*

He shook his head. "You'd have to ask him that yourself."

"Tomorrow we'll pay a visit to the hospital. Maybe I'll get my chance then. In the meantime, is there anything you'd like? I'm here to help."

"If I think of anything, I'll be sure to let you know."

After a moment, Warren returned to the subject of his father. He spoke proudly of the man's accomplishments—part of the CIA's behavioral control program from its very origin. Thomas Warren, Senior, had worked alongside Stanley Lovell, conducting tests with Sodium Amytal, Benzedrine, and electroshock amnesia. If Warren felt any qualms about his father's role in the program, he didn't express them. Yet there was something guilty in his litany, Finney thought. He was all too eager to volunteer details of his father's history.

Warren spoke for nearly ten minutes, drifting from one topic to another: his father's experience with the agency, his hopes for the interrogation with Zattout, his own theories about aggressive questioning techniques. He asked Finney's opinion on the effectiveness of the Page-Russell method, on the administration of psychedelics and microwaves.

"In my experience," Finney said, "aggressive methods often are anti-productive. Better to win the man's trust, if at all possible."

Warren looked nonplussed. "Quinlan seems to agree with you."

Joseph Quinlan was the man conducting the conversations with Zattout—a sallow-faced, tired-eyed agent of about forty-five. Over breakfast that morning Finney had caught a hint of liquor on Quinlan's breath. One of the hazards of the job, he supposed.

"But we don't have forever to get our results," Warren went on. "There's a lot of cooks in this kitchen, you know. FBI, INS, State, Customs, and Treasury . . . all breathing right down the back of my neck."

A field sparrow was singing somewhere—a sweet, slurring note that rose into a trill. Finney looked off across the land, trying to find it. But the bird was nowhere to be seen.

"It seems to me as if Quinlan's dragging his feet," Warren said then. "Do you get that impression?"

Finney looked over. He thought he could read between the lines. Until now Zattout had given them information of only middling value. He had told them of a single sleeper cell unknown to them, in Pakistan, and given some generalities about al Qaeda's recruitment and operational methods. If more substantive results were not secured in a timely fashion, then *aggressive* methods of interrogation—a fine euphemism—would be put into effect. In all likelihood, Quinlan had made it clear that he would not be involved with the implementation of such methods. And so Warren was looking to see how far Finney would go, if push came to shove.

"Quinlan's on the right track," he answered. "Gain the man's trust; learn his strengths and his weaknesses. Make an investment of time and patience, and it will reward you."

"You catch more flies with honey, eh?"

"Something like that."

"What about the possibility we discussed before—that Zattout believes he is telling the truth, but has been programmed with these answers in advance?"

"Highly unlikely."

"But possible?"

Finney shook his head. Iatrogenic creation of multiple personalities was a dramatic idea that, like psychedelics and microwaves, tended to appeal to agency royalists who lived in fear of missing a major advance. But the creation of multiple personalities through artificial means was a tricky business. With Susan Franklin they had not created a secondary personality; they had brought out one that already existed. They had taken a sick young woman and exploited her illness.

For a time, Multiple Personality Disorder had enjoyed a vogue among certain circles of psychiatry. They called it Disassociative Identity Disorder, or DID, hoping to shuck the connotations of science fiction and pulp literature. Believers in the disorder based their conclusions on inarguable fact. Children regularly expressed different sides of their personalities as "imaginary friends"; various manifestations were assigned names, patterns of behavior, sets of manners. But in reality all were facets of the same psyche, and as the child matured, the different personalities were absorbed and sublimated.

Sometimes roots of the personalities remained—particularly in pathological cases like Susan Franklin's. And it was likely that any adult, including Ali Zattout, possessed shades that could be accented through clinical procedure. But unless Zattout was seriously predisposed to disassociative disorder—unless he truly was mentally ill—one would not be able to create separate personalities within him, no matter what methods were brought to bear.

"There aren't any magic solutions," Finney said. "The key to a successful interrogation is patience and flexibility."

"Surely you can bring more to the table than that," Warren said cordially. "You have some experience with hypnosis?"

"Zattout's entire experience here is a form of hypnosis. Every time you become involved in a novel or a motion picture, Mr. Warren, you've put yourself into a hypnotic trance of sorts. The steps we take to promote a suggestible mindset will be considerably more subtle than a swinging watch."

Warren smoked, looking off into the twilight. The quiet drew out around them, interrupted by the occasional sound of crickets.

Then Warren yawned, ground out his cigarette beneath his heel, and checked his watch. "Well," he said. "Another soda?"

"I don't think so. Thank you."

They stood. "It's been a pleasure," Warren said. "Sleep well, Doctor. Good luck nipping that cold in the bud."

Finney gave a tight nod. "Good night."

They went into the house and climbed to the second floor. Finney let himself into his room, then crossed to the window. He stood there, looking out at nothing in particular, wishing he'd had a real drink after all.

* * *

HE DID NOT BELIEVE that the girl posed a threat.

He sat behind the wheel of the coupe, looking at a house a dozen feet away. The house was an unassuming A-frame on a block of similar houses. In the pink light of rising dawn he could make out a single car parked in the driveway, a tired-looking Ford Escort. A flowerpot sat on the A-frame's windowsill; wind chimes tinkled on the porch. The front door needed a coat of paint. An ordinary house, belonging to an ordinary elderly widow.

The resident of number sixty-two Sycamore Drive was named Miriam Lane. According to his information, the woman had lived here for the past fourteen years. According to his information, her husband had died four years earlier. Miriam Lane lived alone.

Now, with his eyes never leaving the front porch of number sixty-two, he thought it again: The girl did not pose a threat.

She simply had a crush; she was only trying to catch his eye. And if she did suspect something, to whom would she report it? Her parents? And what would she report, exactly? Going for a drive in the night was not a crime.

Yet the thought distracted him. The girl had been snooping. His tunic had been in the bag, along with his equipment. She could not have found the secret compartment, he thought. But maybe she had seen enough. What had she made of it?

The front door was opening.

Miriam Lane wore a white uniform and carried a tote bag. As she moved to the Escort, he reached for the coupe's ignition. The clock on the dash read 6:46 A.M.

According to his source, the woman's daily shift at the camp lasted from seven A.M. until four P.M. Today she would be late.

But she surprised him—driving quickly and confidently. When she reached the dirt road leading toward the Marine Corps guard, the clock on the dash read 6:57. Right on time, after all.

He watched as she took the turn; then he continued down the gravel road for another five minutes. He executed a K-turn, heading back to the highway. Thirty minutes later he was stepping into his room at the Sleepy Hollow motel, locking the door behind him.

His thoughts returned to the girl.

Perhaps she would find something else to command her attention. Children had short attention spans. He should leave well enough alone, and within a day she would distract herself with whatever it was that intrigued her besides snooping.

He spread the blueprints on the desk and put the girl from his mind. *Focus,* he thought.

Two fences protected the safe house.

The first was wood, ten feet tall, patrolled at three-hour intervals by men and dogs. The second, a quarter-mile farther on, was stone, eighteen feet high. In addition to barbed wire and searchlights, the stone wall featured two guard towers on each face, set equidistantly—eight in total. Each guard tower contained two marines and a sustained-fire Stoner M63 A1 machine gun, range 2,000 meters, capable of firing seven hundred rounds per minute.

The forest between the fences contained photo-electric beams and microwave sensor motion detectors. The photo-electric beams would trigger an alarm if they were broken. The motion detectors would trigger an alarm if they detected a Doppler shift between 20 Hz and 120 Hz, the frequencies related to the movement of humans.

The fact that the sensors were tuned to humans did not necessarily mean they were impassable. To avoid nuisance alarms—caused by weather, vegetation, and wandering wildlife—the outdoor sensors could not be calibrated to their most responsive settings. Still, he would prefer to bypass them completely.

Both walls used vibration sensors, detecting physical intrusion—a man climbing over the tops—and sending an alarm to the primary guardhouse, located by the steel gate in the second wall.

Between the second wall and the safe house itself was a square mile of wooded ground, equipped with more photo-electric beams and microwave sensors. Motion-activated cameras were scattered throughout the forest, providing another level of redundancy. The beams, sensors, and cameras could be avoided by traveling on the paths—but that meant running into the guard patrols.

The space immediately surrounding the safe house enjoyed still more security. Every time a figure with body heat measuring between 8 and 14 microns stepped off the porch or out the French doors in back, passive infrared cameras switched on to follow it. Here also were more microwave sensors, mounted on trees and buried in the earth. And more guard patrols, staggered at three-hour intervals. The marines on patrol carried modified Tec 9 machine guns, and led Doberman pinschers on chain leashes that could set the dogs free with the flick of a toggle.

You can buy it, and I'll pay you back, the girl had said. *And then I won't tell anyone about what I saw. . . .*

What had she seen? Him sneaking away in the middle of the night. Nothing criminal.

See my earrings? They're on the outside. It wouldn't do a lot of good to have them on the inside, would it?

He leaned away from the desk. It had been a reference to his tunic, he understood suddenly—to the small steel objects sewn into the wrists.

He sighed.

He would need to find out what the girl knew, or thought she knew. But silencing her might be a mistake. It might attract attention.

He would do whatever was required. Nothing could be left to chance.

There was no need for haste. Haste, if he gave in to it, would be his undoing.

Patience, he thought.

After a moment, he leaned forward again and continued his study of the blueprints.

ZATTOUT'S INDEX FINGER moved to a pale, crescent-shaped scar on his right ear.

Finney reached for his notebook. Whenever Zattout felt annoyance, confusion, or fear—a strong negative emotion that he wished to conceal from his interrogator—his hand moved to scratch at that pale scar. In the language of confidence men, it was a *tell.*

Then he began to talk—covering ground that, according to the transcripts of his conversations with

Quinlan, had been covered several times before. The interrogator, Finney thought, was seeking to solidify his dominance by making the prisoner jump through hoops. From a purely rational standpoint it made perfect sense, serving the double purpose of testing Zattout's consistency and cementing Quinlan's position of authority. But such tactics ran a risk of alienating the subject.

The heroin and opium, Zattout reported without inflection, were smuggled through Central Asia, Bulgaria, and Croatia, then hidden in mountain towns outside Macedonia. When an infusion of funding was required, al Qaeda operatives went to the hideouts and retrieved the drugs. From there they were passed to the Albanian mafia, to be channeled into Western Europe. . . .

Joseph Quinlan wore a maroon cardigan and silver-rimmed eyeglasses. Under the harsh light, his pale skin looked almost translucent. He pushed the glasses higher on his nose and interrupted: "This doesn't quite jibe with the intelligence we've received from other quarters. The naval base on Diego Garcia. Among others."

Zattout fingered the scar. "It's the truth," he said. "That's all I can say."

Quinlan turned a page of his file.

"I'd like to return to something else we've discussed before—if you don't mind. The murder of Abdullah Azzam . . ."

Zattout, in a monotone, explained his previous statement. Abdullah Azzam had been al Qaeda's spiritual leader back when the group had been called Maktab al Khidmat lil-Mujahidin al-Arab, or MAK. Azzam, Osama bin Laden's mentor, had founded the group along with his protégé in Pakistan in 1984. The original purpose of al Qaeda, which means "the Base," had been to fight Soviet forces in Afghanistan. But by 1988, the organization had evolved. It had infiltrated and merged with other fundamentalist terrorist organizations around the world, in particular the Islamic Group and Egyptian Islamic Jihad. The purview had been expanded, from targeting Soviet forces—which by then were withdrawing from Afghanistan—to targeting Western infidels. A split had occurred between bin Laden and Azzam. The former had no compunction about targeting civilian non-combatants. The latter did. In 1988, a bomb killed Azzam in Peshawar, Pakistan, clearing the path for bin Laden to assume sole control of al Qaeda.

"You've mentioned shipping operations in the Romanian Black Sea. The ships, you say, change their flags as often as twice a day. The cargo vessels sail out of Constantsa with a Romanian crew. In Morocco, a new crew comes aboard. The ship assumes a new name and flag . . ."

In the back of Finney's mind, a hectoring voice pointed out that he had not yet found time to visit Noble in the hospital. Well, he would get to it soon enough. In the meantime there was work to be done here, starting with an analysis of the Wechsler IQ test that had been administered by Noble, which would shed light on the best way to proceed with Zattout.

Quinlan kept talking. As Zattout listened, a sudden nervous twitch made his right eyelid jump. Finney noted it. For over two weeks the prisoner had been confined to the cell; he had not seen sunlight, nor experienced any

human contact besides his conversations with his interrogator. For years previous he had lived in hiding or on
the run. A deterioration of composure therefore was not
unexpected. As long as Quinlan didn't push too hard,
forcing the man to shut down . . .

The eyelid jumped again. The right leg began to jig
up and down, nervously. Finney watched, taking it all in.

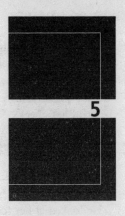

5

"HOUSEKEEPING," Sonya Jacobs called.

She was reaching for the passkey when she became aware of a presence behind her. She turned to find herself facing Simon Christopher: his dark eyes sharper than usual, with an accusatory flash.

Then he raised his right hand, and Sonya saw that he held a liter of Stolichnaya vodka.

A tingle moved down her body, into the pit of her stomach. Why would the man give her a bottle of Stoli now, after he'd caught her snooping? Because he was doing something wrong, here at Sleepy Hollow. She had seen the contents of his bag—the folder, the passport, that odd black tunic with jewelry sewn into the sleeve. And now he was trying to buy her silence.

Her sister would have laughed, had Sonya voiced such a fancy out loud. But the excitement she felt when she allowed the idea free reign was delicious, almost irresistible. Why *not* believe the man was a terrorist? Who was to say he wasn't?

He waggled the bottle. After looking around to make sure her mother wasn't in the vicinity, she reached forward. "Thanks," she said.

They stood facing each other. She could feel a blush rising in her cheeks. "Want to drink it with me?" she asked.

His head tilted a degree to the right.

"I'll show you my secret place," she went on brazenly. "You know—if you want. It's beautiful. Right by the creek."

He looked at her for a moment more. Then he said: "Why not?"

"I have a few more rooms to clean."

"All right."

"I'll be done in a half hour."

"All right."

"I'll knock on your door."

"All right," he said.

BEFORE GOING TO HIS ROOM, she returned to the apartment behind the office and took the pack of cigarettes from its hiding place. She checked herself in the mirror. Her color was high. *Be cool,* she thought. *Be cool. Hold your chin up. Be . . . willowy.*

Presently her color lowered; but the excited tingle remained.

She went and knocked on the man's door, keeping her chin held high.

They walked together into the forest without speaking. It was late afternoon, approaching what in Hollywood was called the Magic Hour. The Magic Hour came twice a day—at dawn and at dusk. It was the time when the light turned golden, when starlets and heart-throbs looked their most attractive. Sonya had read all about it in her friend Paula's magazines. Paula subscribed to *Premiere* and *Entertainment Weekly* and *Teen People,* and last year they had spent most of their afternoons together, sitting in Paula's bedroom, poring over the magazines and talking about their favorite stars. That had been before Sonya had met Jimmy Batterberry, before she had discovered cigarettes and Stoli. Now she and Paula were no longer friends. Paula treated Sonya with brittle condescension, these days. But that was because Paula was jealous. She didn't have a boyfriend. She didn't have older men taking her into the woods at the Magic Hour to drink vodka and smoke cigarettes. All she had were her stupid movie magazines.

Fallen trees and old logs dotted the landscape; the creek wandered down from Devil's Peak, smelling green. They moved for twenty minutes, until the sound of the distant highway was completely lost. Then they reached the small clearing Sonya had been seeking. She sat down on a flat rock by the creek. The man sat beside her, not touching her. She began to work at getting the vodka open.

"This is when they like to shoot movies," she remarked. "Things look their best at this time of day."

He said nothing. Sonya got the bottle open, then took a swig. She managed to refrain from coughing, and passed it over.

In the branches above them, a bird was singing. The creek babbled and gushed. The water was wonderfully clear, with rocks of all different colors forming a mosaic just beneath the surface. Sonya took out her cigarettes and lit one with a pink Bic. This time she did cough—but just a little.

"Last year?" she said. "I only drank beer. I never even tasted vodka until February. But it's much better, I think. And it's not so fattening, either."

He gave a wan smile—which felt like a major victory, to Sonya—drank moderately, and handed the bottle back to her.

"Do you like it out here?" she asked.

"It's very nice."

"I come here to be alone. When I need to think. This is my special place. Is that stupid?"

He didn't answer.

"You're only the second person I brought out here," she said, and then paused significantly.

A beat passed. "Who was the first?" he asked.

"My boyfriend. Kind of. Except he's not really my boyfriend. I don't like him very much, actually. He's very *jejune*. Women mature faster than boys, you know. He's a nice person, though."

Her cigarette had gone out. She lit it again, shielding the flame from the wind with a cupped hand. "What's your deal, anyway?" she asked around the filter.

"My what?"

"Why are you here? Don't you have a job?"

He tossed a twig into the creek and watched as the water took it away. "I'm a researcher," he said.

"What kind of researcher?"

"A geographical survey analyst. I'm surveying the land."

"Why?"

"After I submit my report, they'll come here with a

telescopic ranging pole and a thread adapter—to make a Global Positioning System."

"The things they have in cars, that tell you when to turn?"

He nodded. She drank more vodka and passed him the bottle. "I hate those things," she said with a giggle.

He smiled again.

"That sounds like a boring job," she said. "No offense."

"None taken."

"When I get a job it's going to be something . . . I don't know. Something different."

She dragged on the cigarette and then tossed it into the brook, where it followed in the path of the departed twig.

"Maybe a porn star," she said, and looked directly at him.

His face was blank, impossible to read.

"My friend?" Sonya said. "*She's* going to be a porn star. Not me—not really. Next year I'm going to college. But if I was going to do it, I know what my porn name would be. Ginger Bayard. Do you know your porn name?"

He raised his eyebrows.

"Everybody has a porn name," she told him. "You take the name of your childhood pet, and the name of the street you grew up on. Before we moved here, we lived on Bayard Street, in Philadelphia. And my dog was named Ginger. So I'm Ginger Bayard. Or I would be. If I was a porn star."

"Huh."

"Did you have a pet?"

He nodded. "A dog."

"Named?"

"Ringo," he said.

"And the street you grew up on?"

"Birch Street."

"So: Ringo Birch."

"Huh," he said again.

She felt giddy. She moved an inch closer to him on the flat rock. "Ginger Bayard and Ringo Birch."

He said nothing.

She tilted up her head, inviting him to kiss her. Drunk already, just a little, yes. Her breath drifted onto his cheek. Why wasn't he kissing her? Why had he come out here, if he wasn't going to kiss her?

Maybe he was just shy. She tilted her face away, letting her breath tickle his neck. If he was shy, then she should play hard to get. *Cool and willowy,* she thought.

For several minutes, neither spoke. The sun dropped lower; the shadows lengthened. A chill ran down Sonya's arms, raising gooseflesh. She hugged herself, shivering, and took another sip from the bottle.

He stirred. "Are you cold?"

"A little."

He put an arm around her shoulders. She huddled into him. His arm beneath the sleeve was unexpectedly hard. He had the musculature of a runner or a swimmer: slim and ropy. She offered him the bottle again, and he shook his head. She took another swig herself. Getting very tipsy now. She moved still closer to him. Somehow she felt cold and hot at the same time.

Then she kissed him—a brushing of the lips, lingering.

She leaned away, looking into his eyes.

He looked back at her coolly.

Sonya began to laugh.

At first it was only a nervous chuckle. Then it became a giggle; then a full-blown cackle. "Oh, my God," she said around the cackle. "This is so weird."

He smiled.

"This is crazy," she said. She capped the bottle and set it down, uttering a strange snorting guffaw in the process. The snort only cracked her up more. "My . . . God," she managed.

She drew hard breaths, controlling herself.

The laughter trickled off.

He was still looking at her.

She kissed him again.

This time it was a real kiss; her tongue poked boldly into his mouth, exploring. She straddled him on the flat rock. He did not kiss back actively, but nor did he push her away.

She nibbled on his ear. "Simon," she breathed.

His hands were on her hips. She tugged at his earlobe with her teeth. "Simon," she murmured again. "Why do you have a passport, if you're a—what did you call it?"

"A geographical survey analyst."

"But you're not American?"

He didn't answer.

"You're lying," she whispered, and then pushed him flat onto his back, pressing herself into his body.

She kissed him again. Now he was taking her head in a very particular way, with care. At last, he was going to kiss her back. It would be very different from kissing

Jimmy Batterberry. This was an older man—a knowledgeable man. Some kind of mysterious foreigner, with something to hide. When he removed her bra, he wouldn't fumble around for five minutes, trying to find the clasp. He would be more like Fonzie, from that stupid old show she saw on Nickelodeon. Just snapping his fingers.

She was laughing again.

It was that picture of him snapping his fingers, like Fonzie. She should control herself, she thought. She was going to ruin the moment, just when he had been on the verge of kissing her for real. But she couldn't help herself. The vodka was buzzing through her head, adding to the intoxication of doing something really terribly, horribly, undeniably wrong. Before she knew what she was doing she said: "Ayyyyyy."

Then cracked up again, sagging against him.

"Sorry," she managed between giggles. "I don't know what's wrong with me."

His hands continued to explore the back of her head: finding the lean muscles in her neck, locating the base of her skull.

She returned her mouth to his.

But he wasn't kissing back. She had ruined it. The moment had passed. And it was growing chilly, out here with the sun going down. Her arms were stippled with gooseflesh again. Suddenly she didn't want to be here. Maybe that was why she had laughed, sabotaging the moment. Because some part of her saw this from the outside, and that part knew that what she was doing was wrong.

She began to pull away, but his hands on the back of her head were firm, holding her in place.

"Simon," she said.

He moved her head again—tilting it to a slightly uncomfortable angle.

"I don't know if . . . I don't think I want to."

In fact, she knew she didn't want to. Again she tried to pull away. But he held tight, one hand on the base of her skull, the other moving to cup her face. He was going to kiss her now, whether she wanted it or not.

"Simon . . . please."

"Relax," he said.

She closed her eyes, and braced herself.

FINNEY SNEEZED explosively.

He couldn't find a handkerchief. But Joseph Quinlan was holding out the napkin on which his drink had been resting. Finney took it, nodded his thanks, and blew his nose. He folded the napkin, pocketed it, then looked from one face to the other before continuing.

Behind the octagonal lenses of his glasses, Joseph Quinlan's eyes were cool and neutral. Perhaps there was the slightest flicker of pity there—*spring colds,* that flicker might have said, *they're the worst.* Or perhaps not. The man's air of frigid distance was all but impenetrable.

Quinlan, Finney thought, had cultivated this air as a defense mechanism. Some part of him felt ashamed of what he did for a living—manipulating and interrogating prisoners, treating men like playthings—and he used chilly aloofness as a preemptive strike against criticism. Yet the frigid distance was not enough to salve his conscience. This was why, once again, there was a tinge of liquor on Quinlan's breath, which Finney caught when he leaned in close. If he hadn't been certain before, he was now: the transparent liquid in Quinlan's glass was more than water.

By contrast, Thomas Warren's eyes were hot. He was not pleased by the recommendations Finney was making for the direction of the interrogation. Warren wanted fast progress; after all, he was the one who needed to deliver results to the various agencies involved with the case. If it was up to him, Finney suspected, they already would have progressed to more "aggressive" methods of questioning—torment, or torture. The line between the two was kept purposely blurred. According to the Geneva Conventions, *torture* of a prisoner of war was illegal. But according to the laws of the United States, *torment* was allowable. In this particular euphemism, torment involved a withholding—of food, sleep, water, or medical attention—as compared to an active administration.

Finney sniffled, then continued.

"When dealing with the psychology of the interrogatee, the thing to keep in mind is that Zattout actually *wants* to cooperate with us. He wants this for two primary reasons. First, because cooperation results in rewards—being let out of his cell, allowed more amenities, and eventually allowed his freedom. Second, and just as important, he wants to gratify his captors. Seeking to please a perceived authority is only human nature. Put simply: He wants a gold star."

Quinlan was nodding.

"Yet at the same time," Finney said, "he's been conditioned to believe certain values. To cooperate with us strikes him, deep down, as a betrayal of those values."

"So our job," Quinlan offered, "is to give him an out."

"Precisely. We want to show him a way to cooperate that still lets him feel right about the choices he makes. As the interrogation progresses, we need to convince him that the values on which he's been raised are misguided. This involves gaining the subject's trust. The longer he remains in captivity, the more he naturally will come around to our way of thinking. In this sense, time works to our benefit. Even once the first phase of the interrogation is finished—once it seems that we've gotten everything he knows—the process should continue for at least six months. We must remain in a position to catch anything else that happens to shake loose."

Zattout's pretense of cooperation, he suggested, should be met with concrete rewards. Only then would the subject learn to expect further rewards following further cooperation. Offering the man a nightly glass of wine might be a good start, compensating Zattout for his assistance while loosening his tongue. . . .

Warren's mouth was tugging into a frown. "Wine," he repeated.

"He's role adaptive—able to align himself with a new situation easily. We should take advantage of this natural tendency to conform by making his new situation as pleasant as possible. Furthermore, he's an externalizer. As such he should become talkative with the consumption of alcohol."

He proceeded to explain the Personality Assessment System, developed by Dr. John Gittinger in Norman, Oklahoma, during the 1940s. Tramps and vagrants on their way to California frequently had managed to get themselves admitted to Gittinger's hospital during frigid winters. He had used the opportunity to run psychological tests on these "seasonal schizophrenics," many of whom had worked as short-order cooks or dishwashers before the cold weather drove them to feign mental illness.

Soon Gittinger had seen trends emerging in his data. The short-order cooks demonstrated a talent for remembering numbers, the better to keep track of multiple orders behind the grill. But the dishwashers fared poorly with the digit-span subtest of the Wechsler IQ test. They were better suited to work that could be done alone in a corner, removed from hubbub and distractions.

These observations had become the foundation for the PAS. The short-order cooks were *internalizers,* Gittinger proposed, who could turn within themselves and block out commotion. The dishwashers were externalizers, too concerned with outside stimuli to manage the trick.

As the system developed, other personality distinctions revealed themselves. The block design subtest could be used to define a man as a regulated personality or a flexible one. The regulated person was able to learn tasks easily, but did not understand the task he had learned; he simply executed it. The flexible person was unable to learn a task without first comprehending the various ins and outs.

Observation proved that internalizers tended to withdraw after consuming alcohol; externalizers became more animated and garrulous. And so a man's reaction to drink could be anticipated simply by a study of his performance on the digit-span subtest. The system worked both ways—one could observe a man's behavior after a few drinks and then categorize him with the PAS, anticipating his ability or lack thereof to remember strings of digits.

Warren looked dubious. "You recommend rewarding the subject, Doctor. Yet you've made it clear that in your opinion he's already withholding information—concerning his knowledge of sleeper cells, at the least."

"Zattout isn't stupid. He understands, in his conscious mind, that we are not his friends. So it's hardly surprising that we see some evidence of withholding information. As I said, his entire life has reinforced certain values. Those values are not going to go out the window overnight. You might take some satisfaction, Mr. Warren, from the fact that he's clearly not here as a double agent. If he wanted to provide us with disinformation, he would be considerably more generous with his lies."

"But the fact remains—he is lying, at least by omission."

"To press the issue now is to risk a confrontation. And that would put an end to the trust-gaining part of the cycle. We must show him a way to proceed, and then guide him along it."

"Hypnosis?" Warren said.

"A man cannot be hypnotized against his will. We can increase his suggestibility, to help him attain a state of self-hypnosis. But we must keep in mind that we are allowing a natural desire—the desire to cooperate, to end the interrogation—to come to full fruition."

"Why stop at wine?" Warren said. "Why not a fine cigar? Maybe a visit to a spa."

"I don't like him any more than you do," Finney said tartly. "But do you want revenge, or results?"

"I'm not convinced we wouldn't make faster progress using more aggressive methods."

"When a man is subjected to pain, he'll say anything to make the pain stop. What he says does not necessarily bear any relation to the truth."

"And if we hit a dead end," Warren said. "What then?"

Finney paused.

"Then," he allowed, "we may indeed need to explore more aggressive methods."

"Such as?"

"A worst-case scenario: he withholds completely. Our efforts to develop trust are dashed. Then we might try to access the contents of his mind without his cooperation. But there's no guarantee of results."

"How would we go about that?"

Again, Finney hesitated.

"If coercive techniques fail," he said slowly, "we might consider the implementation of a depatterning strategy. The subject is reduced to an essentially vegetable state, using electroconvulsive shock, sleep deprivation, sensory isolation. Once fully depatterned, he is unable to feed himself; he becomes incontinent; he is unable to state his name or the date. Then we begin to rebuild. The process is called *psychic driving*. But it's hardly an exact science. Far better to secure the man's cooperation, if possible. To work with him, instead of against him."

Warren's frown remained. He did not want to hear

that there was no easy solution, of course. He wanted Finney to wave a magic wand of psychoanalysis and deliver Zattout's full cooperation on a plate. But that was not the way things worked; and torture could lead them only so far.

For the moment, the case officer didn't argue. He looked at his notebook and wrote something down. "Well," he said. "Looks like we've got our work cut out for tomorrow. Let's call it a day."

Finney closed his own pad with some relief. He had been up late the night before, parsing the results of Zattout's Wechsler test. His cold was not only lurking but gaining ground. If he pushed too hard, he would be of no use to anyone.

Yet once in his bedroom, he wasted five minutes looking absently out the window. At last something brought him back to reality: the mournful hoot of a train whistle, from far down in the valley. *The loneliest sound in the world,* his father had called it.

He glanced at the photograph of Lila, her sparkling green eyes competing with—and defeating—the water over her shoulder.

He yawned. Then stood, and went to the bathroom to conduct his nightly ablutions.

AS THE TRAIN whistle receded, the assassin emerged from the forest behind the Sleepy Hollow motel.

He was careful to give the front office a wide berth. Through the window he could see the girl's mother talking on the phone, her voice loud enough to penetrate the glass. "The last straw," she said archly. "It's that Batterberry boy, Tina, I just know it . . ."

In the room he washed his hands and face. He changed his clothes and packed his bag. Then he sat on the floor, cross-legged, and meditated.

Three hours later, he stood. He cracked his spine, neck, and shoulders. His forearms were beginning to burn. He had dug the grave by hand, using a flat rock as a shovel.

At a few minutes past midnight he left the room for the last time. Soon he was on the highway, heading east. Then he turned south, in the direction of New York City.

His return to the city was slightly ahead of schedule. But circumstance had forced his hand. The shallow grave might keep the girl hidden for a day or two—but by the time she was found, he needed to be gone.

It was acceptable. He'd accomplished enough reconnaissance to put his mind at ease. And his presence in the city would afford him an opportunity to visit the mechanic, encouraging the man to deliver on his promises.

At 3:05 on the morning of April 18, the blue coupe pulled into the parking lot of a supermarket. The assassin gathered his belongings and made a quick pass at the car under the sodium lights, removing fingerprints. Then he began to walk.

By the time he reached the Arlington Motel, it was nearly four A.M. The motel was similar to a half dozen others lining the block: dingy and unassuming, with two letters in the neon VACANCY sign winking on and off. The main office was dark. He approached the night window, rang a bell, and waited. Presently a man shuffled to the window, bleary-eyed and bed-headed, wearing a T-shirt and sweatpants.

When the assassin stepped into his new room, the sun was on the verge of rising.

He showered, then set up his laptop on a desk that seemed last to have been cleaned at the turn of the century. He composed a brief letter and addressed an envelope to Miriam Lane, at number sixty-two Sycamore Drive.

He shut down the computer and went to lie on the bed. He closed his eyes, and for ten hours slept a deep, dreamless sleep.

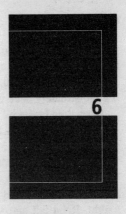

6

WHEN HE WOKE, every joint and tendon throbbed from the exertion of digging the grave.

He showered again—more conscious of his surroundings now than he had been the night before. The bathroom was coated with gray scum and black mildew. Despite the grime he stayed in the shower for nearly twenty minutes, letting the water pound the ache out of his muscles.

By the time he had dressed, his watch read six o'clock: too late to visit the garage. He ventured out anyway, dropping the letter in a mailbox and then taking a walk. The neighborhood featured bodegas, fried chicken outfits with hand-lettered signs in their windows, diners specializing in Spanish cuisine. He was tempted to sit down in one of these diners and buy a meal. Even a few pleasant words exchanged with a waitress might make him feel less dark inside. But lingering in public seemed unwise. He ordered his dinner to go, then brought it back to the room and ate alone, flicking from one weather report to another.

Following the meal, he surprised himself by crawling immediately back into bed.

For a time he stared at the ceiling. A traffic light outside the motel played a light show: red and green, yellow and black.

The girl had reminded him of Rana.

It was true; there was no denying it. Sonya had been fair, where Rana had been dark—Sonya of average height, Rana tall and slender. Yet beneath the surface, something in the girls had struck the same chord inside him. Both had been spirited and rebellious; neither had accepted the rules foisted on her by her parents.

By now Rana Shaykh would be a woman, not a girl. He tried to picture what she might look like. No longer coltish; she would have grown into her legs. But her hair still would be long, still so black that a man felt himself falling into an abyss whenever he looked at it.

Had she married? The last time he'd seen her, she had been engaged. The engagement had happened during her thirteenth year. She'd gone *dabke* dancing with friends, and caught the eye of the derbake player—a village elder with a traditional drum of clay and goat skin. After the dance, the old man had approached her mother and asked for Rana's hand. Her mother had agreed, thinking the engagement offered a chance to remove her daughter from the cinderblock camp in which she'd grown up. But to Rana it simply had offered a different kind of dead end.

I won't marry him, she said firmly.

They were sitting in a lot behind her school, among

the stench of garbage and sewage. From a nearby playground came the singsong chant of playing children: *Sukkar, mukkar, la la la,* delivered without tangible enthusiasm.

At that point, the assassin's parents had been dead for only two years. He had been on his own for only half that time. He had not learned to harden his heart, to be skeptical. He had believed Rana when she continued: *I'm going to run away. In the West, children play all day. They do nothing but play.*

Now he was older, and wiser. Now he knew that Rana must have married the man, despite her protests. It was her only way out, although she hadn't wanted to accept that fact at the time. Why did he even think of it? It had been so long ago . . . she wouldn't even remember him.

The traffic lights played: ladybugs and yellow jackets.

Someone was in the bed beside him.

Are you cold?

A little.

Sonya Jacobs, he thought. Not the girl herself, but her revenant.

She was cold as ice. She had been in the ground for hardly twenty-four hours, but already maggots had grown in her softest spots: eyes, ears, beneath her arms, in her genitalia. Her breath smelled of worms and rot. He could hear the insects that had nested inside her body, preening.

She giggled.

I'm sorry, she said. *I don't know what's wrong with me.*

He closed his eyes. He breathed. When he looked over again, the girl was gone.

In the morning he would go to the garage. He concentrated on that—on work still to be done.

In the morning.

Let it be morning.

ANOTHER SCALDING-HOT SHOWER. Then he headed east, into a neighborhood even more marginal than that of his new motel.

He passed an off-track betting parlor, a vacant lot, a pizzeria with the windows blacked out. Farther on was a weed-choked schoolyard; then an industrial laundry, a warehouse, a store advertising adult novelties and magazines. Fossilized hulks of cars were parked up and down the avenue, balanced on wheel rims and axles.

As he approached the garage, broken glass crunched underfoot. On one side of the building was a storefront reading CHECKS CASHED. On the other, ACE STORAGE. On the garage itself: GOLDEN STAR MOTORS. Parked out front was a lovingly restored 1965 Ford Mustang, incongruously pristine against the ashy surroundings.

Behind the desk in the front office stood an obese man looking over a clipboard. When the bell on the door chimed, he glanced up. "Help you?"

"Is Sal here?"

"Sal!" the man thundered, and returned his eyes to the clipboard.

A few moments passed. Through an open door behind the desk, a radio played tinny Spanish pop music.

The assassin sank into a plastic chair. Stacks of magazines and newspapers rested on a low table to his left. He looked at them, then looked away. He looked back, pulled the *Times* free, and scanned the front page. In the bottom right corner was a headline that caught his eye: "Search Effort Upstate Fails to Find Missing Teenager."

He wet his lips, and bent closer to the page.

An ongoing search has turned up no trace of the teenaged girl who vanished Tuesday night from the small Catskills motel owned by her parents. Officials insist they have not given up hope that Sonya Jacobs, 16, will be found, even as they acknowledged disappointment at the lack of results.

As helicopters, search parties, and bloodhounds combed the woods behind this sleepy mountain retreat, police today released a description of—

"You rang?" a voice said.

The voice belonged to Sal Santiori—a few inches over six feet, a few dozen pounds over two hundred. His clear blue eyes betrayed no sign of recognition.

The assassin set down the newspaper. "I was here a few weeks ago," he said. "The Honda?"

Sal snapped his fingers. "Right. Come into my office."

His office was a corner of the garage visible through the open door behind the desk. A centerfold hung on the wall, above a cup filled with tobacco-browned saliva. Sal flipped through some papers stacked on an engine block. "Honda," he said. "Honda, Honda. Right. The custom job. I sent it out to a friend of mine on the island. . . . Here it is. He says my estimate was a little low."

The assassin waited.

"What did we say—seven hundred? I was three hundred short, he says. So we're talking about a thousand."

"When can I expect it?"

"If I get half the three hundred in cash today— middle of next week?"

He nodded.

"Come into my office," Sal said again.

This time his office was the front office. The obese man had vanished. Sal moved behind the cash register and punched a button. The drawer shot out. "One-fifty."

He accepted three fifty-dollar bills, held them to the light, then marked them with a felt-tip pen and deposited them beneath the tray in the register drawer. "Try me on Wednesday," he said, "and we'll see where we're at."

One week from today. *Delays,* he thought. But would he gain anything by arguing? Doubtful.

"Long as you're here . . ." Sal reached beneath the desk and produced a small spray can. The label read, "Photo Fog: Anti-Flash Photo-Radar Spray."

"Twenty-nine ninety-five. Only takes thirty seconds to spray onto your plates. Invisible to the naked eye. But any camera using a flash can't get your digits; it reflects the light right back. Now here's the beauty part. It's one hundred percent legal."

"I don't need it. But thank you."

"Whatever you say." The spray can disappeared. "So, Wednesday."

"Wednesday."

Sal grinned, showing small uneven teeth like a piranha's. "Pleasure doing business," he said.

ON THE WAY BACK to the Arlington Motel, he stopped at a bodega and bought a newspaper. When he reached the room, he locked the door, moved to the bed, and spread it open.

Police today released a description of a man who was seen with Miss Jacobs shortly before her disappearance. The man they seek is between twenty-five and forty years of age, light-complexioned, with a slight build and no visible scars. A police spokesman said that further details might be released as the investigation progresses.

"If anybody knows where our little girl is," Dorothy Jacobs, Sonya's mother, pleaded this morning, "we ask that they come forward. She never hurt anybody. All we want is to see her again."

Scores of local residents volunteered to join the search, but as this edition went to press the police—

He folded the paper.

The coupe had been abandoned and wiped clean. The identity he had been using no longer existed. The description of him—if it was all they had—was generic and vague. They could not trace him.

But what if the men in the safe house somehow made a connection, between him and the dead girl and Zattout?

The thought was vexing. His breed were silent, unknown, unexpected. If the enemy knew his face, perhaps he needed to reconsider moving ahead at all.

He sat cross-legged on the floor. He exhaled, emptying his lungs, then deliberately refilled them. He repeated this exercise seventy-nine times. On the eighty-first exhalation, he left his lungs empty.

He lowered his chin until it touched his chest, and diagnosed the balance of energy within his body. The path was open: from palate to pulmonary artery, from diaphragm to solar plexus to navel to genitals. Satisfied, he began to breathe again.

He adjusted his position on the carpet, straightening his legs, and leaned forward until his forehead touched his knees. He counted, nine nines. Now the best path to pursue would show itself to him, if only he made himself receptive.

The answer rose from his subconscious like a dreamy spark rising from a crackling fire:

The man on the inside. Quinlan.

If a problem had developed—if they had connected him with the girl, and become aware of him within the safe house—then Quinlan would make a report of it.

He lifted his forehead from his knees, considering. The post office box to which Quinlan sent his intelligence was known to him. The knowledge had come from the first man he had killed, who had spoken at some length before the assassin gave him the mercy of death. That man, Talamous Wahab, had provided information regarding the others associated with the Zattout endeavor: the names, the roles played by each, the methods of communication. Wahab had spoken eagerly, seeming to believe that enough cooperation might somehow save his life. He had not been able to fathom that the assassin—whom he first had met weeks before under polite circumstances—would turn on him so ruthlessly.

Wahab had made a fatal error in judgment. The assassin had no allegiance to these men, nor to their cause. All were tracks that needed to be covered. All except Ajami, who needed to be left alive to arrange the transfer of funds once it was done.

If the death of the girl had compromised the operation, the mole would report it. He would wait a few days and then check the box himself, availing himself of its contents before Ajami ever picked up the letter.

He cracked his neck, his shoulders, his wrists, his knees, his ankles. Now that he had a plan of action, he felt calmer. He found his tunic and donned it, then slipped one of the tools sewn into the right sleeve out into his hand. The concealed tools served a dual purpose. Together, still in the sleeve, they could block a blow, frustrating an attack made by hand or knife. Alone, they fulfilled different needs.

He raised the lock pick he had withdrawn, inspected the soft curve of metal, then returned it to the sleeve with a flick of his wrist.

They had not made the connection, he thought. The men in the safe house would have no reason to pay attention to the disappearance of a girl from a town thirty miles farther down the highway.

But it always was best to err on the side of caution.

MUHAMMAD NASSIF leaned back in the doorway of the coffee shop, trying to suppress a murmur of paranoia.

For five minutes he watched the entrance of the post office with bloodshot eyes. He saw nothing out of the ordinary—and yet the apprehension remained. This would teach him to give in to peer pressure, he thought. This would teach him to act like a child.

Earlier that afternoon he had let himself be convinced to share a joint with two friends from the Queens Bridge Locals. Had he refused to partake, they would have wondered why; so he had taken three hits, being careful not to inhale too deeply. The weed had left him with a dull headache and a fuzzy, insistent sense of unease. Now he found himself here, hunched into the doorway and watching the post office, for reasons he couldn't quite articulate. Just to be sure, he thought. But sure of what, exactly?

After five minutes he pushed out of the doorway and crossed the street, trying not to look like a fugitive as he stepped into the post office.

The place was nearly empty. It felt like a fishbowl, or—more accurately—like a giant empty swimming pool. As he approached the row of P.O. boxes, he felt as if he were walking down a diving board. He slipped the key into the lock, turned it, and saw that the box was empty.

The key went back into his pocket. He spun on his heel and headed for the door. How were the fluorescents so damned bright? The phenomenon was absorbing, uncanny; he walked with his head tilted back, drinking in the light.

When he collided with the woman, his paranoia rose again in a rush.

"Whoa there," she said. "Watch it."

He looked into her face and saw kindly crinkles around the eyes. She was somewhere in her thirties, wearing a postal worker's uniform. A name tag pinned above her left breast identified her as Rose.

"Sorry," he mumbled, and tried to step around her; but she was stepping in the same direction. For a few seconds they bumbled back and forth like characters from a vaudeville sketch. Then he darted to the right, slipping past her. As he left the building, left the fish-bowl, he could feel her eyes on his back. Watching him.

On the street, the paranoia remained. He threw a quick glance over his shoulder. Had Rose followed? No. But a man was there, short, wearing black. The man wasn't looking at him. He was looking through the window of the coffee shop, seemingly intrigued by the menu taped to the glass.

Nassif faced front again. He put on his headphones and switched on the Discman at his waist. Five minutes later he was descending into a subway station. Two minutes after that he was stepping onto a train, lost in the pulse of music, oblivious to the fact that the small man in black was stepping into the next car, a mere dozen feet away.

THE PARANOIA LEFT HIM alone until the moment he was fitting his key into the lock of his front door. Then it returned with a vengeance.

Something was wrong.

He switched off the Discman and lowered the head-phones around his neck. He listened: to the sound of a radiator clacking, to a mid-afternoon cartoon playing in a nearby apartment, to the slow distant thud of helicop-ter blades outside.

The dope, he thought. Why had he smoked it? Now, of all times, when he needed to be ready for any-thing. . . .

He raised the key again and twisted it.

The apartment was empty, and overly warm. He set down his backpack inside the front door. Sometimes, when he stepped through that door, he felt a sensation of coming home. But not this time. This time the apartment felt as it did when he was at his unhappiest—like a temporary way station, a place he and his mother had ended up entirely by accident. This place was not home. It never could be *home*. Home would be Mecca, the place that harbored their roots.

Yet even this thought, at the moment, did not ring true. At the moment the truth seemed to be that he was caught between two worlds, living in neither.

He missed Lisa.

It would have been nice to be with her, this afternoon. To go into his bedroom and lock the door, the way they had so many times over the fall and winter. To lie on his bed, listening to music, cuddling and touching as she pushed his hand away. Each time she'd pushed, she had done so with less force. Eventually her giggles had thickened, as her breathing had slowed. If they hadn't broken up, by now he would have gotten to third base at least.

But he had made his choices. He was a part of something bigger now. And soldiers like himself had to do without the comforts of women.

The paranoia was shading to depression. He gave his head a small shake, and moved deeper into the apartment.

In the kitchen he poured himself a glass of orange juice. He drank it leaning against the counter, feeling the liquid slosh uncomfortably in his stomach. Then he rinsed the glass and went to his room. He returned the P.O. box key to its drawer and sat down on his bed.

The feeling occurred again: Someone was watching him.

He looked at the cracked-open door of his closet. Was that where the eyes were? Or were they under the bed? Or hovering outside his window, belonging to a ghoul unhindered by the laws of gravity?

It was only the weed.

But his eyes stayed locked on the closet door. Suddenly he felt he could sense a monster there, more clearly than he had since the days of his early childhood. It was a man, and yet not a man. It was low to the ground and its eyes rolled as they followed him—even as he stood, taking a step toward the closet door, moving in slow motion, back in the swimming pool now, a swimming pool filled with black water. The eyes rolled and the fetid breath hissed over sharp curved teeth. . . .

He pulled the door open.

A football. A skateboard. A winter coat. A jumble of old comic books, tapes, and baseball caps.

No monster.

His mouth twisted.

This was the last time he would let himself be pressed into smoking anything. Let his friends notice that he had changed; let them think what they liked. He would not open himself to a repeat of this experience. Already his fear was turning to embarrassment.

He shut the closet door.

FOR SIX HOURS the assassin sat motionless.

The boy was puttering around his room—doing homework, talking briefly on the telephone, executing a series of lazy push-ups. As afternoon turned to evening, a woman entered the apartment. His mother, from the look of it. They dined together at a small table in the kitchen. Then she watched television in the living room; the boy returned to his bedroom. He did more homework, then sat before his computer. Yet he did not return to the dresser drawer, the one into which he had placed the key.

Who was he?

The assassin sat cross-legged on the roof across the way, and wondered.

At half past ten, lights began to wink off throughout the building. The mother stayed awake for another hour, watching the monologue of a late-night talk show. The boy stayed awake for another hour after that, still at his computer. Sometime past twelve-thirty, he stripped to boxer shorts. He vanished into a bathroom, then reappeared with his hair standing on end. He spent ten minutes reading a comic book in bed, and switched off the light.

Still the assassin waited.

At last he left his position. His six-hour surveillance had been prefaced by a two-hour reconnaissance of the post office; he felt tired, hungry, and out of sorts. But he rolled his head on his neck, rotating his wrists until they cracked, and then pressed himself into action.

He descended the fire escape and crossed around to the front of the tenement. He reached into the right sleeve of his tunic, withdrawing the slim lock pick. Then entered a foyer papered with take-out menus and smelling of Chinese food.

Four flights brought him to the door that should have

corresponded to the apartment. He paused, listening. The apartment was quiet. The door had three locks. He raised the pick.

Before entering, he returned the tool to his sleeve and slipped out a blade to replace it.

Silently he opened the door. Then dissolved forward, into the darkness. Before him was a kitchen rustling with mice. On his right, the boy's bedroom. He stepped into it, then paused again to listen. The boy was sleeping, his breathing even and regular. The curtains on the window were open, letting in the unnatural light of the city sky at night.

He crossed the room lightly, on the balls of his feet, and opened the drawer where he had seen the boy put the key. After a moment he found it.

So Ajami had tapped this youth to check the box, instead of doing it himself. Why the added layer of caution now? Had something gone wrong? Had they made a connection with the dead girl?

And more to the immediate point: What was to be done about it?

The boy complicated things. Leaving him alive would take control away from the assassin. Was he to spend every moment at the post office, making certain that he gained access to the box before the boy came to check it? He would be noticed. Was he to come to this room every night and conduct a search, to see if the boy had retrieved a message? An unnecessary risk. Besides, a message might be picked up and sent along to Ajami on the same day.

But taking the boy's life might cause problems of its own. The assassin did not know the child's relationship to Ajami, nor the role he was playing. The boy was an unknown quantity.

He disliked unknown quantities.

He made a decision. He would take the key for himself and remove the unknown quantity from the equation. Problems might result, but he would remain in control. He would have the key.

Once the decision had been made, he pocketed the key and closed the drawer. He turned and approached the bed.

As he reached forward, the boy's eyes opened.

The expression on his face was peculiar. He did not look surprised.

For several seconds, their eyes locked.

Then the assassin reached forward, gently covering the nose and mouth with one gloved hand.

ALI ZATTOUT MOVED the glass beneath his nose, inhaling the bouquet. He sipped, rolled the wine around in his mouth, and swallowed. "Taste that?" he asked.

Quinlan arched an eyebrow.

"The hint of *brett*," Zattout elaborated. "A wild yeast, often found in Burgundies. Some sommeliers won't put up with it. But just a touch of it . . . as we have here . . . adds complexity."

For a few moments, they tasted their wine in silence. Zattout's demeanor was more relaxed than at any time Finney had seen him previously. Because they were not interrogating him, for a change. They were simply rewarding him—sharing this excellent bottle of wine, with no questions being put forth.

When the wine had been offered, Zattout had not reacted with enthusiasm. His brow had beetled, beneath the unforgiving light in the cell; a thin sweat had appeared in the hollow of his collarbone. He'd thought it was a trick. But he couldn't figure out just what the trick was. Until Quinlan had consumed the wine himself, Zattout had refused to sample it. Then he'd raised his own glass, suspiciously.

Now, only a few sips later, the alcohol was taking visible effect. The primarily monosyllabic prisoner Finney had observed until now was gone. This was a man who knew wine, and who enjoyed it.

He was drawing Quinlan's attention to the full-bodied robustness. Interesting, Finney thought, that Zattout was so knowledgeable on the subject. Had he been the devout Muslim he often had claimed to be, in his previous life, he would have abstained from alcohol altogether. Clearly, the opposite was true. Since his capture he had not requested a prayer mat or even a copy of the Koran; but he discussed the subtleties of Burgundies with a brio that could come only from experience.

There was a story—probably apocryphal—that enjoyed unfailing popularity among terrorist hunters within the U.S. intelligence community. In the months leading up to the First World War, U.S. forces in the Philippines had been the target of several attacks by extremist Muslim factions. General Black Jack Pershing's response had been to round up fifty suspected terrorists and tie them to posts. Two pigs had been butchered in front of the helpless prisoners. To devout Muslims, pigs are filthy creatures; being exposed to their blood is to be denied entrance to paradise. As the prisoners watched, forty-nine bullets were soaked in the blood of the swine.

These bullets were used to execute forty-nine of the men. Pershing's soldiers dug a hole, and upon the bodies of the prisoners dumped pig flesh, offal, and entrails. The fiftieth man then was released. And for forty-two years, the tellers of the tale concluded, there had not been a single attack anywhere in the world made by a Muslim extremist.

Even if the line of thought was worth pursuing—and Finney had his doubts that it was—Zattout obviously would not be susceptible to such tactics. He continued to declaim about the wine, even as Quinlan struggled to change the topic.

What Quinlan wanted to discuss was al Masada, the Lion's Den. Zattout looked dismayed at the potential detour. Nothing would come for free, he was realizing. But dutifully he answered: describing how the small group of men who had come together there had gone on to form the pillars of an international terrorist organization. These bin Laden loyalists had scattered to Spain, Germany, Bosnia, Saudi Arabia, and the United States. They had planted the seeds of al Qaeda sleeper cells even as bin Laden had devoted himself—and his family construction business—to the creation of a system of underground tunnels beneath the mountains of Jaji.

In any event, Zattout said, hadn't they spent enough time on the subject for one day? To return to the wine . . .

Quinlan acquiesced. For several minutes, Zattout held forth on the topic. Quinlan listened graciously— then, when Zattout paused to breathe, quickly returned to the subject of the loyalists who had scattered to the corners of the earth, to establish sleeper cells. He wondered aloud if there were any specific cells that Zattout, for whatever reason, had neglected to mention.

Zattout looked to his right, toward his strong hand. No, he said after a moment. Upon the subject of sleeper cells, he had told them everything he knew.

But he couldn't speak of it anymore—not without a break. Wine such as this, Zattout explained, was not to be quaffed but savored. . . .

IN ONE CORNER of the living room, Finney had found a shabby recliner. He'd made a habit of coming to it after the interrogation sessions, to pore over his notes in private.

As expected, the wine had loosened Zattout's tongue. Yet Quinlan had failed to skew the conversation in a direction that would benefit them. In the future, a more concrete set of questions should be planned in advance—

When Thomas Warren II stepped into the doorway, something in his body language set Finney immediately on guard.

Noble had taken a turn for the worse, he thought. Perhaps he already was dead. And so Finney had let his last chance to offer forgiveness slip away. No doubt a bigger man would have found the grace within himself to put aside old grievances, at the end, and visit the man's deathbed. But evidently he was not a bigger man.

Warren pressed his lips together. Finney had known he would press his lips together, just that way. He had been here before, perhaps in a dream. He could anticipate the words that were about to be spoken. *I'm afraid I've got some bad news,* Warren would start.

"I'm afraid I've got some bad news," Warren said. *I've just gotten off the phone with the hospital . . .*

But what he said was: "An emergency's come up. Quinlan and I are going to need to go down to Langley. Immediately." A measured pause. "I'd like you to fill in with Zattout in our absence."

Finney said nothing.

"I'm aware that it's not what you signed on for." Warren's voice was reasonable, pitched low. "I'm also aware that we run the risk of setting ourselves back, by changing interrogators. Yet it can't be helped. If we're forced to start with someone new, we'll be set back even further. But you, Doctor, are familiar with the case. And it's only until we return . . ."

He looked at Finney. A bright challenge in his eyes belied the studied evenness of his voice.

"Take a few minutes to think about it," he said, generously.

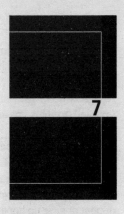

7

TWELVE HOURS after securing Finney's commitment, Thomas Warren II was stepping into the main lobby of CIA headquarters in Langley, Virginia.

As his identification was checked, he found himself looking at the statue of Wild Bill Donovan standing against the lobby's left wall. Donovan had been the director of the CIA's forerunner, the OSS. The statue portrayed him with one thumb hooked jauntily through a loop of his belt, every inch the cowboy. The biblical inscription beside the statue read: *And you shall know the truth and the truth shall make you free.*

He rode the elevator to the seventh floor, then stepped through a door labeled 7d70—director of central intelligence. He passed through another security detail and entered the wood-paneled office of the DCI. The director was standing by an immense polished conference table. Through a window over his shoulder, sunlight danced brightly across the Potomac.

At Warren's entrance, he turned. His only greeting was a curt wave at a chair.

Warren sat, took a deep breath, and then delivered his report as he had rehearsed in the Town Car. The words tumbled from his lips as he tried to get it all out before the DCI could interrupt. Conversations with the director, Warren had discovered, tended to go best when one secured an early lead. If the man saw a chance to assume control, he wouldn't hesitate. Then, operating from a position of power, he would press his advantage until his opponent gave up hope of anything except full surrender.

As Warren spoke, a furrow appeared on the DCI's brow. He pressed on, striving to find optimistic phrasing. The mole within their ranks had been identified. At this very moment Quinlan was undergoing interrogation in a Maryland safe house. This seeming setback might in fact be a golden opportunity. The thing to focus on was not the past but the—

"You're using the specialist?" the DCI interrupted.

Warren nodded. Did the director seem displeased at that decision? Did he consider the use of the specialist overly harsh? He explained—although the DCI knew it full well—that they had no other choice. Polygraphs, instead of detecting lies, detected only changes in heart rate, breathing, and voice steadiness. A knowledgeable man who took the time to train himself could control his physiological responses and deceive the apparatus. Joseph Quinlan, who had received polygraph training from the agency itself, certainly qualified as a knowledgeable man. The usual manipulations that formed the bedrock of agency interrogation strategies would be worthless against a subject who had spent decades mastering them from the other side. So a more aggressive approach was required.

When the tumble of words had finished, the sudden silence felt daunting. The furrow remained on the DCI's brow. "How the hell did this happen?" he asked at last. He seemed to be speaking mostly to himself; his eyes, behind thick lenses, were turned inward. "How the hell did we let this happen?"

He meant the question rhetorically. Warren said nothing.

Then it was the DCI's turn. A lot of people had shown a lot of good faith, he said, in keeping their relative distance from the Zattout interrogation. The FBI, Defense, INS, Customs—all would have liked to have had a hand in the operation code-named KINGFISHER. But too many chefs spoiled the broth, so they had agreed to keep away. Now, however, when it came out that Warren had fouled up—that he'd allowed a mole in his midst to compromise the operation, right under his nose— these people would not be pleased.

At the phrase "fouled up," Warren bristled. "We've been making progress with Zattout," he said defensively. "And the leak hasn't been too severe. Two letters over two weeks. It's not the end of the world."

Furthermore, any information that Quinlan had leaked *before* he was under Warren's authority was certainly no fault of Warren's. For a moment, he let the implication hang in the air. Two could play at the DCI's game; fingers could point both ways. He would not take the entire blame for Quinlan's treachery. And if it wasn't all his fault, then whose fault was it? The director of counterintelligence's, whose job was to ferret out moles? Or might it go higher—all the way to the DCI himself?

"I'd hate to see this end up in the papers," Warren tossed in ingenuously . . .

. . . but hope was far from lost. They still could turn this situation to their advantage. Whatever cell Quinlan had been communicating with could be identified, then, in one way or another, used to disseminate false intelligence straight to the upper ranks of al Qaeda.

The first step would be understanding what had happened, and how, and why. From a review of Quinlan's file, Warren already had come up with several promising speculations.

Seven years before, he reported, Quinlan had gone through a rough divorce. In the time since, there had been a handful of cocktail parties at which he had imbibed irresponsibly and said too much about his work. Eventually, someone at the agency had suggested that Quinlan no longer deserved his top secret security clearance. Then the interrogator had faced a battery of polygraphs and personality tests. In the end, he had run the gamut successfully and retained his clearance. But his callous treatment at the hands of the agency—for that, Warren gathered, was how he perceived it—had added insult to injury. His disenchantment with life had begun to turn into disenchantment with the CIA.

How and when he'd made contact with al Qaeda remained a mystery. But even on this point, Warren could supply a possible answer. With his top secret clearance, Quinlan had enjoyed access to documents concerning mosques, educational organizations, and charities under investigation. By visiting these places on his own time, he might have been able to forge links to al Qaeda. In the near future, Warren would be able to offer more than guesses. The specialist would get answers straight from the horse's mouth.

The DCI looked at him deliberately.

"I would be less concerned," he said, "if I had a concrete idea of how much damage has been done."

Warren rearranged himself in the chair. He gave his reasons for thinking that the damage—at least, the damage that had occurred on his watch—had not been extraordinary.

Once each week for the past fortnight, Quinlan had taken an evening away from the compound. His routine never varied: parking at one end of Main Street, taking a leisurely stroll, then having dinner at the town's sole restaurant, a nice break from the camp food. On the way back to his car, following dinner each week, he dropped off a letter in a mailbox. Mailing the letters was a breach of protocol—while involved with the operation, all correspondence with the outside world should have been vetted with Warren before being sent.

Quinlan had not made any special effort to hide his letter-mailing, but nor had he made a point of reporting it. If Warren had not taken the precaution of having the man followed during his excursions into town, they never would have heard of the letters at all.

He paused, letting it sink in that he *had* been cautious; he had covered his bases; and thanks to his foresight, the problem had been identified before it had gone too far.

The director hardly looked impressed. He folded his hands, tipping his chin down. "But you didn't approach Quinlan himself."

"After looking at the letter, I thought I could see why he hadn't run it past me. There was some pretty personal stuff."

"So you let it go."

"I sent it along. After making a copy for my records."

"Go on."

"Second time—same story. Something wasn't feeling right, but I couldn't find anything classified; so I sent it along. Third time, I decided better safe than sorry."

"Do you have the letters with you?"

Warren reached into his folder, passed the letters across the desk, and then watched as the DCI read the most recent:

April 15

Dear Alexandra,

In the past week I've given some further thought to the questions we discussed before I left. Bankruptcy or estate planning or criminal law—after all this time, you have no clearer idea of what you want to do with your life? The question is not which field of law suits you best, but why, at this age, you still don't know the answer to that question yourself. I'm afraid I see the same old pattern developing here. If I make what we both admit is a risky speculation, you will drop everything; yet you don't even have enough control of your life, nor enough confidence in yourself, to know what branch of law interests you most. If you are asking for my advice, it is simply to look more honestly within yourself, and not turn to others to make your tough decisions for you.

At some point down the line I might be able to afford to keep an apartment in the city and also get a house somewhere not so far away. I agree, it certainly would be a "very nice thing." But the prospect of two such considerable financial drains at once is troubling. Easier to contemplate such a "very nice thing," one suspects, if the proposed drains are not coming from your own bank account.

In all honesty I may be too focused on my own work now to give any relationship the attention it deserves. Beyond any doubt I have no interest in starting a family at any time in the immediate future. But I remain aware of your own concerns in that area, knowing that your age is a factor in any life-affecting decisions you make. I'm also aware we've discussed this already, but judging from your tone before I left, I thought the point bore repeating. I apologize if this sounds cold, as you've so often accused me of being. But better for us both to understand where we stand going into this. Honesty, I know, is the best policy.

For the time being I do not intend on making any major purchases. About the future, I remain undecided. In the meantime, there's no reason for fretting over a market budget or electric bills. I know your concentration is required for more important decisions. I've sent a letter to my business manager authorizing you to withdraw up to $11,500 from my account at JBA, number 540-677821-989.

In spite of many reservations I hope you're well, and

when my latest consultation is finished, I look forward to spending more time together.

Warmest regards,
Joseph

The DCI looked up. "And cryptanalysis said?"

"ARE YOU AT YOUR COMPUTER?" the analyst asked.

"Give me a second," Warren muttered.

He pulled himself out of bed—5:36 A.M. according to his clock radio; the sun just beginning to rise outside the window—and sat before his computer. From the kitchenette came the rancid odor of the milk he had poured down the sink the night before, upon arriving home after meeting with the DCI. The apartment had been empty for nearly six weeks; the spoiled milk had turned solid. Its stench hung on tenaciously, despite the gallons of water he had flushed down the drain trying to clear it.

"I'm sending you an e-mail," the analyst informed him, and a moment later it popped up in Warren's inbox.

He opened it. The e-mail read:

VENI VIDI VICI

Warren stared at it.

"I have to admit," the cryptanalyst said, "it took me a while." He sounded tired but satisfied. Clearly, he was not going to give Warren his conclusions right away. First he needed to describe the path he had followed, thereby securing admiration for the work he had done. It always was the way with technical people, Warren had noticed. They felt the need to lecture.

"I saw right away that there's a code here. Quite an ingenious little system, actually. No equipment required for encryption or decryption, nothing to memorize except a simple key phrase—in this case, VENI, VIDI, VICI. But it does require some trial-and-error work."

Warren kept looking at his computer screen, waiting.

"Each letter contains a string of digits, you realize. The bank-account number in the third, financial details in the second, credit card numbers in the first. The digit strings are the key to decoding. But it's clever. The key for the third lies in the second—do you have the letters in front of you?"

"Right here."

"You see the string of digits?"

Warren saw it. The second letter contained information about a lease negotiation with which Alexandra, it seemed, was involved.

"Take out the dollar signs, the decimal points; reduce it to a list of integers. You get the following."

He could hear the man's fingers on his computer keyboard, crackling like automatic weapon fire. Then a second e-mail appeared on the screen. Warren opened it to find himself facing a list of numbers. 512571023998 2292951, and more.

"Yes?" he said.

"Now look at the third letter. We start at the end. 'Warmest regards, Joseph.' Count back five letters—what do you get?"

Warren counted. "O," he said.

"Right. Next is 'one'—'J.' But if you go ahead and de-code straight, you get a result that makes only occasional sense. Trial and error reveals that some of the numbers are double digits. In fact, the second number is 'twelve'—if you count back, 'M.' I've gone through it all . . ."

More rapid-fire typing. Another e-mail. The man was still talking as Warren read it over.

"They've taken the trickiest letters—Q, J, and V—and replaced them with E, A, and Y. This means that E and A and Y each could stand for themselves, or for their substitutes. Again, only trial and error will tell. They went to a lot of trouble to avoid having Quinlan carry any kind of encryption device or codebook on his person. Eventually, when you apply the digits in letter two to the sentences in letter three, working backward and ignoring the sentence with the account number—that's a 'null' sentence, applying to the next message, not this one—you get . . ."

Warren read the e-mail. "OMQTRLF . . ."

"And so on. And there's your intelligence."

A moment passed.

"Say again?"

"Apply the key phrase to the letters."

Another moment.

"The key phrase," the analyst said. "Look . . ."

Another e-mail, similar to the first:

VENI VIDI VICI

But with the addition:

VENIDC

"You choose a key phrase that's easy to remember. Then you take out the repetition and spaces. Are you with me so far?"

"So far."

"This is your cipher key. Whoever is receiving these letters doesn't need a codebook any more than Quinlan does. All he needs is to know the key phrase. That gives the cipher key. In this case . . ."

A fifth e-mail. Warren read:

A B C D E F G H I J K L M N O P Q R S T U V W X Y Z
V E N I D C A B F G H J K L M O P Q R S T U V W X Y

"And there you have it," the analyst said. "Your digit string: in this case," and then after drawing a breath, "5125710—"

"Got it," Warren said. The numbers had appeared on his screen. 512571023998229295132402818864164516
933191245017203917142412317321725211216368.

"That yields the cipher text—"

Another burst of typographical machine-gun fire: OMQTRLFL JVLMIDNKSTMIBVSQNVQAJEVFRV JQSLNSLKOBRMILVB.

"Then, using your key phrase and some elbow grease, you get the plain text. Which looks like this." PORUSNINBLANODECMTUODHATRCARGLBAI SALRTNCTNMPHSODNAH.

Plain text, Warren thought. He had the beginning of a headache.

"Now it's easy," the cryptanalyst said. "Reverse it."

"Reverse it?"

"Look . . ."

More typing. Warren read: HANDOSHPMNTCN TRLASIABLGRACRTAHDOUTMCEDONALBINS UROP.

"Certain words suggest themselves, if you look closely. For example, a few characters in, there's the word 'shipment.'"

Warren scowled at the screen. SHPMNT, he saw.

"There are others in here, too. Take a gander."

The same text appeared, this time with spaces added. HANDO SHPMNT CNTRL ASIA BLGRA CRTA HD-OUT MCEDON ALBINS UROP.

"I'll tell you what I see," the analyst said. "Shipment. Central Asia. 'HDOUT' could be 'hideout.' 'HANDO,' I can't say . . ."

Suddenly Warren's throat felt as if it were coated with cotton.

"Not HANDO," he said. "H AND O."

Heroin and opium.

All at once he could see the meaning in the code—more clearly, even, than the cryptanalyst himself. H AND O SHIPMENT CENTRAL ASIA BULGARIA CROATIA HIDEOUT MACEDONIA ALBANIANS EUROPE.

The subjects covered during a recent period of Zattout's interrogation, he realized.

Sent off of safe house grounds.

Sent to Quinlan's girlfriend—or to whoever was collecting the letters from the post office box in lower Manhattan.

"Son of a bitch," he said.

* * *

THE DIRECTOR read the letter again.

"There is no girlfriend," Warren informed him. "The post office box is registered to an 'Alan Smith.' There is no Alan Smith, either. The letters must go straight to al Qaeda—telling them everything Zattout tells us."

The director reached up and massaged the ridge between his eyebrows. Warren rearranged himself in the chair again, waiting to hear the verdict.

"Whoever shows up to collect this letter," the director said, "is not to be apprehended."

Warren nodded.

"They're to be followed. I want to know who's in this cell; how they got onto Quinlan; how much he told them before we got onto him."

Warren noticed that "we." He didn't argue. He nodded again.

"I can't sit on this much longer. If the Bureau gets wind of a leak before we go public, someone's going to need to take the fall."

That someone, Warren understood, would be Warren himself. It was within his operation, after all, that the mole had been discovered. It was under his watch that security had been compromised.

"Give me a few days," he said evenly. "I'll turn this thing around."

The DCI leaned back in his chair. He sighed. "I hope you're right," he said. "For your sake, as much as mine."

Warren took the man's meaning. *For your sake,* he meant—and that was all.

"Use the brownstone on eleventh. Take Cass and Moore. Hoyle, too. They're good men. And they won't run their mouths off. We need to keep a tight lid on this."

"Understood."

"Fix this, Tommy. Fast."

Warren smiled blandly, picked up the report, and stood. "No problems," he said.

THE RAIN BEGAN at half past four.

As the assassin walked through the spring drizzle, pedestrians around him unrolled newspapers and magazines, tenting them over their heads while hurrying for subways and buses. Against the darkening sky, a faint rainbow arced over downtown skyscrapers.

He crossed the street, weaving between bumpers of stopped traffic, then paused before entering the post office, checking for surveillance. The street was crowded enough that he would have trouble picking out a surveillance team, if indeed one did exist. Perhaps he had waited until too late in the day to come check the box. But he had wanted to make certain the mail had a chance to get delivered before he visited, to avoid repeating the risk more often than necessary.

He picked out figures that were not moving, who might have been watching the post office. A Chinese woman with a clutch of cheap umbrellas, calling a strident sales pitch to passersby. A homeless man in a corrugated cardboard box that was rapidly becoming drenched. Another man sitting on a stoop, reading a newspaper and ignoring the rain. Yet another man, hunched in a doorway smoking a cigarette.

He registered them all—there was little else he could do without conducting a lengthy reconnaissance, and if he did that every time he checked the box, he would do more harm than good—then pushed open the heavy door and stepped inside.

To his right, a queue led to a row of service windows. To his left, people milled before machines that sold stamps. The people were wet, bedraggled, transparently miserable. Rain drummed against the front window, making squirming lizards on the pane.

The P.O. boxes lined the rear wall, beneath a sign reading RENT-A-BOX. Before approaching the wall, he paused again to cast his eyes around the room. As far as he could tell, nobody was watching the boxes. These were ordinary citizens, miserable and anxious to get home, frustrated and tired.

No cause for concern. And thanks to the boy, he had the key, so there was no risk of drawing attention by picking the lock. He stepped to the box and opened it. Empty. His face stayed blank. He closed the box and began to make his way back toward the street.

The man on the inside had not sent a message to his contacts. No news was good news, he thought. A connection between the dead girl and the safe house had not been made. Things could go ahead as planned. Or perhaps it would be better to wait a few days, to err on the side of caution, and then try the box again. . . .

He stepped outside, and became aware of a man who was not paying attention to him.

It was the man who had been sitting on the stoop with the newspaper. Now he was standing, facing away with such studied nonchalance that he drew the assassin's interest immediately. He was over six feet tall, solidly built, wearing a Yankees cap with matching jacket—

—and he was speaking into his collar.

The assassin turned, heart pounding, and vanished into the drizzle.

They had been watching the box. Expecting him. Or expecting the boy?

Later.

He hurried down the block without looking back.

For a few seconds, he thought he would be able to slip away without trouble. Thunder growled; lightning flashed. Then he heard the sounds of a disturbance on the sidewalk behind him. He shot a glance over his shoulder. The man in the Yankees jacket had collided with a pedestrian. The homeless man was out of his box—holding a pistol.

He moved faster, losing himself in the crowd.

He dodged right, into the street, to avoid a group that blocked the sidewalk. Then left, onto the pavement again. Someone was behind him, reaching forward. But the pursuer was bulky, and hampered by the crowd. The assassin ducked, slipping beneath a couple holding hands. He reached the end of the block, saw an opening in the traffic, and charged ahead as horns blared.

Then he was across the street, crossing a plastic-tarped blanket covered with bootleg videos and DVDs, ignoring the yells of the vendor.

A moment later the neighborhood had changed dramatically: He hastened past fruit and fish markets, grocery stores and small, dim restaurants. Caucasian faces dropped away, with Chinese faces rising to replace them. Signs flashing past read "Acupuncture," "Herbalist," "Live Snails," with Asian characters scrawled beneath the English.

To his right: a muddy alley, stippled by drizzle. He sidestepped into it and then crossed, moving with his lead foot held at a ninety-degree angle to the body, his rear facing 135 degrees away. With each step, the rear foot passed the lead. As a result, his footsteps would appear to move in two directions at once; he could not be traced by his tracks.

Thunder rolled again, distantly.

He came out from the alley and saw a dark sedan turning into the narrow street.

A door was open across the way, leading into the lobby of an office building. He went for it, conscious of the sedan doors butterflying out behind him. A board listed names in Chinese and English. An elevator farther down the hall; beyond it, a door marked *Stairs*.

He pounded up the staircase, his breath coming harder.

On the third floor, he pushed into a corridor. A single door at the end—James Rong, DDS, FAGD. When he burst through it a receptionist looked up from behind her desk. She opened her mouth to speak—

—but he was at the window, working the lock even as the receptionist left her desk, hurrying deeper into the office. In the winding street below was the sedan, doors flung open. Between him and it was rickety-looking scaffolding, edges curled with barbed wire, surface slicked with rain. He put one leg over the windowsill and lowered himself onto slippery metal. Then moved off again, three stories above the city, keeping low.

They had been waiting.

Later.

He reached the end of the scaffolding. Across the

way, a face stared at him from an apartment window—an elderly woman, her mouth sprung.

He pistoned his elbow into the nearest window. He carefully reached through and twisted the lock.

The room was another office, closed down for the night. He glided over pile carpeting. Through a pane in the reception area door was a corridor. Men were there—looking into the dentist's office through which he had passed, with guns drawn. One by one, they entered the office.

He slipped back out into the hallway.

Back into the stairwell. Down the steps, feet clattering, breath rasping no matter how hard he tried to control it. When he reached the door opening into the lobby, he hesitated for a fraction of a second. Then he continued down. They were out there, on the street. They had been waiting.

At the bottom of the stairwell was a basement. On the wall was a light switch; he left it untouched. He crossed to a small window, past stacked crates and a thudding water heater. The window was swollen shut. Too small to slip through anyway, even for him.

A dead end.

His eyes moved to the dark bulb hanging in the ceiling. He jumped up, swiping at it. On the second jump he connected, shattering the glass. It should not have taken two tries. He was tired.

He crept into a corner and lowered himself to the floor. Cobwebs tickled the back of his neck; the gloom felt moist and dense. From outside came the sound of rain, picking up and then dropping off.

He waited, looking not precisely at the door leading to the stairwell, but to alternate sides, one after the other. The cone region of the eye, useless in the dark, absorbs an image when the image is looked at straight on. The rod cells come into play when an object is seen from five to ten degrees above, below, or to the side. For the rod cells to function fully—for a man to see clearly in the dark—the eye must stay in constant motion.

The water heater pounded. Slowly, he regained control of his breathing and his heartbeat. All the while his eyes swept from one side of the door to the other.

After two minutes, the door cracked open—a slab of brown in the black.

He lowered his eyes, so that light would not reflect. One hand reached back to his collar, tugging up the hood. He covered his face and then slipped a blade from his right sleeve, cupping the metal with a hand to prevent a shine. He forced himself to stare at the floor. Here, in the darkness, he was in his element.

The light switch clicked up and down. A muttered curse. Then a flashlight came on. The circle moved across the floor; from the corner of his eye he saw a glue trap, a crate, a hulking piece of equipment. The circle darted in his direction and he closed his eyes.

Five seconds passed.

The sound of the door closing, softly.

He strained to hear beyond the thud of the heater. At length, he stood. His hands wanted to shake. Before moving again, he gave them time to steady. Then he crept back to the door and climbed to the lobby.

The lobby was empty. He stepped onto the sidewalk.

The sedan was gone; the rain was falling harder. Then he saw the car on the next block, pulling away. Sweeping the doorways with light.

He turned in the other direction, losing himself in the rain.

PART TWO

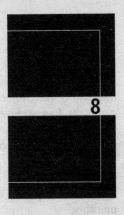

8

INCARCERATION WAS TAKING its toll on Ali Zattout.

When Finney stepped into the cell, the eyes that turned up to absorb him were sunk deep in a face that seemed more angular, beneath the heavy beard, than it had just a day before. A yellowish tint had crept into the man's pallor; his right leg bounced incessantly, trying and failing to work off a surplus of nervous energy. But Zattout retained enough control of himself to conceal the surprise he must have felt at the appearance of this new element. His forehead puckered as he leaned back on the cot and considered his visitor.

Finney turned the chair around, sat, and tried to find the language he would use for his introduction.

With the man's eyes upon him, the words he had rehearsed proved difficult to retrieve. When he had been on the other side of the glass, Zattout had been an object, a collection of traits and quirks that could be analyzed and interpreted. Now Finney found himself facing a man, and the man was looking straight back at him.

This was not a man to be trifled with, he knew. Zattout had inspired other men to give their lives for his cause; he had survived years in hiding. And, despite nearly four weeks of confinement within this sepulchral cell, he had kept not only his wits but also an impressive amount of sangfroid.

Louis Finney himself, however, was no piker. He let a few moments pass. Then he cleared his throat. "Good morning."

Zattout nodded warily.

"My name is Dr. Finney. From now on, I'll be the one to speak with you."

Zattout's face registered mild surprise. He did not ask why Quinlan had been removed from the operation, nor where he had gone. His eyes remained locked on Finney's; his leg kept jigging rapidly up and down.

Finney found a smile. "How are you feeling today?"

Zattout shrugged.

"It seems to me," Finney said, looking around at the cell, "you could use a breath of fresh air."

Zattout leaned forward on the cot. "Yes," he said.

"Why don't we take a stroll outside—and get to know each other in more pleasant circumstances?"

"I'd enjoy that."

"Well," Finney said. "Let's see if we can arrange it."

FOR THE FIRST FEW MINUTES of the stroll, Zattout didn't speak.

He walked with his shoulders thrown back, his eyes drinking in the blue drift of the sky and the green spread of the land. Finney let the silence hang between them, biding his time. They passed a guardhouse, then a pair of marines standing with stone-faced aplomb. They came out into a clearing dotted with trees, with the gravel path winding down the middle. A hundred yards to their left, a creek soliloquized softly. "Can we go to the brook?" Zattout asked.

Finney shook his head. The grounds off the road were covered with security sensors; if they left the path, they would trigger an alarm. But there was no reason for Zattout to know that. "Not today," he answered simply.

Zattout didn't argue. They kept walking, with James Hawthorne—the man who had replaced Thomas Warren as the case officer in charge—trailing two dozen feet behind. For a moment, as the wind shifted, Finney caught the sickly-sweet tang of fertilizer. The sun beat down, warm and lulling. "The sun is nice," Zattout said.

"It is."

From far overhead came the reedy buzz of an airplane. In the forest on their left, the mechanical sound of a Blackpoll warbler: *zi-zi-zi-zi-zi-zi-zi*.

They continued their saunter along the path; Finney's mind rolled, wandering. The warbler, the creek, the man beside him—how had he gotten here?

Thanks to Arthur Noble, he thought.

Noble.

THE YOUNG PROFESSOR had arrived at the classroom five minutes late, puffing slightly, wearing a white shirt with perspiration stains under the arms. Finney still could remember the smells in the room: the faint odor of chalk dust, the mildewy air stirring under a fan. As

Noble arranged his papers on the lectern, the students traded perplexed glances. Could this really be the legendary scion of G. H. Estabrooks?

Then Noble stepped out from behind the lectern to approach the chalkboard. "In less than an hour," he declared in a ringing voice, "a 'normal' man can be conditioned to discard everything he's been taught about morality. This rather disquieting fact has been proven by no less illustrious an institution than Yale University."

He went on to describe the experiment undertaken at Yale, scrawling data on the chalkboard as he spoke. The previous year—1963—forty men in the prime of life had been solicited by newspaper advertisements to take part in a test. The subjects had been told that the purpose of the experiment was to assess human memory. They had been drawn from every socioeconomic background, from every race, color, and creed. They had signed on for a paycheck of four dollars and fifty cents.

Upon arriving at the test center, each subject found himself sitting in a room with two other men. One of these men wore a white lab smock. The other was presented as another subject who had answered the newspaper ad—although in truth, the second subject was in league with the scientists running the experiment. Very little, the lab-coated man explained, was known about the effects of punishment on memory. If a man was disciplined when he got an answer wrong, would he be more likely to get the next answer right? Determining this correlation was the purpose of the test. The two subjects then drew slips of paper from a hat to determine who would be the Teacher and who the Learner— yet neither sheet read Learner. The true subject always became the Teacher, for his behavior was the actual focus of the experiment.

Finney scribbled notes, trying to keep up with the ever-expanding jumble on the chalkboard. Noble paused. He chose three students for eye contact—Finney was one—then continued.

Led to an adjacent room, the Learner was seated in a facsimile of an electric chair. Paste was applied to his skin; electrodes were attached to his body. The paste, it was announced, would minimize burning.

The Teacher was escorted to another room, containing a facsimile of a shock generator and a screen on which multiple choice answers would be displayed. Here he was given a list of questions—word pairs—and instructed to administer a shock at each wrong answer. In addition, he was to increase the charge at each subsequent error by turning a dial on the "shock generator."

As had been previously arranged, the answers given by the Learner were wrong three out of four times. Until a shock level of 300 volts was administered, there came no sound from the adjacent room. At the 300 level, a pounding could be heard on the wall. If at this point the subject displayed an unwillingness to continue, a series of vocal prods was delivered. First: *The experiment requires that you continue.* Second, *It is absolutely essential that you continue.* If the subject still displayed recalcitrance: *You have no other choice. You must continue.*

Of course, Noble said, no electric shocks were delivered, and the connection of memory to punishment could not have interested the experimenters less. The purpose of the test was to see how far the Teachers would go—how quickly, in the face of lab-coated authority, they would turn their backs on the moral conduct they had been taught since childhood.

Another significant pause. Three more calculated instances of eye contact. The scratch of pens across notepads had ceased.

Of the forty subjects, Noble continued after a moment, not one stopped administering shocks before the 300 voltage level. At the 300 level, when pounding was heard from the next room and answers ceased appearing on the screen, only five of the forty refused to go further. In all, only fourteen of the forty subjects—thirty-five percent—eventually disobeyed the experimenter's commands.

Sixty-five percent continued until the shocks being delivered were the maximum that could be produced by the "shock generator."

There had been something smug in Noble's face when he'd finished relating the experiment. Perhaps this had been due to the effect he had created in his students. Or perhaps the man's satisfaction had more to do with his own self-image. In Noble's mind, the experiment proved that morality was subjective. By extension, someone like Noble himself—who, unbeknownst to Finney at the time, already had been working with MKULTRA—could not be blamed for having explored murky ethical waters. Any real scientist would explore these same waters, given the chance; for there was no such thing as true morality. In Noble's mind, the experiment absolved him.

On that day, he'd moved on to a discussion of morality during wartime. War, he said, reversed all traditional values. In Western society, men were raised to *have* and to *hoard*. Yet during war, a man was expected to share his food with a stranger in a foxhole, even to give away his life in defense of a fellow soldier he'd met only weeks before. Surely the rigid rules of "morality" were a construct, and the nature of the construct was an ever-changing one, depending entirely on circumstance. . . .

ALMOST A QUARTER of a century had passed, after that day, before Finney had stumbled onto a more detailed account of the shocking experiment conducted at Yale University. He had been alone in his study, poring through old books after Lila's death. He had found the report titled "Behavioral Study of Obedience," written by Stanley Milgram, the man who led the experiment. And he had discovered that Dr. Arthur Noble hadn't quite told the whole truth, when he'd spoken of that test.

What Noble had neglected to mention was the comportment of the subjects—the "Teachers"—as they proved the flexibility of morality.

One sign of tension, the experimenter wrote, *was the regular occurrence of nervous laughing fits. Fourteen of the 40 subjects showed definite signs of nervous laughter and smiling. The laughter seemed entirely out of place, even bizarre. Full-blown, uncontrollable seizures were observed for 3 subjects. On one occasion we observed a seizure so violently convulsive that it was necessary to call a halt to the experiment. The subject, a 46-year-old encyclopedia salesman, was seriously embarrassed by his untoward and uncontrollable behavior.*

In the post-experimental interviews subjects took pains to point out that they were not sadistic types and that the laughter did not mean they enjoyed shocking the victim.

Farther down the page: *I observed a mature and initially poised businessman enter the laboratory smiling and confident. Within 20 minutes he was reduced to a twitching, stuttering wreck, who was rapidly approaching a point of nervous collapse. He constantly pulled on his earlobe, and twisted his hands. At one point he pushed his fist into his forehead and muttered: "Oh God, let's stop it." And yet he continued to respond to every word of the experimenter, and obeyed to the end.*

To Noble, the experiment offered absolution. To Finney, it implied just the opposite—illuminating everything problematic with the path down which he had allowed himself to be led.

Hadn't the scientists eliminated the need for the experiment, simply by undertaking it? Hadn't they proved with their own conduct—without realizing it—that morality could be bent, warped, and manipulated? Had these men lost sleep because they had pushed innocent subjects to seizures, hysterical laughter, nervous collapse?

Or had they wrapped themselves in complacency, rationalizing their conduct because it had been done in the name of so-called scientific *progress*?

By the time he'd discovered the passage, sitting in his study with the window to the garden thrown open, Finney had been a very different man from the young student who had been so impressed by Noble. He had gained firsthand knowledge of MKULTRA, and through his own research, he had gained knowledge of more. A long, storied tradition of human experimentation had preceded their experiments with Susan Franklin.

In 1950, the U.S. Navy sprayed a cloud of bacteria over San Francisco to test the population's susceptibility to biological attack. Monitoring devices were installed throughout the city to measure the results of the resulting infection.

Three years later, clouds of zinc cadmium sulfide gas were released over Minneapolis, Maryland, and Virginia. The same year, thousands of U.S. citizens in Manhattan and San Francisco were exposed to *Serratia marcescens* and *Bacillus globigii.*

And that had been only the beginning. In 1955 the military released mosquitoes infected with yellow fever into Savannah, Georgia and Avon Park, Florida. In 1965 prisoners at Holmesburg State Prison in Philadelphia were subjected to dioxin, then monitored for developing cancers. In 1990, 1,500 six-month-old black and Hispanic babies in Los Angeles were given an unlicensed measles vaccine. The parents were not informed that the vaccine was experimental. The Tuskegee Syphilis Study, the brain electrode implantation program, the experiment code-named GREEN RUN, in which radioactive iodine-131 was released from the Hanford Nuclear Facility and allowed to drift into downtown Spokane . . .

As part of such a history, it was no surprise that Noble had been able to rationalize the experiments he had overseen. Perhaps it also was no surprise that Finney had allowed himself to do the same. Once a man became caught in a sense of a higher purpose, he compromised his values to an astonishing degree. And war served only to accelerate the process.

* * *

A GUARD DOG was growling, low in its throat.

Finney saw the animal straining at its chain leash. The marine handler restrained it easily, but Zattout— despite the fact that the Doberman pinscher was tightly muzzled—panicked.

Suddenly Finney was a psychiatrist again; and suddenly Zattout was not a man but a puzzle to be solved.

He shied away, moving to Finney's other side. "I'm ready to go back now," he said sotto voce.

In the mental notebook where he kept an ongoing record of the subject's reactions, his drives and fears, his passions and weaknesses, Finney opened another column. "Cynophobia," the column might have been headed: fear of dogs. There was something here. Something that could be exploited.

If, that was, he was willing to exploit it.

Nobody would stop him, he knew, if he suggested tying Zattout to a chair and letting loose a Doberman. Noble was no longer on the premises. Hawthorne was supervising only the mechanics of the operation, not the content. And even if these men had been actively involved, they likely would have welcomed such a suggestion.

As they retraced their steps, Finney tried to return his mind to the present, to matters of consequence. If he could manipulate Zattout into telling the truth, instead of the half-truth, real lives would be saved.

But the experiment still was with him; and he raised a hand, as they walked, to touch the dull ache forming between his eyes.

* * *

ON A LEAFY BLOCK in downtown Manhattan stood a six-story brownstone.

A wrought-iron fence encouraged admirers to keep their distance, although determined bystanders could steal a glimpse of a parlor filled with teak furniture or a third-floor library featuring a grand old fireplace. All onlookers were photographed—by a camera mounted above the front door, by a second camera mounted on the ornate roof, or by a third built into a streetlamp a dozen feet down the block, set between more turn-of-the-century townhouses and cozy French restaurants.

The room into which Thomas Warren stepped possessed none of the charm evinced by the brownstone's facade. It had a low ceiling of flaking white paint, two cluttered metal desks, and smudged walls lined with heavy-duty filing cabinets. At one of the desks sat Anthony Cass, wearing a Yankees cap and matching Yankees jacket.

On the desk before Cass were stacks of folders, with photographs stapled to cover sheets. These were mercenaries, spies, and terror suspects culled from the CIA's records and the FBI's watch list. They were the subjects of Red Notices and Fugitive Diffusions provided by the American branch of the International Criminal Police Organization, which used the radio call sign Interpol. Over one hundred men between the ages of twenty and forty-five were represented by the dossiers stacked on the desk. One of them might be the man who had visited the post office, who had slipped so easily through their grasp.

When Warren entered, Cass looked up. "Any luck?" Warren asked.

Cass shook his head, then raised a hand to stifle a yawn.

He was palpably exhausted. But Warren could not urge him to take a break. Cass was the one who had come closest to the man at the post office; he was the one who had seen the man's face.

"My father used to have a saying," Warren said. " 'Be like a postage stamp. Stick to it until you get there.' "

Cass didn't look inspired. He took off his hat, ran a hand over his brow, and grunted.

For a few seconds, Warren searched for another of his father's chestnuts. *Do not fear opposition; the kite rises against the wind, not with it.* Or maybe—*Great works are performed not by strength but by perseverance.* No doubt that would motivate Cass to buckle down.

Of course, platitudes went only so far. But they had served the elder Warren well enough. By all accounts, Thomas Warren, Senior's career with the agency had been undeniably first-rate.

His career had started in 1951 with CHATTER, a truth serum experiment then being undertaken by the Navy. During the following decades—as CHATTER had gone over to the CIA and become part of ARTICHOKE, as ARTICHOKE had become part of MKULTRA, as the drugs with which they'd experimented had evolved from Dexedrine to THC to LSD—the elder Warren had managed to chart himself an always rising path through a sticky and challenging course. Despite decades of effort, MKULTRA never produced solid results. Yet Thomas Warren, Senior, had come out smelling like a rose.

The son had tried hard to follow in his father's foot-steps. He'd gone to the right school, played the right sport, worn the right varsity letter jacket. He'd mastered Greek so he could study the classics as they were meant to be studied, in the original language. He'd done every-thing as he'd understood he was meant to do it. And still he'd ended up here—in charge of an operation skidding out of control, on the verge of taking a hard fall.

His father would roll over in his grave if Warren were to be pink-slipped.

And rightly so, he thought.

Backbone was required in this world. Thomas War-ren II clearly was not tough enough. Somehow he had absorbed the effete values of the Ivy League intellectu-als, where his father had managed to avoid them.

The junior Warren's shortcomings had become evi-dent during his first major undertaking after graduation. One moment he'd been living in a world of Hasty Pud-ding clubs and white-wine soirees; the next, he'd been dealing in the locations of coastal artillery and mine-fields that might interfere with amphibious landings in southern Kuwait. A timely bon mot, he'd quickly dis-covered, didn't count for much when serving as an agency liaison with the Pentagon's Joint Intelligence Center.

But surely he could motivate Anthony Cass to try a little harder, as he pored over his dossiers. Any compe-tent middle manager could do that much.

Coffee might do the trick.

Without another word, he turned and moved down the wood-floored hall, passing a second low-ceilinged room where Nathan Hoyle was speaking on a telephone.

In the kitchen, he found a Silex bubble full of day-old sludge. He poured it into the sink, then opened a cabinet. As he prepared to sift coffee into a filter, the phone on his belt vibrated. "Warren."

"I'm at the post office . . ."

It was Ron Moore—the agent charged with interviewing witnesses on the scene. Already he had been downtown for hours; Warren had ceased expecting results. He held his breath, not daring to hope.

". . . speaking with a lovely young woman," Moore went on, "who may be able to lend us a hand."

"How so?"

"She's a postal worker. And a few days ago, she noticed someone checking the box . . ."

"Bring her here," Warren said.

THE PHONE RANG twice.

Between each ring came faraway clicking above a subterranean hoot. He was thinking that something might have gone awry—he had dialed the wrong number, or perhaps the woman had gone out, although where she might have gone he couldn't imagine—when a breathless voice said, "Hello?"

"Ms. Miriam Lane?"

"Yes?"

"This is Jack Atelier, calling from Atelier Discount Auto Parts. I'm pleased to report that you've been selected as a final runner-up in our greater New York promotional campaign. You've been selected to be in the top three, Ms. Lane."

"Top three?"

"Yes, ma'am."

"In what?"

"As per our previous correspondence," he said smoothly, "your name has been selected for a promotional event. Atelier Discount Auto Parts is the premier discount automobile part supplier for the greater New York area. Having reached the final runner-up stage, you're now guaranteed a cash reward of five hundred dollars, and a chance at the grand prize: a brand-new Honda Accord."

Silence on the line.

"Ms. Lane?"

"Yes?"

"The final drawing will take place tomorrow night, here at our home office. If you win the grand prize, you'll also receive the chance to take part in a television advertisement. We'll fly you down to New York City to arrange the taping. Three nights and two days at the Parker Meridien Hotel, where a team of hair and makeup specialists—"

"What is this?" she asked.

"The promotional campaign," he said. Had she even opened the letter?

"Have I won something?"

"Yes, ma'am. Five hundred dollars, at the least. And a chance at the grand prize. A brand-new Honda Accord."

"Oh my."

"As I said: The final drawing will take place tomorrow night. After that, I'll contact you again with the results."

"Oh my."

"Yes, ma'am. It's very exciting."

"What do I need to do?"

"Not a thing. I'll contact you again with the results of the drawing. The day after tomorrow."

"The drawing?"

"To see if you've won the grand prize."

Again, silence.

"A brand-new Honda Accord," he said.

"That would be wonderful."

"Well," he said. "Let's keep our fingers crossed."

After hanging up, he sat on the edge of the bed and stared into the middle distance.

So he was going ahead.

Something had gone wrong. They had been watching the post office. Yet he was going ahead.

He would be cautious. With patience and vigilance, he would discover if Ajami had been identified by their enemy, or if he was colluding with them. With the information he gathered, he would make an informed decision about how to proceed. But he would go ahead regardless of what he found.

He moved to the floor. To escape the notice of the enemy—if indeed they were watching Ajami's building—a calm mind would be required. A man without serenity could not be invisible.

The car would not be ready until Wednesday, the thirtieth. So there still was time. Tomorrow he would conduct surveillance of Ajami's building and find out how they had learned of the post office box.

He would not hurry. Haste, if he gave in to it, would be his downfall.

His eyes drifted shut; his head bowed.

9

"SOMETIMES," SAID Ali Zattout philosophically, "I wonder how things ended up this way—if this is truly Allah's will."

His tone was that of a man sitting with distinguished company before a fireplace, discussing poetry after a fine meal. But his physical appearance belied his carefully measured voice. His cheeks had continued to hollow; his right leg vibrated up and down more rapidly than ever. His eyes had achieved the yellowed, bloodshot intensity of a trapped animal.

Louis Finney made an encouraging sound.

Zattout indicated the cramped cell around them, managing to convey a world of disdain with a single gesture. "Once, I would have had no doubts. Life was much simpler then. But now . . ."

He paused. Had they been sitting before a fireplace, he might have used the opportunity to sip at his glass of port.

"Do you regret being here?" Finney asked.

Zattout stroked at his beard.

"In one way," he said at last, "I'm thankful. Being here gives me the opportunity to correct my past wrongs—or at least to make a beginning." Another pause. "But I don't know that any man could be entirely satisfied living in a cell. It would be dishonest to say that I have no regrets."

"Understandable."

"Of course, I realize the arrangement is temporary. But it can be difficult to keep that in mind when the walls start to close in. Do you think I might be allowed outside today?"

"If we make some progress this morning—perhaps this afternoon."

"I hope so," Zattout said earnestly.

Finney waited to see if elaboration was forthcoming. When it was not, he turned a page in his notes and then described a smuggler's route along the 1,500-mile border between Afghanistan and Pakistan. Recently, unmanned spy planes had noted increased activity on this desert route: convoys on horseback and foot, apparently composed of refugees. But the path was known to have been used by al Qaeda in the past. Could Zattout offer any information regarding it?

He could. The borderlands were dominated by ethnic Pashtuns who possessed no loyalty to the Pakistani government. These tribal leaders might well be harboring al Qaeda fugitives. In fact, Zattout said, the wrong question was being asked. Until the Americans understood that their enemy and the tribal leaders were two sides of the same coin, they would continue wasting their time.

The answer was both repetitive and evasive. Then Zattout used it as an entrée to a subject that was of no interest to Finney: the balance of oxides present in that region's stones. Some of the world's most brilliant sapphires came from this area, he reported, and from the legendary Himalayan mines on the opposite border of Pakistan, near India. Did Finney know that the word *sapphire* came from the Hebrew *sapphir,* meaning to tell a story? In ancient times a sapphire was believed to be an unripened ruby, and the Kashmir sapphires were the most coveted of all. . . .

Finney changed tack. "Let me jump to another subject, if you don't mind—the connection between al Qaeda and the Syrian Muslim Brotherhood."

Zattout nodded. He proceeded to speak of the decades-long war between the Syrian Muslim Brotherhood and the secular Syrian government. One result of the war had been a confluence of the SMB's interests with al Qaeda's. Before 9/11, members of the two organizations had worked together out of cells based in Aachen and Hamburg.

More insight into information they already had. And Zattout knew what he was doing, Finney thought. As he spoke, a louche smile flirted around the corners of his mouth.

"Interesting," Finney allowed when he'd finished. "But dangerously close, I'm afraid, to ground we've already covered."

"Is it?" Zattout asked blandly.

"I'd like nothing more than some fresh air myself, you know. But I have superiors to whom I must answer.

I'm obliged to give them something of value in exchange for such a reward."

"What do you call what you've been giving them—worthless?"

Finney shrugged.

"Is it the quantity of the results that concerns you," Zattout asked, "or the quality?"

"I'm not the one who's concerned. But it's safe to say that they would like more quantity *and* quality. You know how it works. Nothing comes for free."

Zattout gazed at him with a jaundiced eye.

"Speaking of fresh air." Finney turned a page; the paper whispered secretly beneath his fingers. "During our last walk, I noticed your reaction to the Doberman. How long have you suffered from fear of dogs?"

"Fear of dogs?"

"Yes. You shied away."

Zattout reached for the scar on his ear. He shook his head. "You must have imagined it."

"Do you think so?"

He touched the scar again. "Most definitely."

Finney moved on. With ironic courtliness, he invited Zattout to share any knowledge he possessed of a German arms dealer who had been selling rocket launchers to undercover CIA agents. Unfortunately, Zattout said, he did not know of the man. But this was hardly surprising. His organization was highly compartmentalized. This was its greatest strength—but then, Finney doubtless understood that fact already.

"I do understand that. But you occupied a high position in the hierarchy. You must have theories, if nothing else."

"Guesses? If that's what you want—yes, I can offer guesses. Whether or not they'll satisfy your superiors . . ."

"Let's return to the subject of sleeper al Qaeda cells on American soil. If you could recall something on the topic that hasn't yet come to light . . . guesses, or anything else . . ."

"Are you implying something?" Zattout asked.

"Pardon me?"

"Twice already I've told you what I know of the sleepers. All I know."

"I'm just making sure nothing was missed."

"Nothing was missed," Zattout assured him.

"Well, it's good to be sure."

"Of course."

"If something does occur to you, please don't hesitate."

"Of course," Zattout said again.

As Finney asked his next question—a long one, involving information gained from prisoners at Guantánamo Bay about possible methods used by future hijackers—the man's attention drifted visibly. When he finished speaking, there was silence.

Finney moved an inch forward on his chair. Zattout was there, but not there. His nervous movements ceased, one after another, like a clock winding down. First his leg grew still. Then his hands stopped moving, lying fallow in his lap. He muttered something beneath his breath.

"Could you repeat that?" Finney asked.

Zattout's eyes sharpened.

"My mind is wandering," he said.

"Is it too much for one day? We can end the session, if you like. Although I'm afraid we haven't gained enough ground to justify a walk today."

"Let's continue."

"Future hijackings. We've heard rumors of edged playing cards . . . plastic weapons hidden in children's toys . . ."

Again Zattout was drifting; his eyes turned hazy. They focused on the light and stayed there, transfixed.

Half a minute passed. Finney made a notation in his pad.

Then Zattout blinked. "I'm sorry," he said.

"No need to apologize."

"I can't . . . I'm having trouble concentrating."

"Hm."

"If you want me to think clearly, you'll need to let me out of this cell."

His tone was dull. But his eyes, Finney noticed, were hostile and shrewd.

"Without better results," he answered, "I'm afraid a reward is impossible."

"If you're displeased with my results, perhaps you should consider changing the quality of my environment. As you said yourself, Doctor: Nothing comes for free."

They looked at each other.

"We seem to have reached an impasse," Finney said.

"I'm doing the best I can. But without fresh air, once a day . . ."

"Perhaps it can be arranged."

"Twice a day would be better."

Finney said nothing.

"After a long day of cooperating, two walks hardly seems too much to ask for."

"You're absolutely right. I'll look into it."

"And another set of clothes wouldn't hurt. No need for designer labels. Anything clean."

"Hm," Finney said.

Zattout stroked at his beard again. "Perhaps a newspaper, once in a while. And the soap I've been given is hardly of the highest quality. . . ."

FINNEY CAME OUT of the cell and literally bumped into James Hawthorne.

One of Hawthorne's eyes was glass; it gleamed disconcertingly in the shadows. For a second time, Finney felt a flash of déjà vu. He had been here before. He had seen the dusky glimmer of that glass eye. And he knew what Hawthorne would say, even before the man opened his mouth to say it. *Interesting approach, Doctor. Give the prisoner every luxury he requests. It's becoming increasingly difficult to tell exactly who is in charge of this interrogation. . . .*

"It's Noble," Hawthorne said.

He put a hand on Finney's shoulder. "There's still time."

THE WOMAN'S NAME TAG identified her as Rose.

After a brief interview, Warren invited her to speak with a forensic artist he'd drafted from the NYPD. Now she sat with the man in the sun-flooded parlor. The sketch in the artist's lap was only half finished; he had interrupted his work to deliver an impromptu lecture on the importance of his profession.

"—the most overlooked job in law enforcement," he was telling Rose. "When most people think of a police sketch artist, they picture some cop who wanted to be a painter and failed. But that couldn't be farther from the truth. It takes five years of experience with a law enforcement agency, two hundred hours of composite art training, a written and verbal exam, multiple letters of recommendation. It's not a hobby. It's a passion. Without forensic artists, they never would have caught Ted Bundy. Without forensic artists, they never would have caught Richard Allen Davis. . . ."

Yet another expert who felt the need to lecture, Warren thought darkly. But beggars couldn't be choosers. He stood outside the door, smoking a Camel Light and trying to refrain from interrupting. Beside him, Ron Moore was rubbing his own shoulders with nicotine-stained fingers.

". . . I'm rambling," the artist said. "Let's finish this up. Did you see him smile?"

Rose shook her head.

"That's too bad. I'm also trained in odontology, you know. The study of teeth. It takes that kind of all-around education to make a really good forensic artist. It's not just about bone structure. I've studied odontology, I've studied anatomy, I've studied psychology . . ."

Warren checked his watch. He finished the cigarette, dropped the butt in a foam cup, lit another. Beside him, Moore continued kneading his own shoulders.

Finding Rose was a start. But they needed a break—a real one. Without it, the shuddering train that was Warren's career would derail. Even now he could sense the wheels flirting with the tracks, losing purchase. And it was all he would deserve. Some men were cut out for greatness. Others were doomed never to fulfill their potential. . . .

The break came two hours later.

EVEN BEFORE the forensic sketch had been printed up as a "Wanted" poster, a detective second-grade recognized the boy: perhaps sixteen, olive-complexioned, raven-haired, large soft eyes glistening with sensitivity even in two-dimensional black and white.

Ten minutes after the detective recognized the face, Thomas Warren II was holding a police report concerning the death of one Muhammad Nassif. The report had been written by the same man who was on the other end of the phone connection. Three mornings ago, he told Warren, Nassif had woken up dead, ha ha. The cause of death was *positional asphyxia*. This meant, as unlikely as it sounded, that the boy had slept wrong. He had slept so wrong that he had neglected to turn over, and had suffocated against his own pillow.

"You're shitting me," Warren said.

"I shit you not. The autopsy might tell a different story. But in this city it can take ten, twelve days to get the report."

"His own pillow?"

"According to the ME—yeah. You ask me, it's probably pills. A kid like this, some drug history, some vandalism . . . he gets high and takes some scripts and chokes on his own vomit during the night. Except there was no vomit in the windpipe."

"Weird."

"I'll try to put a rush on the report. Big important federal case like this. In the meantime . . ."

In the meantime, he gave Warren an address and a name belonging to the boy's mother.

HE FOUND THE BUZZER he wanted—apartment 49— and leaned on it. A moment passed. The speaker crackled. Then a woman's voice, lightly accented. "Hello?"

"Mrs. Nassif?"

"Yes?"

"It's Tom Warren. We spoke on the phone . . ."

The speaker buzzed. Thomas Warren exchanged a glance with Ron Moore, then pushed forward. They ascended four flights of stairs that smelled of cooking odors and Lysol.

The boy's mother met them at the apartment's front door. She was pretty in a grief-stricken way: pale and drawn, lovely in her vulnerability. She led them to a threadbare couch in a dark living room, offered coffee and tea, barely seemed to hear them when they declined. Then she told her story, working her way through a box of Kleenex as she spoke.

Moore took out a pad and made notes. Warren simply listened, nodding sympathetically.

Muhammad had passed three days before, very suddenly, in his sleep. The police thought it was drugs, she said. Nobody had stated this out loud, but she had read it in their eyes. But it had not been drugs. Her boy did not do drugs. It had been something else . . .

. . . she trailed off.

"Take your time," Warren said gently.

He had been a good boy. A few scrapes with the law, but nothing too serious. It was tough to grow up in this neighborhood and not have a few scrapes with the law. Vandalism, a pot bust. But he had been a minor; the judge had shown leniency; his record had been clean. His grades always had been good. And recently he had straightened up, she said. Over the past few months, however, he had started to get involved in something else. And this was what had killed him. She didn't know how, and she didn't know why. But she knew it nevertheless.

Warren tried to make his eyes glisten with some of the sensitivity he had seen in the sketch of the boy. "Go on," he said.

She drew a hitching breath, wiped at her nose with a Kleenex, and continued.

A few months before, Muhammad had discovered a sudden interest in his Muslim heritage—thanks to his older brother, no doubt, who had gone back to Saudi Arabia in October of the previous year. Muhammad had revered his older brother. So he had taken to hanging around a mosque out in Brooklyn. He had met people there, she said. The same people his brother had met. The same people who had been responsible, in a roundabout way, for the death of her husband in Syria in 1994. Mossad had pulled the trigger, in that case. But she did not blame Mossad. She blamed whoever was at the mosque, sucking her family into this cause, this horrible, terrible, murderous cause. . . .

"Do you know who he met, at the mosque?"

She shook her head, dabbing at her nose.

"Do you mind if we take a look around?"

"Like the detective?" Her eyes flashed. "He spent five whole minutes looking around. He couldn't care less about my boy. They say his pillow killed him." She laughed hoarsely. "His pillow."

They left the woman crying softly on her couch.

The room where the boy had died was a typical teenager's bedroom, with a garish poster on one wall and a closet door hanging open to reveal jumbles of comic books and sporting equipment. The bed itself had been stripped down to the mattress.

Ron Moore moved to search the closet. Warren went to the dresser and opened a drawer. Below neatly folded T-shirts he found a rumpled twenty-dollar bill, a key chain in the shape of a skull, and a glossy photograph. The photograph pictured a slim unsmiling boy with overwrought eyes, his arm draped across the shoulders of an appealing-looking blonde.

He pocketed the photograph. The postal worker—Rose—would need to make a positive ID.

From the living room, he could hear the woman still crying.

A computer rested atop a makeshift desk. As Moore dug noisily through the closet, Warren reached out and nudged the computer's mouse. The monitor remained dark. So the computer was not in sleep mode. Was it turned off—or had someone sabotaged it? He would bring the tower back to the brownstone, where the technicians could have a look. Even if the boy had cleaned his cache, removed his cookies, deleted his e-mail, and scrubbed his file allocation table, the techs could recover magnetic shadow images of the lost files.

He opened the desk drawer and found envelopes,

floppy disks, rubber bands, stamps, Elmer's glue, pencils, and a resin-stained roach clip.

Then, having nowhere else to turn in the little room, he found himself standing before the dresser again. He reached for another drawer and dug through rolls of FUBU socks. Then another drawer: underwear. At the bottom was a slip of paper. He raised it to the light. On the paper was an address and a single name.

The name was *Iqbal Ajami*.

WHEN IQBAL AJAMI stepped off the elevator, Pegasus was waiting, meeting him with a series of high terrier yips.

Ajami bent, scratched behind the dog's ears, then set down his briefcase and moved into the kitchen to find a rawhide bone. He watched as Pegasus carried it protectively to a bowl by the refrigerator, feeling an almost painful stab of affection. This little dog, he realized suddenly, was the closest thing in the world he had to a friend. If he did decide to run, Pegasus might be what he missed most.

He showered, fixed a drink, and settled down before the evening news. A terror suspect in New Jersey had been arrested by the FBI. For a moment, as Ajami sipped at his drink, his spirits sank. He rubbed at the dark semicircles beneath his eyes. Fatigue and depression competed inside him. But he would not give in to either. The thing to remember was that more *shuhada* were waiting to take the place of this captured man. Just as others would replace Ajami, if he were to fall.

The movement had many members, wearing many faces. There were the infantry, the rank-and-file foot soldiers. There were the sleepers like Ajami himself, who had mingled so long among the enemy that they had, on the surface, become indistinguishable from them. There were the American Arabs who went overseas to train in Afghani camps, and the Arab mothers who came to America specifically to have their babies, so that the children would be U.S. citizens and in twenty years could cross the border with impunity. There were zealots and cynics, puppets and puppeteers, members of other organizations that had been absorbed into the Base. They were thousands strong, with millions more waiting in the wings. Their strength only would continue to grow.

And despite the assassin's turning to bite the hand that had fed him—despite the man covering his tracks, and disturbing Ajami's sleep—there was no cause for concern. Quinlan's letters had informed him that Zattout had given up only a single cell in Rawalpindi. He had thrown his captors a bone: a few men, a few chemistry textbooks and bombs using Casio watches as timers. He had not revealed the cell to which Ajami belonged. Nor had he exposed the other sleepers of which he knew. Zattout would hold out . . . long enough for the assassin to reach him and end this, before genuine damage could be done.

His attention was drifting. He found himself looking not at the news but at the room around him, furnished with walnut antiques and a towering grandfather clock, decorated with George Stubbs hunt scenes and phalenopsis orchids. From the kitchen came the sound of Pegasus gnawing on his bone, audible even over the television.

He drank more vodka, replaying the events of the day in his mind, wondering if he had made any fatal mistakes.

The FBI already was overwhelmed with lawsuits from non-profit religious charities. The 501(c)(3) organizations he had accessed during the day therefore enjoyed some measure of relief from federal supervision. Yet somewhere inside himself, Ajami knew they were watching. And moving such large amounts of funds in so short a time only increased the chances of raising eyebrows.

Despite the risks, he had no other choice. He needed to set up his offshore account—all of his instincts clamored for this safety measure. He also needed to finish preparing the second half of the payment, so that the assassin would not have reason to come after him. And he needed to do it all without letting his performance at the law firm suffer, or otherwise drawing attention to himself.

He heaved a sigh. That afternoon he had lifted seventy-five thousand dollars from a charity called Kindness Without Borders, to put toward the assassin's numbered Swiss account. From a business called Digital Imperatives he had borrowed fifty thousand, freshly laundered, for transference to his own nest egg. Was it too much, too fast?

His dream of the night before occurred to him—the same dream he had been having ever since the assassin had started murdering the members of the cell. In the dream, Ajami was mounting the steps of a stage. He was a young man, in his twenties. His mustache was black as pitch. He had forgotten why he was mounting the stage. He had nothing to perform. The auditorium before him was filled with white light and suffocating stillness.

He tapped the microphone, coaxing a whine of feedback, and drew a breath. For one more moment there was only silence: silence, and the overpowering glare of the hot white lights.

Then he began to recite. Later, after he'd awoken, Ajami couldn't remember a single word of the poem. He didn't know if the poem had used any words at all. But it had been elegant, and it had been passionate; he remembered that much.

When the recitation was finished, the final echo of his voice dribbled away. There was more quiet, heavy and thick—

—and then a mordant patter of applause from a single pair of hands.

He left the stage, descending the steps carefully, and made for the auditorium's exit. He could sense a man coming to his feet, but continued moving at an even clip. To hurry would betray fear. And that, he understood suddenly, would be the end of him.

He reached the door. At the same instant he heard the thin, sibilant whicker of a blade leaving a sheath. But he would not turn. To turn would be to seal his fate.

He felt the sharp, swift pain in his rib cage. Then the slipping forward, his body folding onto the ground with his heart catching in his chest. In the distance, the eerie sound of the muezzin's call to prayer, reverberating through the old city. . . .

Just a dream.

He tried to focus on the news again, to distract himself. But even here, forty stories up, he did not feel safe. The assassin was a *stealer-in*. He was a *ghost wind,* an *eye of God.* If he was to come for Ajami, nothing in the world would stop him.

At quarter past six he stood, clicked off the news, and trudged wearily into the bedroom. He would have liked to stay home tonight, to catch up on some of the sleep he had lost over the last few weeks. But his dinner plans could not be canceled. Tonight he would be asking David Goldstein for the kind of favor that could be requested only in person.

As he buttoned his cuff links, he ran through the words he would use. He planned to ask Goldstein to hold a bit of money for a few days and then funnel it back. The man owed him a favor, thanks to Ajami's wise (and complimentary) counsel during his divorce; he would not refuse. So a Jew would help to further the cause. A Jew would help, albeit unknowingly, to sate Ajami's hunger for justice.

He had trouble with the cuff links. He was exhausted. And the terror of the dream would not leave him.

Was he weakening, after his two-decade journey toward justice? Had he lived with the seductive comforts of the West for too long?

Ajami's hunger for justice had begun when he was a child, surrounded by the squalor of the Sabra refugee camp. But it had crystallized when he was twenty-seven years old: holding his mother's head in his lap, both of them soaked through with her blood.

It had been September of 1982. The Israelis had

invaded West Beirut, targeting the PLO Research Center and the Palestinian camps at Sabra and Shatila. But the Zionists would not dirty their own hands in the camps— not when they had others willing to do their bidding. Phalangist militiamen were eager to avenge the 1976 Palestinian massacre of Christians at Damour, and so Phalangists were charged by the Israeli general staff to enter the camps and weed out PLO supporters. In this world, there was always a past massacre to be avenged. And this day in 1982 would see yet another—the massacre for which Ajami, more than twenty years later, now was seeking justice.

For seventy-two hours the Israeli army had turned darkness to daylight with their flares, illuminating the camps for their willing executioners. The militiamen had worked their way through the settlements, slaughtering every human they came across. Had Ajami's mother been a terrorist? No. She had been a widow and a mother. Yet she had been gunned down in cold blood.

Ajami had not been there to protect her. He had been out looking to see if the rumors were true—if death was sweeping through their camp, indiscriminately. The calamity had been real, indeed. And his mother, an innocent, had become part of it.

At twenty-seven, Ajami already had been too old to become a foot soldier in the great holy war. That was for the fortunate young, the mujahedeen, who could extinguish themselves and their enemies in a blaze of glory. Instead, Ajami had needed to assume a more administrative role in the organization—a less satisfying position but a necessary one. As the Zionists had perfected the art of staying behind the scenes, dangling their marionettes on jerking strings, so too did the cause need to master such skills.

He had worked hard to make opportunities for himself, pulling himself from a life in the camp to a life in the city, moving west, from one relative to another. He had reinvented himself as a student, and in time had been awarded a law degree in London. There he had begun to attend services at a local mosque, where he had met recruiters for al Qaeda. Then he had gone to al-Masada, the Lion's Den, the first training camp of its type in Afghanistan. He had been introduced to the American woman who would marry him, thereby securing U.S. citizenship. Once the marriage was dissolved, he'd moved to Manhattan and started the long slow rise to his current position.

During these years, for the first time in his life, he had begun to understand the meaning of a certain phrase: *Revenge is a dish best served cold.* The meaning could not have been simpler. Revenge easily attained would be unsatisfying. It was only after the dish had been set aside, to cool down over the course of years, that it attained its full flavor.

But there was a risk, when one let revenge cool for too long. The hunger might abate, and the dish never would be consumed at all. Over the years, Ajami had felt himself many times to be in danger of losing his faith. For he had been surrounded by men who had turned out to be good men, despite their Americanism.

For too long he had been here, in the midst of the enemy camp. Their rhetoric had started to make some sense to him. From time to time, over the years, he had felt an urge to call for compromise. Compromise, peace, an end to the ancient cycle of bloodshed. Was it so impossible?

It was. The desire for peace, he knew in his deepest heart, was a betrayal of his mother's memory.

He selected a pair of Italian loafers. He was bending to remove the shoe trees when he sensed a presence standing behind him.

He whirled around, his eyes raking the gloom.

Nobody there. Not even Pegasus.

Nerves, he thought.

But suddenly the dream was with him again: the faceless figure, with eyes deep and dark.

He shook his head. Then he leaned down again, removing the shoe trees and stepping into the loafers.

In one corner of the closet was a packed suitcase. He could take it and run, this very moment. Enough money had been shuttled into the account. But Ajami knew the assassin would find him—wherever in the world he went.

At that instant, Pegasus erupted into urgent barks.

FOR A MOMENT he considered meeting the intruder with words.

He had transferred the money. He had done his part. And unlike the others in the cell, he never had seen the man's face. There was no need for him to die.

Yet he would not have time to get the explanation out. He would be dead before he ever saw the man—just as in the dream.

He stepped to the nightstand by the bed. The Glock

he withdrew contained seventeen rounds of 9mm Para-bellum ammunition; any one would do.

He hefted the gun, wondering if he should go to the assassin or let the assassin come to him. Let the man come to him, he decided. Place his back against a wall and he would survive this, *Insha-Allah* . . .

Pegasus continued to bark. Ajami heard the front door of the apartment buckling; a moment after that, the thunder and flash of a concussion grenade.

He trained the gun on the bedroom door. A dark form in the doorway—

He fired.

The form ducked away.

Then another blast: this one closer, inside the bedroom. A starburst filled his vision. He staggered backward, stunned. Yet when the dark figure reappeared, he managed to squeeze off another shot.

The figure returned fire.

Ajami took another step backward. He hit the wall and sagged down onto the floor, his shirt raking up his back. He had been kicked by a horse, he thought. The horse had kicked him in several places at once—in his arms, across his chest, nicking the side of his head.

He remembered the dream. The call to prayer, echoing; the sharp pain of the blade slipping between his ribs. He had never imagined it would be like this: pummeled by multiple hooves, his shirt hiked inelegantly up his back.

He could hear the call to prayer. Distantly, thinly, but there beyond any doubt.

Two men wearing body armor entered the bedroom, sweeping their firearms back and forth. Two more followed. Then Thomas Warren II, holding his own pistol at shoulder level with both hands.

By then, Ajami had followed the muezzin's call into the light. When the men approached him his eyes were cloudy marbles, staring into eternity.

10

NOBLE LOOKED LIKE A CORPSE.

Finney and Hawthorne moved quietly into the sick-room. Each took a seat in a hard-backed plastic chair.

There were no condolence cards in the room; no cards, no flowers. Just a sick old man, dying alone. So Finney wasn't the only one Noble had managed to alienate over the years. In fact, he had driven them all away— all the students and the patrons and the fawning acolytes. And now this was his reward.

Then Finney sighed, and rubbed at the bridge of his nose with thumb and forefinger. Who would be at his bedside, when the time came? Thomas Warren II? James Hawthorne? Not bloody likely. He would be as alone as Noble. More alone, he thought then. Because he himself would not be here to pay a visit.

Hawthorne remained seated for all of five seconds. Then he said, "Coffee?"

Finney shook his head. Hawthorne stood, gave an oddly ceremonial bow, and left the room.

Noble had two black eyes. The skin there was purple; dark veins stood out in a sunken road map. His breathing was papery and shallow.

An odd disassociation descended on Louis Finney. He had felt much the same sensation watching Lila die. Before the end had come many emotions—wrenching, conflicting emotions. But by the time she had drawn her last breath, the guilt and anger had given way to resignation and relief . . . all of it thinned by that supernatural, oddly comforting sense of disassociation.

One hand moved for the doubloon inside his pocket. "Arthur," he murmured.

No response.

"Arthur," he said. "It's me."

Noble produced a sound: a cooing burble.

His mouth opened, gaping unevenly. In the next moment, he began to shake. His knees drew up sharply, almost to his chest. Finney half stood in his chair. He looked for a call button, found one, and stabbed it.

The young nurse who breezed into the room looked at Noble, looked at Finney, and donned a well-worn expression of sympathy. "What's happening?" Finney asked.

"Electrolyte imbalance. Just reflex. He's not in any pain."

Noble's eyes fluttered open.

"How about a drink?" the young nurse asked politely. She found a cup and tilted it to Noble's lips. The water dribbled immediately down Noble's chin. She picked up a napkin, dabbing primly.

Hawthorne was stepping into the room again, holding a cup of coffee. He halted, absorbing the scene.

"Valium should relax the muscles," the nurse said. "If you gentlemen wouldn't mind stepping outside for a moment . . ."

Finney followed Hawthorne into the corridor as a second nurse stepped past them and closed the door.

Three minutes passed. The nurses came out of the room, easing the door shut. The younger turned to Finney, still wearing the worn expression of sympathy.

"It could be tonight, or tomorrow . . . or he could rally. It might be days yet."

"You'll keep us posted?" Hawthorne said.

"Of course."

Hawthorne turned to face Finney. "Well," he said.

Finney was watching himself from the outside: watching an actor playing a character, in a motion picture about some other hospital, in some other world.

"—come back in the morning, if we don't get a call," Hawthorne was saying. "In the meantime, there's—"

"I'll stay here," Finney said.

THE DOCTOR SHOWED HIM how to use a cotton swab to apply water to Noble's parched lips. Then, once again, Finney and Noble were left alone.

Noble's mouth made a shape resembling a starfish. Whenever Finney dabbed moisture onto the lips, the starfish puckered open and shut.

The day passed. Finney visited the cafeteria once, to force down sustenance. He carried a cup of coffee back to Noble's bedside and left it untouched.

When evening arrived, Noble's calm fractured again. His body shuddered; his knees drew up to his chest.

Finney caught a glimpse of the man's penis beneath the gown, shriveling into his body. It seemed the ultimate invasion of privacy. But Noble, he knew, was past caring.

He reached for the call button. A nurse came and gave Noble some Valium. Then he rested. Every few minutes Finney dabbed water onto his lips.

At eight o'clock a woman he hadn't seen before peeked into the room. "Visiting hours are over," she informed him.

Finney looked at her balefully. She backed off, closing the door.

Before midnight, Noble stirred only one more time. His eyes opened. Then his mouth opened. He was trying to speak. Finney leaned closer, straining to hear. But no sound came. Noble's mouth closed; then his eyes closed.

At last, Finney moved two plastic chairs together. He sat in one and put his feet up on the other. Not much of a bed, but it would have to do.

He remained awake until the small hours of the morning, listening to the shallow breathing. Each time the breathing paused, he left his jerry-rigged bed to check on his mentor. Each time it started again, he returned to the chairs.

Sometime past one, he drifted off.

OUTSIDE THE WINDOW a bird was calling: a distant, nasal *pitty-pit-pit*.

The call belonged to an Antillean nighthawk. Usually the nighthawk was found in climates far to the south. If one had ventured this far north, it would be one for the magazines.

He climbed stiffly out of the plastic chairs. He had been dreaming of a cemetery: Lila standing beside him, urging him to place a stone on a grave. *Forgiveness isn't a gift you give someone else,* she'd said. *You don't need to carry this burden any longer. Let it go, Louis.*

In the dream, a dog had been watching them—the Doberman that had frightened Zattout, fawn-colored and sleek. But now the dog, like Lila and the nighthawk, was nowhere to be seen. Beyond the window was only a parking lot, deserted in the gloomy predawn.

He turned to look at the bed, feeling mired in deep frost.

Suddenly he missed Lila so fiercely that his knees turned weak. She had been a wise woman, he thought. And beautiful—beautiful in a way that went far beyond her dazzling emerald eyes. In the mornings, he had lain beside her and counted the growing lines around those eyes. He had watched her change from a girl to a woman to a lifemate, her fate entwined with his. There had been bad times with the good; and he treasured even those. In a way he treasured those the most. Was it possible that she really was gone? Had she truly left him alone, twisting in the wind?

Behind him lay Arthur Noble. This would be Finney's last chance to offer forgiveness.

He could do it.

He would do it.

He left the window and approached the bed. But he knew the truth before he had reached it. His throat closed to a whistling pinhole. He reached out a hand to steady himself against the bed frame.

Arthur Noble's eyes remained closed. His mouth had

opened again, crookedly. One hand was raised into a grasping claw.

Arthur Noble was dead.

OF THE SIX NAMES on Thomas Warren's list—six of Iqbal Ajami's closest acquaintances, taken from an address book beside the man's bed—three now had lines drawn through them.

The names came from the Arab world. The men to whom the names belonged, however, had been as well integrated into American society as Ajami himself. It was a sleeper cell—a wider-ranging one than Warren had expected. These were powerful men, well entrenched. Ajami, it seemed, had been a part of something big.

But the cell no longer existed. As the names were checked, Warren discovered again and again that he was too late. Someone had been eliminating these men as methodically as a Vegas poker dealer raking in his chips.

The brownstone around him was filled with raised voices. The control post had been expanded to include another half dozen men: videographers and cryptanalysts and experts whose exact roles Warren did not even know. The director would not be thrilled, he knew, to see the operation expanding. The director was most concerned with keeping things quiet, with covering his ass. But Warren was most concerned with finding the man in black who had eluded them at the post office—and to do that, he needed more than three agents and a forensic artist borrowed from the NYPD.

He looked back at the notebook, trying to block out the noise. Past the room's window was a cedar terrace overlooking a garden. It would have been nice to take a few minutes off, he thought, to go out on that balcony and soak up a little sun. Or—even better—to crawl into one of the brownstone's bedrooms and curl up to steal a few moments' sleep. But he could not afford that, not now.

Nathan Hoyle was standing in the doorway. He came forward and flashed a gregarious smile.

"Go ahead."

"The woman at the post office ID'd the photo. Muhammad Nassif was the one checking the P.O. box."

Warren nodded.

"Still no autopsy report. But we're working on it."

When Hoyle had gone, Warren looked back at his notebook. Three of Ajami's closest acquaintances, dead. The boy, dead. No doubt news of more would come in as the investigation progressed.

Perhaps they were suicides, he thought.

Perhaps he had stumbled onto some new breed of mujahedeen, and these men had taken their own lives to cover their tracks. But if they were suicides, they had been of the assisted variety. One man had died during an attempted mugging, another during an interrupted burglary. The third apparently had been taken by a heart attack. The fourth, whose name he just had received over the phone, had suffered an especially bizarre accident: losing his footing as he rode in his own elevator, and falling in a particularly awkward way that had broken his neck. And then there was the boy. Killed by his own pillow.

He thought of the small man at the post office. The

man who had managed to elude a trap that should have been inescapable. This man had not suffered the fate of the others. Because . . .

. . . because he had been the one to kill the others.

Had something gone wrong inside the cell? Had someone hired this man to dispatch the sleepers, and make it look like a series of accidents? Or was the man on his own, serving a personal agenda?

Perhaps word of Quinlan's capture had leaked. That was why somebody was cleaning up the sleeper cell—so that Quinlan's insight would lead the agency nowhere. There was another mole somewhere, still reporting . . .

. . . no. Most of the deaths had occurred before Quinlan had become known to them. And who was to say anybody was cleaning up anything, after all? The series of deaths might have been just what it seemed—an extremely unlikely coincidence.

He got the specialist on the phone. The man's voice was thin but calm as he reported that Quinlan had revealed nothing. It would take time, he explained. Quinlan had spent decades mastering this game. . . .

Warren hung up, then looked at the notepad again. One of the remaining names on the list might provide a clue. If any of the men still lived. Which he doubted.

The dead men. Ajami, with a packed suitcase in his closet and an offshore account ready and waiting. Why?

Because he'd been scared.

Because he'd feared a visit, Warren presumed. A visit from their man in black.

He leaned back in his seat, looking out at the cedar terrace.

The phone rang. He answered, listened, then reached for the pen and crossed out the next name on his list.

Not suicides. These men had been eliminated— methodically, pitilessly.

By the man in black. He knew it now.

The man had visited each of them, in turn.

He must have left some evidence of his visits. He was not invisible, after all.

Warren reached for the phone again.

"STOP," HE SAID.

The analyst froze the image. The digits in the lower right-hand corner of the monitor ran backward, to 07:31:26-4-12.

He ran the sequence again. The video had been captured by a security camera in the lobby of Al Guhrair's apartment building. Onscreen, a man moved past the front desk with his face turned down. He had come from the stairwell, and within three seconds had vanished through the door leading to the street.

"Let me clean that up," the analyst said.

As he worked, he explained what he was doing in more detail than Warren needed to hear. He tweaked the luminance signal, increasing the overall brightness of the image, and then adjusted the chrominance signal, sharpening the contrast of the relative color values. The video imaging analyst was a pudgy man, redheaded, with green Irish eyes. He studied the grainy image onscreen for a few seconds; the mouse in his hand clicked metronomically.

"We've got a signal-to-noise ratio of thirty db, which

makes this a good candidate for enhancement. Let's apply a filter to emphasize the motion. A mathematical routine estimates the velocity and acceleration of the subject, and the computer compensates at the level of individual pixels. . . ."

The clip replayed. The figure with the downturned face became the most noticeable object on the screen: a wiry man, dressed all in black.

The analyst zoomed closer. Now the face onscreen looked like an abstract portrait of a face, blocks of gray and white, the kind of optical illusion that might assemble itself meaningfully if the viewer backed away and relaxed his eyes. The analyst tapped a fingernail against his two front teeth. "And for my next trick . . ."

The image sharpened. Warren found himself looking at a photograph of a man that might have been taken with any disposable drugstore camera. The dark eyes faced down, pointedly avoiding the camera.

Warren waved Anthony Cass forward. Cass approached, holding his baseball cap in both hands.

He studied the screen.

He nodded.

11

FINNEY'S NOSE was running.

He raised the handkerchief to blow it. His hands were trembling slightly, making the task more difficult than it should have been.

They reached the town. They climbed the hill. They passed through the log gate, then through the checkpoint at the stone wall. When the Town Car disgorged them before the farmhouse, Finney headed immediately for the front door. He took the staircase to his room.

His hands wouldn't stop shaking. He pressed them together, twisted them into a knot. At last, the trembling subsided. He kept his hands tightly entwined, to forestall a recurrence.

Distantly came the sound of a train whistle. *The loneliest sound in the world,* he thought.

Then a tentative knock at the door. Finney didn't answer. The door opened; James Hawthorne peeked in.

"I hope I'm not disturbing you."

Again, Finney didn't answer. Hawthorne came to sit

next to him on the bed. He was a short man, but solidly built; the frame creaked when he lowered himself onto it. He sat facing the window, looking out at the purpling twilight with his glass eye drifting off to the left.

"I wanted to offer my condolences," he said after a moment.

Finney nodded.

"I'll speak with Warren about arranging the funeral. But it might be some weeks yet. You don't happen to know if the man had a plot . . . ?"

To the best of Finney's knowledge, Noble's faith would not condone the delay of a funeral. But he only shook his head.

Hawthorne folded his hands and rubbed the thumbs together, aping Finney's behavior, consciously or not. Then he began to speak—expressing, with a modicum of subtlety, that if KINGFISHER did not move faster, they would do irreparable damage to their own cause. Hawthorne knew the Arab mindset. It was a tribal mentality. In the Arab world, kindness equated to weakness. . . .

Finney knew from Warren that the man's background was with the clandestine operations directorate. He had worked in Afghanistan twenty years before, arming rebels to fight against the Soviets. Now those same rebels had coalesced into al Qaeda. Their attention, along with their CIA-funded weaponry, had been turned from the Soviets to the Americans. It was no surprise, Finney supposed, that Hawthorne believed he understood the intricacies of the tribal mindset. He had toiled alongside these people. He likely had lost his eye toiling alongside them.

". . . every time Zattout receives a glass of wine or a walk outside, he takes it as evidence that we're soft. I don't mean to step on your toes, Doctor. You have your expertise, and I have mine. But you can't deny that our progress has been disappointing, at best."

Finney was remembering a passage from a book he had read, comparing the religious symbols of the West and the Muslim East: the angular compositions of the cross and the Jewish star versus the softness of the crescent moon. The symbols of the West were straightforward, clearly defined. But the crescent moon was an ambiguous arc, turning back on itself. In the Arab world, the author had stated—in the world of *tribal mentality,* as Hawthorne put it—men could sit down and break bread and still consider one another mortal enemies when the meal was done. Because the Arab world was flexible, uncertain, ever changing. One leader held power only until another stronger leader came along to depose him. By trying to deal with these primitive clans as modern city-states, the author had concluded, the West was painting itself into a corner. For the Arab leaders would pretend to play by the rules of diplomacy; but it was only a pretense. And as soon as backs were turned, the knives would come out.

But during war, of course, one depersonalized the enemy. And writing off the entire Arab culture as possessing a *tribal mentality* hardly offered a balanced picture.

"I've had a chance to read your report," Hawthorne was saying. "These sleeper cells, about which Zattout continues to hide his knowledge . . . their victims won't be soldiers, Doctor. They'll be innocents."

Finney grunted acknowledgment.

"If you're willing to do what needs to be done, you could make faster progress with Zattout—isn't that so? Coercive techniques are not proving effective. It's time to proceed to the next step."

Finney didn't answer.

Tribal mentality or no, there was truth in Hawthorne's words. For whatever reasons, Finney had not pressed Zattout as hard as he might have. Because he had been afraid of the consequences, perhaps. Afraid of where confrontation might lead them.

"It's important to go after them where they live. We can't wait for them to come to us. An ocean between America and the people determined to compromise our freedoms doesn't keep us safe—"

The wall between the past and the present had become a transparent scrim. He could feel Susan Franklin standing just on the other side of it. Lila was there too, watching. And somewhere in the shadows behind them, Arthur Noble. It was Noble as he once had been, callow and criminally self-assured, his chin thrust out with arrogance.

"How do you train a dog? You slap him across the nose with a newspaper when he misbehaves. These people are the same way. They'll get away with whatever they can, for as long as they can. At some point, if you want them to understand who is in charge, you need to give them a slap."

Finney thought of Black Jack Pershing, slaughtering forty-nine suspected Muslim terrorists with bullets soaked in pig's blood—and forestalling extremist attacks for over four decades. "I agree," he said.

Hawthorne did a slight double take.

"You do," he said after a moment.

Finney nodded.

He would not proceed to depatterning. Depatterning was the last resort. But there were weapons in his arsenal that had not yet been brought to bear. If Zattout were to be drugged, he might become more susceptible to manipulation. Then Finney might make some headway in identifying the trauma underlying the cynophobia. He might isolate and exploit the child-identity within the man. The issue of his evasion on the sleeper cells might be confronted directly, from a position of power.

"The kid gloves," Finney said, "are off."

AS HE FOLLOWED Police Chief Hank Reps into the woods behind the Sleepy Hollow motel, Thomas Warren II tried to keep his mind from telling bad jokes.

He couldn't help himself. In the safe house he had felt removed from his surroundings, living in a generic stretch of backwoods northwestern America; in the Manhattan brownstone he had been surrounded by modern technology. Now, with the night rustle of leaves all around, walking into a pitch-black forest, following the bobbing light of the police chief's flashlight, he was acutely aware that he was in the Catskills.

Or perhaps his mind was serving up the bad jokes for another reason—to provide distraction. Although the girl's body had been removed twelve hours before, they were entering a killing ground where a child had met her end. The black forest was filled with a plangent, insinuating wind. In this atmosphere it was all too easy to imagine that the girl's spirit would continue haunting the ground where her body so hastily had been laid to rest. And it was all too easy to imagine, as he and Police Chief Hank Reps approached the shallow grave, that the wind would gain strength; then the flashlight would begin to flicker as the batteries died . . .

When I was born, my father spent three weeks trying to find a loophole in my birth certificate. Thomas Warren, Senior—otherwise a man of impeccable taste—had loved that borscht belt shtick. Whose had that been? Jackie Vernon's? Or maybe Shecky Greene's?

Ahead, the bright yellow of police tape strung up between trees caught the flashlight. Beside him the police chief was talking in a laconic drawl, evidently not sharing Warren's unease.

"My brother-in-law," he was saying. "He's the one who gave me a ring about your BOLO/APB. Few days ago, we were at a barbecue and I was telling him about our prime suspect in the case. He thought the fellow in your photo looked like the fellow I'd described . . . so he sent it on, and I showed it to the girl's parents. Beyond a doubt, they say. That's the guy, they say. Simon Christopher."

They reached a flat rock by a streambed. As the light passed over it, the police tape trembled in the breeze. "You can see there was a little scuffle here . . ."

Warren looked; but he saw no such thing. All he saw, in the moving circle of light, was a rushing creek, patchy grass, bare dirt. Some marks were in the dirt—squiggles and scribbles—but how was one to know they had come from a teenaged girl fighting for her life? Police Chief Reps, he thought, was a regular Sherlock Holmes.

If he had been better rested, perhaps Warren could have read the scribbles in the dirt himself. He had reached a stage of sleep deprivation where it was difficult to connect one thought to another, let alone make brilliant leaps of deduction. Driving up, he had become so entranced by the sunset in the trees—the sun minting the leaves into gold, alchemy at its most real—that he had nearly plowed right off the road, through the guardrail and into a ravine.

After a moment, the man led him still deeper into the forest. Warren lit a cigarette; the nicotine gave his system a jolt, sharpening his edges.

"He left the motel the same night the girl disappeared. Nobody saw them together . . . but that don't mean a thing. The girl was keeping to herself, more and more. It's the way with teenagers, ain't it? I've got two girls of my own. Eleven and thirteen. The thought of them—to tell the truth, I can't even face it. Now here's where we found her. Sometimes she'd come into the woods back here, alone. But she must have brought him along that night. We found a bottle of vodka in the grave. So that's what they were up to, we think. Grave was dug by hand. Hard to see, since we took it up again using a Cat . . ."

More police tape, flapping importantly. The Caterpillar that had dug up the grave had deposited the earth in two thick wedges shaped like oversized orange slices. As he looked over the scene, Warren wondered: Why had the man killed the girl? Perhaps she had seen too much. Or perhaps he was a rapist, along with everything else. He wondered if there had been evidence of molestation.

"Didn't touch her," Hank Reps answered before the question had been asked. "Except to break her neck, that is. With his bare hands, according to the coroner. What kind of man can break a little girl's neck with his bare hands? I don't mean what kind of man, physically. I mean what kind of man, inside."

They stood looking at the upturned earth. Warren shivered, and thought of another joke:

A musician played in Key West. It was the first time I knew what key he was in.

Ah, Uncle Miltie. He'd had a million of them.

Suddenly, Warren felt nauseated. He turned away from the shallow grave, ground out his cigarette on the sole of his shoe, then conscientiously pocketed the butt.

So the man had been within thirty miles of the safe house. Because he'd been receiving intelligence from Quinlan? Had there been more avenues leading away from the compound than just the P.O. box in New York? If they had taken Ajami alive, they could have asked him for their answers. Alas, it wasn't meant to be.

Perhaps Quinlan would break, and provide illumination. But Warren wasn't betting on it.

Yet they had a name—*Simon Christopher.* They had a photograph. And now they had evidence that the man was a killer.

"You've got to ask yourself if he did this before," the police chief remarked. "Just because we only found one body doesn't mean there aren't others. In my experience, these guys don't usually stop at one."

His experience, Warren thought. Hank Rep's experience with serial killers, despite his Holmesian skills of deduction, probably began and ended with the Saturday-afternoon matinee on Channel 9.

Absently, Warren put another cigarette in his mouth. The police chief continued staring at the grave, his lips twisting. Because he had two girls of his own, as he had said. To a man like this, a child killer was personal.

He did some rough math. They had a photograph in the hands of the NYPD, an All Points Bulletin to Be on the Lookout—which meant that several thousand pairs of eyes were looking for the suspect. But how many men were there like the sheriff, with teenaged girls of his own? Many more than several thousand. And their eyes would be hungrier than the eyes of the police.

Another joke occurred to Warren, unbidden. *Never raise your hands to your kids. It leaves your groin unprotected.*

He smiled, very slightly. That was Red Buttons, he thought. The one and only.

But you couldn't get away with a joke like that these days. Violence against children, of course, was no laughing matter. Men like the police chief beside him— and countless others—would cry bloody murder at a joke like that.

He thought of all these men, with all their teenaged daughters and all their eyes . . . just waiting to be put to use.

Bloody murder, he thought again from nowhere, and lit the cigarette.

THE ASSASSIN sat on a bench on Central Park West, his face turned up to catch the bright morning sun.

His head didn't move; but his eyes tracked steadily back and forth, from the awning across the way—Iqbal Ajami's building—to the government agents who also were watching the building.

On the northern corner of the block, a man lingered with a dog on a leash. Taking his bulldog for a turn by the park, one might have thought. Except the man had been lingering for fifteen minutes; the dog clearly had no further business to do.

On the southern corner was a second agent, manning a shoe-polish station. During the quarter-hour that the assassin watched, the agent was approached twice by pedestrians requesting a shine. He begged off, making some excuse that hardly seemed to satisfy the frustrated customers.

So they not only were watching the box; they were watching the money man, too.

How had they gotten onto him? Through Ajami's own negligence? Or had they found him through the boy?

Presently, the assassin stood. He wandered down Central Park West, moving unhurriedly. At Sixty-sixth Street he turned west. Perhaps a newspaper would offer more information about the disappearance of the girl. Perhaps there would be a clue, there, as to whether or not a connection had been made between her, and him, and Ajami, and Quinlan.

The city around him was cacophonous: car alarms, sirens, blaring radios, whirring portable generators. The air felt heavy and humid, clinging to the back of his neck. He approached Broadway and saw a kiosk. As he angled toward it, a man selling snow globes featuring miniature Twin Towers followed him with a flat, chary glare.

He matched the gaze with one of his own; but the man kept staring. Finally, as the assassin walked past, he looked away. No wonder the man stared, the assassin thought. He was not at ease with himself. Apprehension was radiating off him in waves. He needed to calm down.

Upon reaching the kiosk, he took a coin from his pocket and then turned his eyes to the stacks of newspapers.

CHILD KILLER, read twenty-point type on the Newark *Star-Ledger*.

Below the headline, a photograph of his face filled the entirety of the front page.

Fear touched the base of his spine.

Beside the *Star-Ledger* was the *New York Post*. Here the headline was an interrogative: SERIAL KILLER? The photograph was smaller; he was sharing the front page with a picture of Sonya Jacobs. She was wearing a field hockey uniform and grimacing into the camera, her cheeks pouched with baby fat that had been gone by the time he'd met her.

Beside the *Post*, *USA Today*. The headline concerned a rash of tornadoes in the Midwest. Beside *USA Today*, *The New York Times*. Again, the headline concerned tornadoes. But just above the fold was a hint of another story: "Police Identify Suspect in . . ." If he reached out and turned the paper over, to see the front page below the fold, the same photograph would be there. Where had they gotten it?

A family was squeezing around him on the sidewalk:

husband, wife, toddler. The husband's eyes glanced across his face without pause. Then they returned, glinting.

His paralysis broke. He started moving again, continuing down Broadway. His gait felt stiff; his knees were trying to lock. Was the husband still watching him?

On the corner he was approaching stood two policemen.

On a stoop to his left—a man reading the *Post*. The man looked up. He looked down at the paper. Looked up again.

The assassin turned back toward Central Park West.

The man on the stoop was bringing a cell phone to his ear. He was dialing a single number. *0,* of course. For operator.

He moved faster, heartbeat accelerating in his chest.

On Central Park West, he turned south. To look over his shoulder would draw attention. And with his face on the front page of every newspaper, he could not afford that. Yet he needed to get off the street. He needed to find a taxi, immediately. He looked back—

—and saw the pair of blue-suited policemen following.

They moved at a fast walk, the same pace used by the assassin. Directed to him by the man on the stoop, he thought. The police were not accelerating, not forcing his hand. So they were backup. Backup implied something that needed backing up. A moment later he saw a police cruiser idling at a traffic light, half a block ahead. Then another cruiser, approaching the intersection from a cross street, prowling steadily forward.

He turned to his left, into the park. One of the cops

was yelling something. He missed the words, but the tone was unmistakable: an urgent imperative.

He adjusted the bag he was carrying so that it hung tight across his chest, out of his way. His right wrist flicked and then there was a blade in his hand, concealed from sight.

The park was relatively empty. He continued south, moving at a trot. A leafy glen lay to his left. He ducked through it, coming out onto another path running parallel to the first. Moving farther from Central Park West, deeper into the greenery, he could hear the echo of the policeman's voice.

A helicopter was crossing overhead. He paused, making certain he was concealed beneath an overhang of leaves. After a few seconds, the sound of the rotors receded. He continued south.

Through foliage on the left, he could see one of the roads that ran through the park. A taxi there idled at a stoplight. Tempting—but no good. Traffic might choke to a stop. Then they would have him. Before getting into a taxi, he needed to throw off the pursuit.

He tossed a glance over his shoulder. Distantly, he could see a spot of blue.

When he looked front again, a policeman was there.

The man looked ludicrously shocked. He promptly backed off, reaching for his holster. The blade whipped up, landed quivering in his throat.

The assassin was past the body before it hit the ground, then under a canopy of branches, around a woman pushing a baby stroller.

He was nearing the southern flank of the park. He heard the rumble of eighteen-wheelers, the squeal of air brakes. At least one man was behind him, shouting. The helicopter was back, blades pounding.

He dodged left, through a group of tourists. Then, suddenly, he broke out onto Fifty-ninth Street. Across the way, before the row of premier hotels, was more blue—a phalanx of police, no doubt notified by radio of his imminent appearance.

Behind him: more police. Above, the circling helicopter.

Another wave of tourists broke, offering a few precious moments of cover. He looked around desperately. This southern end of the park was thronged with pedestrians, hot dog carts, caricaturists. A line of old-fashioned horse-drawn carriages waited to provide couples with romantic turns through the trees. Soon enough the pursuit would spill into this crowd. He could not hide here for long.

If he could change his appearance, he might have a chance. But drawing up the hood on his tunic only would attract more attention. And there was no time to reach into his bag, to apply a proper disguise.

He moved from reflex, his body ahead of his mind.

He stepped toward the first horse-drawn carriage in the queue, flicking a fresh blade into his hand. He reached for the nearest woman passing in the crowd—a pretty redhead of about his age, wearing a belly shirt and cut-off blue jeans, with a scattering of freckles across a pale nose. Not even a remote resemblance to Rana.

He put one hand around her wrist; her eyes widened. He moved closer, shielding the blade from view as he pressed it against her ribs. "I'm not going to hurt you," he said into her ear.

Around them, pedestrians streamed past in a bustling flow. Where were the cops? Almost here.

"Don't scream," he said. "Stay calm. I'm not going to hurt you."

Then he was ushering her into the back of the carriage. At first she refused to move. The knife poked into her side, hard enough to break the skin. She moaned. He lifted her forward and she half climbed, half fell into the seat below the canopy. Two bouquets of flowers mounted on the carriage roof shivered in a gust of wind.

He turned to face the driver, who was turning himself at the sudden weight, and found a smile. "Once around the park," he said.

The driver grinned back. "Beautiful day for it," he answered, and shook the reins in his hand as the assassin settled into the wagon beside the young woman.

The horse began to clip-clop forward on the pavement.

The woman had gone deathly pale. A small pink tongue came out to brush across her lips. "Please," she said. "Please don't hurt me. I'm pregnant. I'm two months—"

He angled the blade up into the chest cavity, finding the heart. Her mouth made a sound like a popping bubble.

He let go of the blade and took her face in both of his hands. Then leaned forward and pressed his lips against hers, keeping the back of his head facing the park.

He could hear feet pounding. Police—looking for a single man on foot, wearing black. Not looking for a couple on a romantic carriage ride through Central Park, a couple so in love they couldn't keep their hands off each other.

Blood was refluxing up the woman's gullet, gushing from her nose. He gagged, but didn't lean away. The blood warmly coated his mouth and chin.

Five seconds passed. They kept clip-clopping north. He forced himself to hold still.

The lower half of his face grew wet and tacky. He pulled his head back a few inches, and chanced a glance out of the carriage.

Still more police—spilling down from inside the park, weapons drawn.

He kissed the dead woman again.

When the kiss broke, he risked another glance out of the carriage. For the moment, the coast was clear. The police were behind him, in the place he had been moments before.

He pushed the redhead away. She fell back into the seat, ichor streaming onto her chest.

He slipped silently out of the carriage, wiping a sleeve across his face, vanishing into the trees.

12

THE HYPODERMIC NEEDLE penetrated the cork smoothly. Slowly, Louis Finney depressed the plunger; a cocktail of Nembutal, Thorazine, and Seconal moved from syringe to wine.

He withdrew the needle with care, then searched for evidence of tampering. There was none. Ali Zattout would not know that the wine had been doctored until it was too late. The Thorazine would produce lethargy and sleepiness. This would be balanced by the Nembutal, which fostered anxiety and confusion. The Seconal would smooth off the edges, blending the effects. Even as Zattout came to suspect that he had been drugged, he would have a hard time knowing for sure—and if all went well, he would have a hard time caring.

Then he would be at a marked disadvantage. Finney would explore the regression associated with dogs. He would press hard on the matter of sleeper cells, about which he knew Zattout had been less than honest. And he would send a clear message: lack of cooperation resulted not in rewards but in refined tactics. There was no percentage to be gained by continuing to hold out, for the prisoner was entirely at their mercy.

He sniffed, wiped a hand across his nose, then carried the bottle and a glass of cut crystal down the shadowy staircase.

"IN MY *HAMULA*," Zattout said, "a man with your beard wouldn't last a day."

He was sitting on the edge of his cot with the glass of wine—still untouched—held in both hands. His eyes were cloudy; a small fleck of saliva glistened near one corner of his mouth. He raised the glass, then lowered it without drinking.

"The neighborhood children would hunt you down and shave it off. Then they'd press their feet in your face. A man shouldn't wear a beard like that, they would think. And so you would be punished, and insulted."

Finney managed not to reach self-consciously for his beard. "I'm glad I don't live in your *hamula*."

"So thin and gray. Hardly a beard at all."

"Cultural differences," Finney said.

Again, Zattout raised the glass. Again he lowered it.

"If you could see what I see," he said. "When I'm alone at night—my grandmother comes to visit. She tells me how ashamed she is. How I've been disavowed by my family. Is McDonald's such a horror? That's what they fear more than anything, you know. Chicken Mc-Nuggets. Insanity."

Finney made no comment.

"I'm the *shohet,* she tells me. And she's right. I have no problem with McDonald's. Would I be here if I did?"

He shook his head, two quick shakes like a dog coming out of a lake. The next part of Zattout's conversation occurred internally. His brow furrowed; one tapered finger compulsively traced the rim of the glass in his hand. His eyes closed. For thirty seconds they stayed that way, as he swayed gently back and forth on the cot.

At last he blinked, and looked at Finney with unexpected keenness. He raised the glass; Finney's eyes followed it. He lowered it; Finney's eyes followed. He raised it again. Lowered it.

Then he barked a sour little laugh, and held the glass forward. "You drink it."

Finney didn't move.

"Go on," Zattout said. "Humor me."

"I don't drink."

"It's drugged."

"You saw me take out the cork with your own eyes."

"Then you drink it."

He kept holding the glass forward.

Finney reached for it. He took a small sip and tried to hand it back.

"Drink deep, Doctor. Life is too short to deny yourself such pleasures."

"I appreciate the offer. But what I'd really like to do is return to—"

"Until you drink, I'm not saying another word."

Finney sighed. He took another, larger sip.

"All right," he said. "Now. I'd like to get back to the subject of shipping operations in the Black Sea. There seems to be some confusion about communications. Are the ships in active contact with al Qaeda? If not, how are they made aware of changes in protocol?"

Zattout's eyes were frostily calculating; he didn't answer.

"Did you hear me? I want to know how the ships stay in touch with al Qaeda. What arrangements have been made in advance, and how changes are communicated."

No answer.

"Perhaps it's not the best day," Finney said. "You don't seem in a mood to cooperate. Perhaps some time to yourself . . ."

"Finish the wine."

"What will that prove?"

"Everything."

Finney hesitated.

Then he raised the glass.

Backing down now would shift the power position in their dynamic, perhaps irrevocably. Zattout would have won his bluff; the pretense of mutual trust would be lost. But if he could convince Zattout by example to quaff his own glass, they would be on equal footing.

No, not quite equal. For Finney would have the advantage of knowing what to expect from the doctored wine. He would concentrate, then cut the interview short and escape without losing face.

"If I drink it," he said, "you'll be satisfied?"

"Completely."

"Then you'll join me in a glass?"

Zattout nodded.

Finney felt a bit reckless. It would be all right, he thought. Zattout would follow his lead. The session would be salvaged. But if the man refused to drink . . .

. . . why did he feel so reckless? Could it be the effects of the drugs, even after only two sips? Impossible.

He drained half the glass.

"There," he said.

"Finish it."

"I can't. As I said, I don't drink. But why don't you . . . ?"

"No, thank you."

"It's excellent. I recommend it highly."

"Not right now. Thank you."

"Suit yourself." It would not do to show desperation. Finney set the glass aside. "Shipping operations in the Black Sea. What lines of communication are used?"

"I've explained this already. Have you not been paying attention?"

"I've been paying perfect attention. But I require clarification on this point."

"Or what?" Dark mirth danced in Zattout's eyes. "I'll be locked in a cell and drugged?"

"You know what the repercussions might be. Transferral to Diego Garcia. No more walks outside, no more wine."

"Did you have a bad night, Doctor? You seem on edge."

"Don't concern yourself with me. Answer the question, please."

"If I do—what reward might I expect?"

"Wouldn't you like to go outside again?"

"I'm looking farther than that." The leg started to jump; Zattout pressed both hands on his knee, stilling it. "When this is all done—what can I expect?"

"That's not for me to decide. Have a drink." Finney reached for the bottle. The bottle was not just where he expected it to be; it was an inch farther to the right.

He got his hand around the neck, then deliberately re-filled the glass. When he offered it, Zattout shook his head. Finney held it tightly, being careful not to spill.

"Let's talk about dogs," he said. He needed to regain the offensive. But his mouth seemed filled with flannel; before continuing, he swallowed. "Do you remember any incident that might explain your fear?"

"I have no fear of dogs."

"You may not even be conscious of it. But I believe there is a part of you into which this fear has been sub-limated. I suspect a trauma . . ."

A grin slanted Zattout's face. "Do you feel all right, Doctor?"

"Fine." Finney could feel himself squinting, as the bare bulb in the ceiling burned his eyes. "Drink the wine."

"I don't think so. It doesn't seem to have agreed with you."

"What do you mean?"

The words were not as clearly articulated as he would have liked. He wanted to return to the line of question-ing, to regain the upper hand—but suddenly he could not remember the line of questioning.

"Should I expect to spend the rest of my life in de-tention centers, Doctor? Or will my responsibilities be discharged, at some point?"

Finney's vision had turned blurry; a warmth had risen inside him. "I'd expect the latter," he managed. As he spoke, he consulted his notes. He kept squinting, try-ing to make out the word there. Yemen. He would press Zattout on the connection between—

"But you will never be convinced that I've given full

cooperation. There always will be doubt in your mind. I do not believe that I will ever enjoy freedom again."

"You've got to trust me."

"After you just tried to drug me?"

The Seconal headed off Finney's alarm, spreading it thin. Yes, this was bad. But he felt so comfortable, floating away on wings of forgetfulness . . . how could one be too concerned?

"Who do you report to? Who will decide my fate?"

Finney shook his head. "My . . . superiors."

"I'd like to speak with these superiors. Can that be arranged?"

"I can't say."

"I see right through you," Zattout said crisply. "You don't sleep very well at night—do you, Doctor?"

Finney couldn't answer. Now his head felt filled with sunshine, bright and blinding. He closed his notebook and put it under his arm.

"Bring a message to your *superiors* for me. Tell them I won't waste any more time speaking with a fool. If they want to talk to me, they can come do it themselves."

He stood up and moved past Finney, to address the one-way mirror directly.

"Do you hear me?" he asked his reflection. "Send me someone who knows what's going on—or finish this. No more games."

Finney gained his feet unsteadily, picked up the bottle.

"Go sleep it off," Zattout told him scornfully. "And don't come back here, Doctor. Send me someone with real authority." Then to the mirror: "That's two. Who's next?"

Finney staggered past him. He opened the door,

slipped out, and then dropped both bottle and glass. As they exploded on the floor—*pow POW*—he leaned against the door, closing it.

Zattout continued to face the mirror. Hawthorne was looking at Finney with an expression disconcertingly close to Zattout's—derision.

HE SAT facing the limestone fireplace in the living room, head in hands.

Presently he became conscious of a soft whirring sound. Inside his head, he thought. The drugs were buzzing around in there. Or was it the cold? He wanted to lie down on the couch, to fall asleep right here.

No. The whirring came from the mantel above the fireplace. He focused blearily on a pair of candlesticks. The candlesticks were humming. *Cameras,* he understood suddenly. *You may notice that the house is wired,* Arthur Noble had said. He had mentioned one-way mirrors and hidden microphones. But he had neglected to mention hidden cameras.

Or was it only his imagination?

James Hawthorne stepped into the room. He said nothing; but Finney could feel his opinion without needing it spelled out. *You don't have what it takes,* Hawthorne was saying—without ever opening his mouth.

Finney forced himself to concentrate. He drew curtains in his mind, blocking off the sunshine. "We're going to refine our focus," he said.

Hawthorne waited.

"A change from coercive methods to behavioral conditioning. If necessary, depatterning."

Hawthorne nodded.

"Twenty-four hours without food or water," Finney said. "Then a meal with thirty cc staph enterotoxin. Let's see him avoid drugs when his only other choice is starvation."

"Staph enterotoxin?"

"To produce nausea. He'll throw the food right back up. But the toxin will remain in his bloodstream for six hours. He'll suffer."

Hawthorne nodded again.

"We'll interrupt his sleep. Break down his defenses. He'll come to understand who's in charge. And if he doesn't, we'll wipe him clean. Then we'll see what's in his mind, with his cooperation or without."

"Whatever you recommend, Doctor."

Finney felt that there was something else to be said. But he couldn't get his mind around it. He rubbed at his temples. "I'd like to lie down for a few minutes," he mumbled.

Hawthorne nodded once more, and vanished from the doorway. Finney tried to get himself off the couch, to climb the stairs to his bedroom. But he couldn't make his legs move. Instead he lowered himself onto the cushions, drawing into the fetal position. As he drifted away, he heard the whirring again, subtle but steady, both within his head and without.

HE WAS NOT a large man.

Studying his face in the mirror above the filthy sink, he considered this fact.

His most striking characteristic, like it or not, was his

diminutive stature; the rest of his features tended toward indistinctiveness. People tended to project their own suppositions onto a face like his. One observer might describe him as handsome, another as epicene, even gamine. He might be considered Caucasian or Hispanic or Asian or Middle Eastern. His age could be guessed at anywhere between twenty-five and forty.

But everyone considered him short.

A sound came from behind him—a rattling doorknob. "Open up," said a male voice.

"One minute," he said.

"It's a public freaking bathroom," the voice said.

If it had been that public of a bathroom, the assassin thought, there would not have been a lock on the door. He returned his attention to the mirror.

He was short, and slight. So the best disguise would address these traits. Lifts for his shoes; multiple layers of clothing. He should become a large man, a bulky one.

Except all he had to work with were the tools within his bag. The disguise kit there could change his features, but not his build.

He considered himself for another few moments, and then went to work.

He would play an older man, tending toward puffiness. He opened the kit and lined its contents on the rim of the sink: a mixing dish, a mirror, brushes, scissors, cotton swabs, tweezers, spirit gum, all contained in a case no larger than a videocassette.

He used a stippling technique to design a foundation that suggested pockmarks. A 6mm sable brush applied the foundation, emphasizing the roundness of his cheeks and the swelling below his eyes. He washed the brush and then applied red-tinted shadows, using horizontal lines to lend maximum width to his bone structure. When he had finished, the face looking back at him was no longer that of a clean-featured young man. It was a round-faced fellow on his way into late middle-age . . . but an unfinished one, a halfway-real person.

No further complaints from outside the door. The man had moved on, he guessed, to find another public restroom in the park.

He added a layer of translucent face powder. Then some broken veins, using a coarse sponge. A dark brown pencil intensified the shadows beneath his lower lip, focusing on the center to imply fullness, creating a small, well-rounded mouth that gave the impression of bitterness and age. He considered his efforts, wiped off the pencil, and tried again. Better.

White lining color on a mascara brush lightened his eyebrows. He applied the color against the grain, thickening and fluffing.

Now the hair.

He used whitener with a tinting brush. False hairpieces, he knew, raised suspicion. If one was looking for a man in a disguise, wigs and handlebar mustaches were liable to catch the eye. Instead he worked with what nature had given him, striving for subtlety. Gray around the temples; a few streaks on top. He used gel to pull the hair away from his forehead, emphasizing the slight receding hairline. Late middle-age, not old age. Don't overdo it, he thought.

When he'd finished with the hair, the cipher in the mirror looked back at him levelly.

He pressed the latex piece into position. The nose

was larger than his own, with a bulb on the tip. The man he was playing was a habitual drinker, he decided. A wealthy man, a city dweller. Going upstate for a fishing trip, more likely than not—an excuse to drink during the day. He trimmed away the excess latex, keeping the outline of the nose as irregular as possible. Straight edges would be difficult to camouflage.

A thin film of spirit gum went around the false piece. He fit it carefully over his face and used a dampened paper towel wrapped around his fingertips to press down the edges. He dabbed liquid latex adhesive along the joints, then paused to let it dry.

When he looked at himself again, a stranger was looking back. But the stranger was clearly a construct. He slowly and painstakingly applied light makeup to the false nose, blending it into the mottled complexion. Better.

Three moles of Derma Wax—two by his mouth, one in the center of his right cheek.

He looked away, then looked back. His eye picked out flaws in the disguise: uneven coloring, too smooth skin. He fixed it.

At last the face in the mirror looked almost genuine. Seen from a slight distance, under less-than-direct light, it would suffice.

AFTER LEAVING THE CAB he spent ten minutes watching the door of his room at the Arlington Motel. Then he found his courage, and moved forward.

Inside was no evidence of intrusion. He gathered together his laptop computer and the few belongings not already in the bag. Two minutes later he was outside again, walking rapidly away. He hailed another cab, slipped inside, and hesitated. He had nowhere to go—but he could not stay here.

"Leonard Street," he said, pulling the address from thin air. "Greenpoint."

The driver reached for his meter. They drove for about eight minutes, past laundromats and fast food joints. Then they were passing elevated railroad tracks; a weedy cul-de-sac beneath a trestle caught the assassin's eye. He would be safe there long enough to figure out his next move. He let a few more seconds pass. As they drew up to a stoplight he told the driver, "I forgot something—let me out here, please."

Then he backtracked toward the cul-de-sac. The place smelled of urine and rotting garbage. Before entering, he searched the darkness for vagrants. Then he advanced, crouching to avoid cobwebs, and found a fairly dry spot to sit among empty bottles and cans—an old wooden platform, rotting but stable.

The twenty-ninth of April, he thought as he sank down onto the dirty wood.

He could not pick up the Honda until tomorrow. If he even could do it then. What if Sal Santiori had seen a newspaper? Then it would not be safe to show his face, disguise or no.

The post office box was under watch. Ajami's building was under watch; the chances of the second payment being delivered seemed slim. His face was known. It would be trouble enough just getting out of this country without being arrested. Why go ahead?

Because he needed to prove something. To himself, more than anyone else. At the temple he had been known as *little mouse*. Yet he was capable—more capable than the others there.

The difficulty of the assignment had been a large part of its appeal. He would not pretend to be more than he was, but nor would he pretend to be less. He was indeed *little mouse*. And that would be enough—if he was true to himself.

Once he had proven his value, the accomplishment would show on his face. Inner peace created outer power. Once he had completed the challenge, his face no longer would blur into indistinctiveness. Then when he finally did find Rana again . . .

. . . she would be stepping out of a limousine, he thought, on a shopping trip of some kind. Her husband would be extraordinarily wealthy; she would be attended by servants and chauffeurs. But the trappings of money would not make her happy inside. Rana was too complicated for that, too good.

When she first saw him, she would not remember. To the assassin, she had been the one person who had given him kindness in a cold world. But to Rana, he had been just another urchin. She would not remember; but she would be impressed by the bearing of this man, who would approach her as she stepped out of her limousine, asking for a moment of her time. She would see, even without the riches brought by the second payment, that this man before her was a greater man than all others. He never even would remind her that they had met once before, decades earlier, in a world of squalor and misery . . .

. . . it was too fragile. Thinking about it would make it go away. Then he would be left with nothing.

He focused on concrete things, on the immediate future.

He needed to pass another night in the city. With the disguise, he could manage it. He would avoid motels and public thoroughfares. He would become, however briefly, a part of the community of drifters. Then he would pick up the Honda. That in itself was hardly a risk-free proposition. Would Sal have reported his illicit customer to the authorities? Or would that have put Sal himself in a bad light? The nature of their business, after all, had been illegal.

Somehow he would manage it. Then he would get out of the city. He would need to hear another weather report before proceeding. Without proper cover—without a guarantee of twenty-four hours of rain—he would not attempt to penetrate the compound.

First, however, he needed to get through tonight. That was the priority.

A sound from outside the cul-de-sac. A wino—even from here reeking of body odor. He was peering owlishly into the gloom. "Who's there?"

The assassin took his bags and stood. "Just moving on," he said.

"That's right," the man said, with tattered arrogance. "Just keep right on moving."

He did—stepping outside and then pacing the train tracks, looking for a place secluded enough to settle for the night.

THOMAS WARREN II lay on a queen-size bed in the brownstone's parlor studio, trying to block out the noise from the next room so he could grab some sleep.

When he had spoken with the director earlier that day, he had expected to be chastised for letting the operation grow out of control. But it seemed the director now was less concerned with blowback—negative publicity resulting from clandestine operations—than with results. On his own initiative, the DCI had put in calls to the Defense Secretary and the National Reconnaissance Agency, securing surveillance planes and satellites to lend a hand with the hunt.

The director's efforts to secure recon assets was doubly reassuring. He must have been feeling more heat than he had let on, during their meeting at Langley. Evidently he wasn't at all certain that he would be able to throw the blame for a botched operation into Warren's lap; and so now, at last, he was extending himself.

Elsewhere in the brownstone, someone was watching a tennis match on television. Warren could hear the faint sounds of the game: . . . *pop* . . . *pop* . . . *pop* . . . applause. He found himself slipping into an uneasy doze. Perhaps he would achieve a few minutes of real sleep, after all. The rhythm of the tennis was soothing—the long, suspended pause of the ball over the net, then the pop of the racquet making contact. A rhythm like that, he thought vaguely, could help a man fall asleep.

One of the voices from the next room was talking about the body they had found in the carriage in Central Park. A young mother named Liz Halloway; identification had been made by her husband. Their target had used the woman's body as camouflage, slipping out of the park right under their noses.

A nice trick, Warren thought. But the last nice trick the man would manage. Thanks to the DCI, they had access to twenty-four military reconnaissance satellites traveling in six orbital planes, with four satellites focused on any part of the world at any given moment, flashing images to the NRO at 186,000 miles per second. They had two PR9 Canberra aircrafts equipped with SYERS. The Senior Year Electro-Optical Relay System cameras possessed a range of over one hundred miles, allowing the Canberra to travel at altitudes that guaranteed it would remain out of eye- and earshot of civilians. With so many resources, the man would need to be a true magician to escape them.

But he *was* a magician, Warren thought. Look at the tricks he had played already. Despite everything, the man would manage yet another feat of sleight of hand, and leave them with nothing.

That was exhaustion talking. Sleep would cure that nagging voice. Even just a few minutes'.

Two other voices—he recognized them as belonging to Nathan Hoyle and Anthony Cass—were discussing the media. The media wanted to know if the incident at Central Park had involved a terror suspect, and how it had turned out.

Cass made an executive decision: no statement at the present time. He asked if Hoyle had contacted the State Police yet. Hoyle confirmed that he had. Roadblocks had been established at twenty-mile intervals, feeding out from the city in every direction. They were reluctant to keep the roadblocks up for more than four hours. Six at the least, Cass answered, and don't take no for an answer.

Good man, Warren thought. He listened to the tennis match. *Pop . . . pop . . . pop.* A suspended moment; then applause.

A ringing phone. Hoyle made more executive decisions, audibly. The husband of the dead woman—Liz Halloway—was to be given their sincere condolences, but no further explanation. Searches of area motels should continue. Warren was to be disturbed only in the event of a major breakthrough. . . .

He rolled over. The tennis match continued. For the first time he wondered: Who the hell was watching tennis?

A magician, he thought. He pictured a rabbit coming out of a hat. The small man in black, holding it by both ears, thrusting it forward. *And for my next trick, ladies and gentlemen—*

"Now?" Hoyle was asking.

Something in his tone made Warren's eyes open.

Then Hoyle was in the doorway, a cell phone at his ear. "Tom," he said, but Warren already was out of the bed.

13

THE OWNER of the Arlington Motel was a man named Ted Mudgett. In the thirty-odd years he had run his establishment, he had seen a lot of things. But he never had seen anything like the activity he had witnessed in the past twenty minutes.

The activity had begun when a tall man in an ill-fitting jacket stepped into his office and showed him a photograph. The tall man, Ted understood, worked with the government. He hadn't needed to see any identification to understand this plain fact. He had seen it in the man's brusque demeanor, in his self-important air, and in the bulge that fanned up the ill-fitting jacket just above the right buttock. Ted had taken one look at the photograph and then nodded, slipping the toothpick from one side of his mouth to the other.

"Yeah," he said, and then leaned forward to check his registry. As his finger moved over the names, the toothpick switched back to the other side of his mouth. "John Wilson. Room twenty-one."

That had been twenty minutes before. Since then, Ted Mudgett had seen a great many things that he previously had seen only in movies. The government agent had gotten on some kind of glorified walkie-talkie and spoken a cryptic string of words. Within four minutes, the first van had appeared on the street outside the motel. VERIZON, the van read between blacked-out windows. By then the government agent had shucked off his ill-fitting jacket, revealing the holster on his right hip, and replaced it with a Kevlar vest.

By the time ten minutes had passed, two other black vans had joined the first by the sidewalk. Ted Mudgett stayed behind his desk, the toothpick switching steadily from one side of his mouth to the other, taking it all in. From each van came an emissary. They clustered around his desk, poring over blueprints of his motel.

They were going to break into John Wilson's room, of course. He had seen enough movies to recognize a SWAT team when he saw one. Remotely, he wondered what John Wilson had done to deserve such attention. He also wondered who had put in a call to report John Wilson's presence at the motel. Ted Mudgett had not seen a recent newspaper.

Then the government agents were working out a plan of approach, right in front of his eyes. The tall one announced his intention to make the primary entrance himself. Backup teams would cover possible routes of escape. One would be stationed in the alley behind the motel; another, with rifles, on the rooftop across the way.

"What's the best way onto that roof?" the tall man asked Ted.

Ted shrugged. "Fire escape, I guess."

They ignored him again.

Seventeen minutes after the tall man had stepped into the motel office, the black vans opened their doors at precisely the same moment. Men armed with riot guns streamed out, splitting into two streams—one heading into the alley, the other for the fire escape of the building across the way. The two who had been poring over the blueprints were putting on their own Kevlar vests. As he watched, Ted realized he had chewed the end of the toothpick to a pulp. He tossed it into a trash can, then took a fresh one from the pack in his desk drawer.

The tall man produced a shotgun, into which he fit a three-inch Magnum shell.

Ted Mudgett followed them onto the sidewalk. He watched the ensuing drama from a spot a few feet in front of the first van, the one marked VERIZON.

The three men climbed the stairs to room 21. Two, including the tall one, put themselves to the right of the door. The other stood to the left. On the rooftop across the way, a sniper's scope flashed in the sun. Ted caught a brief glimpse of the sniper himself, half-concealed behind a billboard featuring Joe Camel.

Then the tall one hefted the shotgun, stepped forward, and emptied it into the door at the height of the knob.

The boom rolled into the alley and then back onto the street. By then the tall man had kicked in the door.

It was exciting, Ted Mudgett thought from his spot on the sidewalk. It may have been the most exciting thing he had ever seen. He was so excited that it didn't even occur to him to worry about the property damage.

The men entered the room. A woman in 24 peeked

her head out, then vanished. The men who had gone into 21 reappeared. The tall one spoke urgently into his fancy walkie-talkie. Even from the sidewalk, Ted could surmise that the room had been empty.

His fresh toothpick was already pulped. He spat it out, watched the agent yell into his walkie-talkie for another moment, then went back to the office and opened the desk drawer. As he was digging for the pack, he suddenly realized that they had kicked in a perfectly good door, when he'd had a passkey right at hand.

He frowned. His excitement diminished with surprising rapidity, as he tried to figure out how in hell he was going to get money out of these men.

SAL SANTIORI began his last day on earth by meeting a new client from Baltimore.

They went through the usual preliminaries, sipping coffee and feeling each other out while sitting in the grungy front office of the garage. They discussed the game last night, then the neighborhood around the garage, then the weather. It had been a hard fucking winter and a bad fucking spring, the client from Baltimore said. Raining almost nonstop. Sal politely agreed. But the last couple of days hadn't been so bad. And April showers, he remarked, brought May flowers.

They traded stories of the man who had put them in contact. The stories were delivered in an offhanded manner, as if they were coming to mind only as they were spoken. In fact, they were carefully calibrated to indicate that both realized the nature of their business would be illegal.

With such bona fides established, Sal assured the

man that they could work together. His team could strip a vehicle's serial number and give it a new identification, down to forged computerized chips and bar codes, with a turnaround time of under forty-eight hours. For twenty minutes, they discussed volume and percentages. Then Sal leaned back in his chair, letting a pensive look come into his eye. He snapped his fingers. "You know," he said. "Long as you're here . . ."

He brought the man out back, where the modified Honda was waiting. He leaned into the backseat, searching for the loose corner of upholstery.

"I did the work myself," he said. "I like a challenge, every once in a while. Guy who commissioned this tells me he wants a compartment so long by so wide. Give me a Chrysler, I say, no problem. Big cars are filled with wasted space. But it has to be the Honda, he says. Because compacts aren't going to catch your profiler's eye, you know. State troopers are looking for a sedan or a van, when they're looking for contraband. You take a little car like this, nobody looks twice. You can't hide anything in there, they think. But *voilà* . . ."

He lifted the corner of upholstery, worked loose the screws on the panel, and removed it to reveal the hidden compartment.

The client from Baltimore leaned forward, looking impressed.

"I pinched some space from the trunk. Some space from the backseat. But nobody's going to notice a thing unless they take out a tape measure. They can hold a mirror beneath the chassis, they can search the trunk and the interior, and they'll never look twice."

"What happened to the guy who commissioned it?"

"Funny story." Sal inserted a pinch of tobacco into his lip. He refitted the panel, then left the car and spat onto the asphalt. "Little guy. Colombian, or maybe Cuban. So the car's going to carry heroin, or maybe coke. I don't ask, you know. I don't stick my nose into other people's business. I just do the work. But in the back of my mind, while I'm doing the work, I'm thinking heroin or coke . . ."

The man from Baltimore nodded.

". . . then his face gets splashed across the papers. He's a child molester. A pervert."

"No shit."

"The compartment's going to hold drugs, I thought. But now I see—it's just about the right size for a little girl."

"No shit."

Sal nodded. He spat again. "So fuck 'im," Sal said. "He shows his face to pick it up, I'll beat him clear into next week. I've got a little girl myself, you know. But it means I'm left with this vehicle on which I've done, if I do say myself, one hell of a job. I need to get it off my hands. So it's a bargain."

"I don't know if I can use it."

"I'll make you a deal you can't refuse."

"I'll think it over."

"You do that."

They shook hands. Then the man got into his Range Rover and spun into the street, tooting the horn once. Sal watched him go, then moved back into the office. He checked the clock hanging on the wall. Eleven-forty.

When he stepped outside again a military helicopter was crossing the noontime sky.

* * *

HE TOOK HIS GIRLFRIEND to a matinee.

They sat in the last row, making out like teenagers. Audrey did something to him, and there was no denying it. It was similar to what Krista had done to him when they had first been married. As they kissed, his hands moved up and down her blouse; his head spun with dizziness.

On the movie screen, two Italians were discussing a hit. They were meant to be part of the Mafia. Sal, following along with half an ear, found the portrayal utterly unconvincing. Worse, it reinforced negative stereotypes. The real gangsters these days were not the Italians but the blacks, the Colombians, and the Russians. And the real gangster movies were not this warmed-over shit—gangsters reheated from decades of stereotypes, a practice that had been losing steam until *The Sopranos* had hit. The real gangster movies were the ones about hungry kids. He had seen a flick called *City of God,* about child gangs in Rio . . .

Then Audrey had his zipper open. She was bending down. He leaned back in the seat, closing his eyes, half-listening to the lousy actors on-screen portraying reheated Italian stereotypes as his head continued to spin.

BY QUARTER PAST TWO he was back in the office, with less than three hours to live.

His final afternoon passed drowsily. He sat behind his desk, reading a newspaper and absently spitting tobacco into a cracked mug.

He had skipped lunch to see Audrey. At three-twenty he went to the deli down the block for a roast beef sub.

After eating behind his desk, he felt the need for a nap. He moved into the cramped back room, off the garage, and lay down on the cigarette-burn-scarred sofa.

When he woke up, the quality of the light had changed. He sat slowly, rubbing at his eyes. Gradually, his synapses began to fire. He returned to the office and looked at the clock. Ten to five. He had slept the second half of the afternoon away.

Then he realized: He needed to pick up Phil from soccer practice, on his way to pick up Trish from her friend's house.

He was late.

Big Tony was nowhere to be seen. But the shop was closing at six. Until then, they could do without him. He found his keys, left the office, and slid heavily behind the wheel of his Mustang convertible.

HIS FIRST INKLING that something was wrong came a half-block from the auto shop.

The inkling involved a presence in the backseat. Before Sal had registered it consciously, the presence moved in a fluid way. A length of wire looped over Sal's scalp and dropped to his throat, pinning his head to the pony interior upholstery.

"Keep driving," a voice hissed into his ear.

Sal's body informed him that doing as he was told would be a good idea. The wire was pressing against his windpipe, and if he disobeyed the order, then the man in the backseat easily could cut off his air—if not his head.

His eyes moved to the rearview. The shape behind him was dark and low. Behind the shape he could see the shifting lanes of rush-hour traffic—not too terribly thick, out here in the boroughs. In the city, the traffic would have been thicker. If the traffic had been thicker, someone in another car might have glanced into the interior of the Mustang and seen the large man behind the wheel with a wire looped around his throat and a figure skulking in his backseat. But they were not in the city.

"Watch the road," the voice commanded.

Sal's eyes slipped away from the mirror, to face the road again.

For several moments, they drove in silence.

"You're making a big fucking mistake," Sal said then.

He was surprised by the evenness of his voice. Fear and anger were competing inside him—for the moment, anger seemed to have the upper hand—and either emotion might be expected to make his voice shake. But he spoke with the calm determination of a man stating an inarguable fact. "A big fucking mistake," he said again.

No answer from the backseat.

"You trying to scare me?" Sal said. "Well, I'm not scared. You're the one who should be scared. I'll split your skull for this. You motherfucker."

"Turn left," the man commanded.

Sal didn't reach for the turn signal. The wire pinched harder into his throat, cutting off his air. He cursed, hit the turn signal, then spun the wheel. They moved off the avenue and onto a side street, heading in the direction of the bridge.

The wire let out an inch of slack; Sal drew a burning breath.

"You're with Liguori," he said.

Michael Liguori had been threatening Sal for about eight months now, ever since Sal had started to cut into his territory. Sal wasn't afraid of the wannabe gangster, who was strictly nickel-and-dime, and didn't understand his place in the scheme of things. He hadn't expected this, however. He had thought that Liguori was all bluff. Evidently he had been wrong. The wannabe gangster had sent this man to put a scare into Sal . . . or something worse than a scare.

He looked in the rearview again. Except for the eyes, the face there was cloaked in shadow. The eyes were cold as dead ashes.

"I'm not afraid of you," Sal said.

But his hands on the wheel were white-knuckled, giving lie to the statement. Sweat had broken out on his brow. He shifted in his seat, and the wire dug into his flesh. "Goddamnit," he said, "let up a little."

"Turn right."

This time he obeyed without argument. They turned into a parking lot behind a seafood restaurant. The lot was empty. Beyond it was the waterfront; towering over them, the bridge sparkled like tinsel in the late-afternoon light.

"Park behind the Dumpster."

Sal slid the Mustang behind the Dumpster. Now they were hidden from the parking lot, hidden from the eyes of everyone except the commuters in their cars on the bridge above. To those commuters, the Mustang would not attract attention. All they would see was a car parked by the water. A couple of teenagers looking for a quiet place to make out. He remembered kissing Audrey in the movie theater, the way his head had spun.

If only he had taken down the Mustang's roof, he

thought, then they would not be hidden from view. But he had been waiting for summer. It had been a hard fucking winter and a rainy fucking spring, and for the first time in a decade, he had reached the end of April without taking down the Mustang's roof.

"Raise your hands," the man said.

"Fuck you," Sal said, and then spun in the seat, meaning to get his hands around the man's throat. He would show this cocksucker what it meant to fuck with Sal Santiori. He would send a message to Michael Liguori, not open to interpretation. For a fraction of an instant, he was pleased that this had happened—he had found a chance to bust a head today; he had found a chance to send a clear message to everyone who thought that Sal Santiori could be bullied into giving up even an inch of his territory. They thought he had grown complacent, fat, soft. They were wrong. As soon as he had his hands around his man's throat, he would show them all—

He managed to turn halfway around in the seat. Then the wire was biting into his windpipe so harshly that the sparkle of the bridge brightened, washing out everything else. An exquisite pain blossomed in the precise center of his skull. The entire world was pain and light, his throat and his skull.

When the wire loosened infinitesimally, Sal was no longer angry. Now he was only afraid.

"Christ's sake," he managed.

"Hands."

He raised his hands, trying not to breathe because breathing made the wire slice deeper into his windpipe. Then a second length of wire looped around Sal's wrists, pinning his hands together above his head. The man in the back pulled it tight without mercy.

Reflexively, Sal tried to lower his wrists into his lap—that would be more comfortable—but the man stopped him with a sure hand. Sal caught another glimpse of the eyes in the rearview. Now the cold ashes in those eyes were smoldering.

For several seconds, they held each other's gaze.

He realized with a dull thud of surprise that he recognized those eyes.

The face around them had changed—aged, softened. But the eyes belonged to the little man who had commissioned the modified Honda. The child molester.

"I'm going to ask you a question," he said.

"Christ's sake," Sal said again.

"Did you tell anyone about me?"

"Fuck—"

The wire around his throat tightened. Something in the sleeve of the man's tunic jingled softly, like the chimes on the door of the auto shop.

When the wire relaxed, Sal was seized by coughs. A dollop of bloody mucus hit the center of the steering wheel and clung for a moment before beginning a long, slow downward slide.

"Did you tell anyone about me?"

Sal's throat felt as if it had been torn open. A single tear ran down his cheek. He shook his head; the motion brought a flare of agony.

"Not the police?"

"Nobody."

"Is the car ready?"

He nodded, as tightly as possible.

"Keys?"

"In . . . the office."

A low rasping burr reached his ears. He knew that sound—a strip of duct tape coming off a roll. A gloved hand came forward and slapped the tape across Sal's mouth. Somehow the wires around the wrists and throat never loosened.

Another burring rasp, as a second strip of tape was pulled free.

The second strip went over Sal's eyes.

Then he was being tossed into the passenger seat like so much luggage. Enough rationality remained for him to be surprised at the little man's strength. A moment later, the man had climbed behind the wheel. Sal was riding shotgun, trussed around the wrists, blindfolded and gagged. He could go for the little man, he thought. He could dive across the seat, bound wrists or no, and try to pay back a little of the strangling. But his chances would be better if his hands were free . . .

. . . he rotated the wrists, exploring. The wire was tight, but there was some slight give. He kept rotating his wrists, striving to loosen it.

"Stay low," the voice said. A hand pressed on his head, forcing him down into the seat.

He stayed low, moving his wrists in quick, tight circles.

When sixty seconds had passed, they turned again. By then Sal had gotten his left wrist half-loosened from the bonds. But from the crackle of gravel beneath the tires, he knew that they had reached the garage. Was Big Tony still inside? Would Big Tony look out and see what was going on?

The engine died. The door opened. The man was going to check on the Honda, Sal understood.

He kept trying to tug his hands free. His wrists were slicked with blood. But the blood served as a lubricant. Five seconds passed, and he felt close to slipping the left hand out. Give him ten more seconds . . .

The man was in the car again. "Looks good," he said mildly.

He took Sal's hands, tugging the wire tight. Sal uttered a muffled cry into the duct tape over his mouth. Then more tape was coming free.

The tape was slapped over his nose—cutting off his air.

Not good, Sal thought.

He began to whip his head from side to side. His lips beneath the tape worked like a horse's chewing cud. A terrible heat began to burn in his temple. He jerked his hands with such strength that they tore out of the man's grip, then reached up to claw at the tape on his face.

The man firmly took the wire between Sal's wrists and restrained him.

Ice was filling Sal's belly in great, cumbersome chunks. It spread out through his veins, chilling him. He kicked at the dashboard. He began to try to climb out of the car—his feet padding up onto the wheel, kicking at the windshield. Big Tony, he thought, what the hell is wrong with you, look out the window for Christ's sake—

Purple slashes cut the darkness. The need to breathe was passing. The need for anything was passing.

Beneath the tape, his eyes bulged. A shuddering tremor passed through his body as his bowels evacuated.

For another thirty seconds the assassin continued holding Sal's wrists, making sure.

Then he let go. The bound hands fell into Sal's lap. Sal rolled bonelessly onto one side, spearing his ribs on the gearshift.

The assassin left the Mustang, bringing his bags. He turned to look into the car. Sal was sprawled facedown in the passenger seat. The pony interior was splotched with blood, mucus, and pungent shit.

He spent two seconds looking down. Then he turned and made his way toward the office. Three miles away, Sal's son watched as his last teammate climbed into his parent's car. Phil Santiori gave a sigh. He set down his shoulder pads and checked his watch. Where the hell was Sal?

14

APRIL 30, 2100 HOURS

At 1630 dinner was served. Until 1705 the subject left both food and water untouched. During this time he faced the one-way mirror, clearly meaning a show of rebellion. Subject's willpower proved short-lived and at 1705 he began consuming both food and water, completed at 1715 hours.

Nausea occurred at 1740 and was more pronounced than expected. (Lower dose of staph enterotoxin recommend for future use: 20 cc?) For twenty minutes he expelled his dinner into the latrine, with shivering and extreme perspiration. Shortly past 1800 he crawled to bed, where he remained motionless for nearly an hour.

At 1855 subject began talking to himself. Verbalization was slurred and slow, the words themselves inaudible. Yet increased agitation and distress are unmistakable. Disassociation is evident in many mannerisms, including shaking of the leg, compulsive touching *of the beard, occasional touching of the scar on the right ear, and a contortion of facial features in a child-like manner.*

At 1940 subject's nausea apparently returned. He lay down on the cot and soon fell into an uneasy slumber. Cell lighting has been discontinued, coaxing the brain from a waking alpha state to a beta state, reinforcing an environment conducive to trance. The sleep will be interrupted at two-hour intervals throughout the night, increasing disassociative tendencies.

In the early morning a conversation will be initiated to determine whether behavioral conditioning is proving effective. If not, commencement of depatterning is feasible at any time, as subject's deterioration is pronounced.

"MS. MIRIAM LANE?"

"Yes?"

Behind him, a mother was scolding her children. He hunched farther into the phone nook, raising his voice to cover the sound. "This is Jack Atelier, calling from Atelier Discount Auto Parts."

Tension hissed over the line. The woman was holding her breath, he realized.

"I've got good news," he said. "The final drawing of our promotional campaign has indicated that the winner of the grand prize is—you, Ms. Lane!"

She exhaled with the force of a wind tunnel. "Praise the Lord," she said.

"How do you feel?"

"Praise the Lord," she said again.

"You've won five hundred dollars and a brand-new

Honda Accord. Subject, of course, to final confirmation by the division of promotional compensation. Atelier Discount Auto reserves the right to revoke or amend this gift if fraudulence on the part of the rewardee is discovered. Other terms and conditions may apply."

Silence.

"Ms. Lane?"

"Yes?"

"Within no more than twenty-one business days, you'll be receiving a check for five hundred dollars. Within no more than seventy-two hours, you'll be receiving a brand-new Honda Accord. Can you use a new car, Ms. Lane?"

"Lord knows I can."

"We'll deliver the car directly to your door. We'd like you to begin using it immediately, if that's not a problem. Because in two weeks you're going to be flown down to New York City, where you'll take part in the filming of a television commercial. It would be nice if you had spent some time behind the wheel, so you can talk honestly about what a fine vehicle it is."

"It's so exciting," she said.

"It certainly is. In New York you'll be staying at the Parker Meridien Hotel, located at One-eighteen West Fifty-seventh Street. But I'll be back in touch next week, to provide more details about that. This call is only to inform you of your status as grand-prize winner, and to arrange the delivery of the car."

"I've never won anything before in my life."

"There's a first time for everything," he said with a smile in his voice. "Within the next seventy-two hours, as I said, the car will be delivered to your door. There's no need for you to be home to receive it; the key will be left in your mailbox—or, if you've got a mail slot in your door . . ."

"Yes, I do."

"If you're not there to receive it, then the key will be placed through your mail slot. As I said, please begin using the car immediately. So that when it comes time to tape the commercial, you'll be able to talk about driving it."

"This is wonderful. So wonderful."

"To be honest, this is the part of the job I enjoy most. Giving something back to the community."

"I don't know what to say."

"That's all right," he said. "Just as long as you've figured something out by the time we go to New York. And if you haven't, maybe I can help you find the words."

"Thank you, Mr. Atelier. God bless you."

"Well," he said. "God bless *you*. I'm looking forward to meeting in person, Ms. Lane."

"Please—call me Miriam."

"Miriam," he said.

He gave her a telephone number to call in case she had questions, then mentioned that they had been having trouble with the line. If she was unable to get through, she might want to wait awhile and then try again.

After hanging up, he turned from the phone to face the travel plaza: a domed building of steel and glass, with magazine stands, fast food stalls, and coffee shops surrounding a tiled atrium. He crossed the dome with his head lowered, then moved through the parking lot.

Before departing the rest area, he filled the Honda's gas tank.

At 8:14 P.M. he got back on the highway, driving north for what would be the last time.

The overcast sky turned the road into a monochromatic ribbon. He put the Honda in the right lane, pegged the speed at fifty-five, then dialed the radio until he found a weather report. More rain on the horizon, the announcer said ruefully. The system was coming from the northwest and would arrive tonight, staying through the week. For the next few days it would be a tough slog, but by the weekend—

He snapped it off, satisfied.

He began to navigate the preliminary steps of his meditation ritual. He would not go too far, not behind the wheel; he would not put himself into a trance and risk piling the Honda into the surrounding traffic. But he would lay the groundwork, so that when the time came he would be able to achieve the necessary state.

At nine sharp the first drop of rain hit the windshield. He rolled up the window, switching on the wipers.

ONCE THE IDEA had planted itself in Thomas Warren's mind, he couldn't get past it.

If he hadn't been half asleep, he would have been able to bathe the idea in rational light. He would have dragged it out into the open sunshine, where it would shrivel and die. But here in the shadow realm, the idea held on. The thing they were chasing was just that—a thing.

He rolled over, muttering. He wanted to get up, back

to the action to oversee the hunt. Without his guidance they would not apprehend the man, no matter how many satellites and reconnaissance planes, front-page articles and multistate manhunts. Because it wasn't a man at all, he thought. Dressed in black, leaving knives in police officers' throats, slipping through dragnets like water running through cracks. It was like nothing they ever had seen before. Not a man. An avatar.

His mind kept working, like a tongue poking at a loose tooth.

From the knife recovered in Central Park had come fingerprints. The fingerprints had not been on file with IAFIS in Clarksburg, nor with any foreign agencies to which they had access. Because the man was not a man . . .

Trying to sleep was pointless. The longer he lay here, the more the idea gained strength.

He went to find Hoyle, to ask if anything had come in. He found the agent in the kitchen, scraping yogurt from the bottom of a cup. Hoyle informed him that, as of five minutes ago, nothing was new.

Warren went back to the parlor studio. He returned his head to the pillow. Rest. Who knew when he would find another chance?

He drifted.

Once he had gone on a walk with his grandmother—his mother's mother. She had lived in Georgia, on what once had been a plantation. As they walked, Warren noticed a strange creeping plant he had never seen before. It was ivy, but not ivy. And it was everywhere, climbing drainpipes and rock faces and the sides of barns with equal disregard.

Kudzu, his grandmother said. *It's a weed. You can't get rid of it. It hangs on, Tommy.*

Like the idea in his head. He tried to push it away; but it grew back immediately, hanging on. The man was not a man . . .

His phone was ringing.

He found it on an end table without switching on the light. "Warren."

It was the specialist.

The specialist was telling him that Quinlan was gone.

A heavy silence followed the announcement. Did the man expect to be reprimanded for letting the interrogation go too far? Warren didn't have the energy. He muttered something obliging and terminated the connection.

Then he stared into the darkness, thinking. Quinlan was gone. Another avenue closed. But it was all right. They didn't need Quinlan. They would apprehend the man on their own. To escape now, he would need to vanish off the face of the earth.

Which he would.

Because he was not a man.

He turned his head to look at the clock. One minute past midnight. The first day of the new month, he realized. On the first day of a new month, it was good luck to say *rabbit, rabbit* before any other words passed one's lips.

"Rabbit, rabbit," he said to the darkness.

He pictured rabbits coming out of hats. Knives lodged in throats. Men who were not men, vanishing off the face of the earth. Abracadabra. Presto.

He sighed, pushing his head deeper into the pillow.

* * *

ALL NIGHT the rain had been playing a cat-and-mouse game with him. Now it picked up, whipping against the car in sheets.

He saw the exit looming in the headlights. After taking the ramp he drove for twenty miles along a rural route leading west, into black farmland. Tractors hulked on the tilled fields in prehistoric shapes. Lightning slashed the sky, freezing a million silver raindrops in mid-flight.

He pulled into a shaded coppice, then cut the ignition and the headlights. Night closed in to swallow him; rain turned the Honda into a thundering drum.

Mechanically he removed his disguise, returning the pieces to the bag and wiping the makeup from his cheeks, working by touch.

He left the car. A white ash was there, shivering in the storm. He would be able to find it again easily. He put the laptop behind the tree, then covered it with loose brush. The computer might become ruined by the rain. That would be all right, as long as the damage was severe enough that no clues could be recovered from the hard drive.

Back in the front seat, he interlocked his fingers and placed them on the nape of his neck, palms covering the ears. His thumbs applied gentle pressure to the base of his skull. He felt the beat of his pulse. He breathed shallowly, in and out, nine nines.

He placed his hands on his thighs. His upper body turned left, then right. Twenty-six times. The hands moved to his kidneys. He began to breathe more deeply, saturating his blood with oxygen. As his blood turned alkaline, his heartbeat slowed.

Part of his mind was visualizing escape routes. The primary route emphasized stealth; it avoided sensors entirely, minimizing proximity to guard patrols. The secondary route emphasized speed. If something went wrong, he would need to get off the compound grounds quickly . . .

. . . he wasn't concentrating.

He emptied his lungs, refilled them. He was nothing—no body, no mind. He and the material world did not intersect.

He was a ghost wind, a *stealer-in*.

The storm cycled from drizzle to downpour and back again.

ALI ZATTOUT hid the knife at 2:14 A.M.

Until now, Zattout's food trays and all their contents had been collected immediately following his meals. This time, he had been left alone since the delivery of the dinner containing the nauseating agent. The tray had remained in the center of his floor, along with its plastic silverware and paper napkins. At nearly quarter past two—shortly after the bulb in his cell was switched on—he stirred on his cot. One hand fell loosely off the mattress, seemingly the result of a disturbed sleep. The hand moved across the floor. From behind the one-way mirror, Finney watched. The hand picked up the knife, concealing it behind the wrist, and casually slipped it below the mattress.

To all appearances, Zattout continued to sleep.

Finney looked over at Hawthorne. Hawthorne had seen it too.

"You see?" he said. "Give him half a chance and he'll stab you in the back."

Finney looked at the prisoner again: pale as window glass, curled on the bed with flecks of vomit speckling his filthy beard.

"With a plastic knife," Finney remarked.

"If he gets that plastic knife in your eye, you'll be sorry."

"I wonder if he could manage it."

"Maybe. Maybe not. Do you really want to find out?"

Finney thought about it.

He shook his head.

HAWTHORNE PRECEDED HIM into the cell.

He pulled Zattout off the bed, applying a choke hold. Finney stepped forward, raising the syringe. Zattout cursed bitterly. He kicked; Finney dodged. He kicked again, sending the plastic dinner tray spinning against a wall. Then Hawthorne tightened the hold; Zattout flushed an acute shade of crimson.

Finney grabbed the man's left arm. As he injected the sedative, Zattout wailed. When it was done, Hawthorne spun him viciously onto the floor. He and Finney retreated through the door.

Zattout was on his feet again immediately, facing the mirror.

He spat.

He punched the reinforced glass, right fist then left fist. He let out another hoarse cry, and punched again: right fist then left fist.

Finney and Hawthorne waited.

For two minutes the prisoner tantrumed, assaulting the glass, spewing epithets and howls. Over the following two minutes, both blows and cries weakened. Finally Zattout gave up. He moved in lost circles, muttering beneath his breath, eyes shifting from side to side. Presently he slumped down onto the floor. He stared at the one-way mirror with eyelids lowering to half-mast. His back was against the cot—very close, Finney noticed, to the place where he had hidden the knife.

Finney counted to thirty. He looked over at Hawthorne.

They went back into the cell. Hawthorne dug beneath the mattress and promptly found the plastic knife. "What's this?" he asked, brandishing it in Zattout's face. "What is this?"

Zattout grinned lethargically.

"Let me handle it," Finney said.

Hawthorne didn't back off. He held the knife, glowering.

"Let me handle it," Finney said again. "Give us a minute."

No reaction.

"I'll be all right. Go on."

Hawthorne gave Zattout a final glare. Then he turned, picked up the dinner tray, retrieved the plastic fork from a corner, and left.

Finney took a seat. Zattout remained slouched on the floor, still grinning stupidly.

An amateurish performance ensued. Slackness crept onto the prisoner's face; the smile vanished. His eyelids fluttered dreamily. He exhaled a stertorous breath. His eyes drifted closed. They opened, flickering. Then closed again, as the man feigned unconsciousness.

"I know you can hear me," Finney said.

Zattout's head sagged, chin against chest.

"I'm here to give you one more chance. Cooperate voluntarily. Things will go better for you."

From far away, through the forest and the house and the pantry and the staircase and the one-way mirror, came a low roll of thunder.

Finney inched forward on the chair. Zattout was faking—exaggerating the effects of the drugs. But was it because he hoped to avoid a conversation, when his defenses were down? Or did he still plan a last, desperate effort at escape? If the prisoner came for him, Finney would defend himself. Zattout was weakened; Hawthorne was just outside the door.

"Tell me something of value," he said imploringly. "Something I can use."

The smile crept back. *"Kaffir,"* Zattout muttered without opening his eyes.

"In English."

"Infidel," Zattout translated.

"This is your last chance. After this you won't be able to call a halt, even if you decide to cooperate. Because you won't be able to talk."

"Khasioon."

"Your head will be shaved. The electrodes require clean contact."

"Whoremonger," Zattout said.

"This doesn't have to happen. We still can be civilized. The decision is yours."

Zattout's eyes opened.

"Go fuck yourself," he said clearly.

Finney stood. He tugged his shirt straight, and left the cell.

THE FIRST REITER electroshock machine was commissioned in 1942 by a psychiatrist named Paul H. Wilcox.

The Cerletti-Bini alternating current device then in favor for electroconvulsive therapy administered a level of electricity far higher than was necessary to induce grand mal seizures in a patient. Dr. Wilcox theorized that ECT's therapeutic effects could be achieved by administering a much smaller jolt. He found an electrical engineer named Reuben Reiter who was willing to build a machine to his specifications.

To be considered an effective treatment for schizophrenia or depression, a seizure needed to last twenty-five seconds. The original Reiter machine used a cumulative approach to create such a convulsion; the operator flicked a switch on and off during treatment, modulating the amount of current being delivered. Once an acceptable seizure occurred, no additional electricity was administered. To refine the procedure, a method was developed in which electrodes were placed on the subject's head, allowing particular lobes of the brain to be targeted.

Introduced in 1943, the Wilcox/Reiter machine gained immediate acceptance. But in 1956, at the Second Divisional Meeting of the American Psychiatric Association, a doctor named David Impastato announced that clinicians who used ECT as a regular part of treatment had found that the Wilcox/Reiter machine produced an unsatisfactory change in their patients' demeanor. The now-passé Cerletti-Bini AC device—which administered electricity at a much higher voltage—had, perhaps unsurprisingly, created more observable effects of docility and apathy in subjects.

The next year, Wilcox, Reiter, and Impastato joined forces to introduce a new model of the Reiter machine. The Molac II—the last ECT device ever produced in America—was the machine now resting on the table outside Zattout's cell.

Like the Cerletti-Bini before it, the Molac II administered shocks at a much higher level than was necessary to create convulsions in the patient. An initial 190 volt current rendered the subject unconscious. Jolts of 100 volts followed, at the operator's discretion. Unlike earlier machines, there was no failsafe to limit the length of the shock; it continued for as long as a black button was depressed.

Until his arrival at the farmhouse, Finney had not seen a specimen for over two decades. But the Molac II looked just the same as ever.

It was not torture, he thought.

No. It was worse. For Zattout could not agree to cooperate, once the treatment was under way, and put an end to it. He would be rendered unconscious by the first shock. Then the depatterning would commence.

Hawthorne stood beside Finney, watching.

Behind the one-way mirror Zattout sat motionless on the floor.

Finney reached for the doubloon inside his pocket. He squeezed it so tightly his hand cramped—

—and nodded.

PART THREE

15

THREE A.M.

His eyes opened.

He started the engine.

He switched on the windshield wipers and drove to number sixty-two Sycamore Drive. He slipped the Honda's key through the mail slot, moved to the Ford Escort, allowed himself entrance, opened the hood, and snapped the ignition wire.

In the backseat of the Honda he raised the loose corner of upholstery. He unscrewed the bolts, pocketed them, and pulled the panel free.

The compartment looked small.

He strapped the bag across his chest, settling it into the hollow of his sternum. Then he reclined on the backseat, knees raised. Inhaled, forcing the belly out. Exhaled, drawing the navel to the spine. Six times, finding his center.

From the center he journeyed up. His presence weighed upon each rung of the ladder, pushing the vertebrae farther apart, opening and separating them as he went.

Tension lingered in his chest and shoulders. He examined it. He massaged the mental knots, freeing the tension, then climbed again. Seven cervical vertebrae brought him to the brain stem. Once inside the compartment he would need to retain position for nearly sixteen hours, until the three o'clock patrol had passed. The brain would come into play then. For now, he turned away.

On the path down he paused to breathe air into the throat, the heart, the solar plexus, the center itself.

He arranged himself in a triple fold—lying face-down and extending his arms above his head, then arching the back until his buttocks touched his shoulders. Another push brought knees to elbows and he was doubled over on himself, folded in half.

Without untangling his limbs he carefully lifted his body, forearms trembling with strain, and lowered himself from seat to floor.

He began to insert himself into the compartment.

The buttocks went first. Then a period of repositioning: finding the proper angle to continue. His pelvis lifted, and he moved another two inches. His hips were tight against the walls. The compartment smelled oddly medicinal.

He pressed on. His knees, already touching elbows and ears, were forced farther down. Another interior journey up the spine, seeking openness. Down again. He moved another two inches. He rested.

Claustrophobia could come now, at any time. But he was not here. He was somewhere else—in the place he had spent the past hours reaching. It was a quiet place, icy and still.

Another push forward; and he was inside up to his chest. The bag pressed tight against him. His back, legs, and hips all flush against the compartment's boundaries. He breathed. Pushed again—inserting himself up to his shoulders.

Two minutes later, a final effort. The last of his body disappeared beneath the seat.

His right hand still could achieve limited motion. It found the panel, fit it back into place, jiggled it until it fell into the grooves.

He closed his eyes and found the icy place again.

Outside, the leaves hissed teasing riddles. A thunder-clap cracked. Then lightning flashed, sending ragged shadows japing across the porch of number sixty-two Sycamore Drive.

THE STORM DIED DOWN, ruminated, and gained force.

Thomas Warren II looked again at the red numbers of the clock: ten minutes past three A.M. He forced his eyes closed, and returned to the half-dream.

In his mind's eye, the man who was not a man was pulling rabbits from a hat. Behind him, kudzu draped a dilapidated barn. Before him knelt Ali Zattout. Zattout was wearing a navy blue business suit, tugging at his collar like Rodney Dangerfield. Thomas Warren, Senior, had loved that hoary old bit: *I don't get no respect.*

But Zattout wasn't tugging at his collar to get a laugh. He was doing it to expose his throat. Then he was laying his exposed throat on a tree stump—a makeshift chopping block. The small man who was not a man kept pulling rabbits from his hat. But his last and best trick, Warren understood suddenly, would be to produce an axe. Then he would whip the blade down, decapitating Zattout. Abracadabra, presto.

Why? They were part of the same faction, this man and Zattout.

No—not quite. The small magician in black had killed the others in the cell. The small magician murdered his own.

But that wasn't exactly right, either. He did not murder his own; for he was not one of them. He was something different. An outsider.

From the hat came small pink balls. The magician began to juggle. Three balls, then four, then six, then ten, until the air was so thick with bobbling pink projectiles that Warren could no longer see the man who was keeping them aloft. Smoke and mirrors, he thought. A plane passed overhead; above it, a beeping satellite. But the balls kept the magician concealed, from planes and satellites and Warren's own eyes.

He still could see Zattout, however—his throat exposed on the chopping block. Waiting patiently. For he had nowhere to run. He could not get away.

The magician in black had killed the others in the cell. And now he would kill Zattout, just as soon as he had finished his juggling trick.

Then the balls were tumbling to the earth. The magician's performance was wrapping up. The wind gusted. The kudzu fluttered against the barn. The dark magician gestured over the hat, then began to withdraw something else. Warren saw the glitter of a blade, razor-sharp.

Zattout watched his executioner with disconsolate eyes.

Did he know this man—this wicked thing that was about to take his life? Not precisely. For the magician was not one of them. He was something different. An outsider. Yet he dealt with the Arabs. He dealt with al Qaeda . . .

Warren's eyes opened.

Right in front of his face. So close he hadn't even seen it.

Zattout already was in custody. Quinlan was gone; but a description of the fugitive could be put to the prisoner—

—and perhaps Zattout could offer some insight into the nature of the beast.

He clawed for the phone by the bedside, sending loose change and cigarettes scattering across the floor.

FINNEY POURED.

He handed the first glass to James Hawthorne. Hawthorne, clearly rattled, bolted the drink without waiting for Finney to fix a second.

The tempest lashed at the windowpanes but made no observable impression on the men. They sat opposite each other in a room lighted by a single weak lamp, with candlesticks on the mantel whirring softly.

Before administering the first shock, Finney had injected propofol and succinylcholine chloride—anesthesia and muscle relaxant—to reduce the risk of fractured bones. The Molac II delivered a current hundreds of thousands of times greater than the usual electric activity of the brain. Violent muscle spasms resulted. Until ECT administrators had started using muscle paralyzers, broken bones had been a common occurrence during treatment, with cracked spines a particularly frequent injury.

Electrodes had been attached to Zattout's bilateral frontal lobes. The first shock, at 190 volts, continued for three seconds. The resulting convulsion lasted forty-nine seconds. Before proceeding, Finney checked for life-threatening complications: apnea or cardiac arrest.

Cerebral atrophy, heart arrhythmia, ventricular tachycardia, epilepsy; thanks to the treatment, Zattout might manifest any of them in the near future. All in a day's work, Finney thought bitterly. Hippocratic Oath? He supposed he had heard of it. But he couldn't quite bring it to mind at the moment.

The second shock, at 100 volts, lasted two seconds. The third, four seconds.

One could live a full life, the doctor in him thought, after receiving ECT.

Witness Susan Franklin. Eight months after she had been released from their care, Finney had gone with Noble to pay their ex-patient a visit. Their purpose had been to determine the extent to which her conditioning remained intact. Perhaps Noble had conducted similar follow-up visits in ensuing years; but by then Finney had separated himself from his mentor, and he had no way of knowing.

The clinic was set behind gothic iron gates, on a sprawling lawn dotted with daylilies and hydrangea. After a brief consultation with a sour-faced Dr. Young, they were led to the game room. There they found Susan

Franklin absentmindedly doing needlepoint before a flickering television. She had gained a surprising amount of weight; her appealing face had gone from gaunt to fleshy. But Finney recognized her immediately. He recognized her eyes.

If the recognition went both ways, she gave no sign. Thanks to a combination of posthypnotic suggestion and electroshock amnesia, it was entirely possible that she had no conscious memory of the experiment. When sour-faced Dr. Young introduced them only as his "colleagues," she reacted with nothing more than a remote flicker.

They bade the doctor good day. Then Finney, Noble, and Susan Franklin took a walk around the clinic's garden paths. Noble talked softly, reasonably, soothingly. He remarked on the mild weather, asked about the clinic's food. Susan Franklin listened, answering quietly whenever a question was put to her. She seemed painfully shy, but cogent.

As the stroll continued, Noble's questions became more searching. Had she been feeling well over the past eight months? Was she satisfied with her treatment here at Carter Clinic? In reply, she spoke of patterns in illnesses, patterns in therapy. With the help of Dr. Young, she was learning to identify her patterns and change them. The speech was delivered with a cadence that struck Finney as exceedingly familiar. Then he realized that it had belonged to Young himself; she had memorized not only the words, but every inflection.

They kept walking, past a gardener with a hose, then a stand of golden forsythia. Noble casually began to

whistle beneath his breath. It was the lilting opening
notes of an aria of Mimi's from *La Bohème*—the "signal cue" used to access Robin, the strongest of Susan
Franklin's secondary identities.

They had found seven discrete personas within the
woman's psyche. All had been formed during early
childhood, initially taking the guise of imaginary
friends. Susan had put faces to these identities, visible
only in her bedroom mirror. With time, Robin—an un-
usually sharp-tongued and observant personality—had
forced the other identities to recede. She had become the
primary repository for Susan's negative feelings, of
anger and sorrow and grief. And she had held obsti-
nately onto childhood, remaining forever young even as
Susan Franklin and her other personas aged.

Noble finished whistling, then looked at Susan sideways. Searching for nausea, Finney knew. Paleness,
shortness of breath, rapid blinking. But the woman kept
walking, undisturbed. The aria was only an aria to her.

The damage they had inflicted, it seemed, had begun
to wear off.

Noble returned to small talk. He tried to forge a connection by broaching the subject of handsome box-
office stars of the day: Paul Newman, Steve McQueen,
John Wayne. Susan responded politely but distantly.

Then Noble was whistling another tune. This had
been the signal cue for an identity named James. Again,
Susan Franklin manifested no obvious reaction. Noble
stopped whistling. He commented on the beauty of the
gardens they were passing. A poem was brought to his
mind: *A song of the good green grass! A song no more*

of the city streets; a song of farms—a song of the soil of fields.

If Nina—the identity they had accessed using the stanza's final line—heard the words, she kept it to herself. Susan Franklin merely listened, then nodded. Indeed, she agreed, the gardens were lovely.

By the time they returned to the clinic Noble had attempted to contact four of the seven personalities. At each turn, he had failed. When they thanked Susan for her time and took their leave, Finney had allowed himself to believe that she might enjoy a full recovery. They had damaged her, but perhaps not irrevocably.

In the years since, he sometimes had wondered if Noble had left it at that. At the time of the visit, he and Noble had been within months of their split; tensions were running high. His mentor would not have pushed Susan Franklin too hard, in Finney's presence, risking an argument. But perhaps he had gone back to the clinic on his own, that year or another, seeking to uncover the personalities they once had accessed so easily. Perhaps he even had removed Susan Franklin from Carter Clinic, returning her to a cell and a regimen of electroshock, hypnosis, and drugs . . .

. . . or perhaps she had recovered completely. And lived a full life, despite the games they had played inside her head.

A phone was ringing.

Hawthorne had poured himself a second drink. He set it down, found the phone at his belt, and flipped it open. "Yes," he said.

He listened.

"I think we're making progress," he said.

Finney found the bottle and refilled his glass.

"Right here," Hawthorne said, and handed over the phone.

COLD FIRE had blossomed in his extremities.

It might have been pain, he thought. If he still had been occupying his body, that cold fire might have burned hot. But he was somewhere else, somewhere high in the mountains south of the Caspian Sea. Counting heartbeats.

His heart rate had slowed to barely forty beats per minute. After counting twenty thousand, he entered back into himself just enough to take measure of the situation. The rain, playing an intricate tattoo on the car around him. The blood not moving fast enough through his hands and feet; the cold fire blooming. But it was to be expected. When he moved again, the blood would move with him.

He counted another ten thousand heartbeats.

His leg pulsed. The leg wanted to distract him, to pull him back to reality. But without meditation, he would lose his mind to claustrophobia. He isolated the pain in his leg and set it cautiously outside himself, on the window ledge of his consciousness.

The air was surprisingly cold. The sensation was a curiosity, nothing more. He was calm, patient. He was a quiet little mouse. He had all the time in the world—all the heartbeats in infinity.

Still the rain fell.

The next time he returned to himself, something had

called him back. A sound; a sensation. The engine of the Honda had turned over, he realized distantly. It was thrumming all around him, vibrating in his bones.

So it was morning.

A moment later, the car was moving.

He couldn't tell if they were turning right or left; he was thrown both ways, one after the other. Something sharp jabbed into his temple, not quite hard enough to draw blood. The rear tires whispered smoothly, close to his ears. Then the engine was opening up. He retained enough awareness to tighten his grip on the panel, to hold it in place. He couldn't feel the hand, nor the panel. But he could see them through the gloom: black and ghostly.

Air leaked into the compartment through invisible cracks. There was wetness, amid the cold.

Time passed—unknowable time, time without qualities.

They were idling again.

Then moving again. He heard a sound like blatting geese. Too close to this world, now. He needed to return to his spirit state, to shut himself down for another few hours. He went back to the place he had been, high in the cold mountains.

Yet part of him remained aware: of another turn, then of the pavement beneath the tires turning to crunching gravel. And then, as they pulled to a stop again, of voices, coming to his ears through bolts of cotton.

". . . new car, Miz Lane?"

"You won't believe it, Ray. I won it in a contest."

"You're right. I don't believe it."

"I never won anything in my life," she said.

More conversation, lost to the wind. Then: ". . . hate to do this, but . . . out of the car?"

The trunk was opening. Then closing. The back doors were opening. Then closing.

"Sorry about that, Miz Lane. Just needed to be sure . . ."

"Have a good day, Ray."

"You too, Miz Lane. Looks like a lousy one. But I'll do my best."

Once again, the car moved.

He deepened his breathing, saturating his lungs with oxygen, returning his heart to its frigid half-beat. More hours of stillness lay ahead. More hours of calm and patience. He could not give in to the leap of excitement in his belly, not yet.

But the excitement was there. For the car continued to roll through the rainy morning that he could not see. He could not see, but he knew: He had done it.

He was inside the gates.

FINNEY FINISHED SPEAKING, and watched closely.

He had doubted that the description would produce any discernible reaction. Therapy had been conducted recently enough that the subject, even if he achieved consciousness, would remain in a state of catatonia. But there was a response to the words he had used, etched clearly into Zattout's face.

It was the child-contortion again: the brow tightening, the nostrils flaring. *A small man,* Finney had said, using words provided by Thomas Warren. *Dark clothes. Wiry build. Skilled at the art of evasion . . .*

Zattout moaned.

He tossed his head to the left.

Finney leaned back, considering.

The depatterning already had begun to take hold. The childlike fear in the subject's face—the same fear Finney had seen in Zattout's reaction to the guard dog—indicated that his regression had accelerated. As the adult persona broke down, the child-identity was coming to the fore. And the child-identity was very afraid.

But it was not rational fear. This was something else. Fear of the words he had used, Finney thought. They meant something to Zattout—something more than they meant to him.

It was another path that could be explored. Or could have been explored, if he'd had the information hours before. Now, however, depatterning had commenced. Zattout no longer was capable of speech.

But until the second treatment was administered he still could hear, and react.

"I want you to find a good feeling inside yourself," Finney said.

The subject's face twitched. "A good feeling," Finney repeated. "A feeling of strength, and comfort, and fulfillment. Locate it within your body."

Zattout gave another moan, low and unhappy.

"It's all right," Finney said gently. "Let yourself feel good. There's been enough suffering, hasn't there?"

More signs of distress. Zattout was determined to resist. *Let it go,* Finney thought. *Continue with the depatterning.*

But the process of psychic driving would consume months; and Thomas Warren's need for information had sounded urgent. The man on whom he required insight was a fugitive, a member of a sleeper cell that he thought might be known to Zattout. Along with the brief description, Warren had offered a startling detail. This man had been eliminating the members of his cell, one after another. In fact . . .

. . . here Warren had hesitated, as if aware that the possibility he was about to voice sounded preposterous . . .

. . . it was possible, he added, that the man in black would seek to dispose of Zattout himself.

He'd quickly rushed on. Security forces would make short work of any intruder at the compound. But it was something to keep in mind, when Finney put his description to the prisoner—a possible fulcrum from which leverage might be gained.

Finney went over it again.

A man was eliminating members of his own terrorist cell.

Zattout may have been next on the list of targets.

When a description of the man had been offered, Zattout had reacted.

He had reacted with a child-part of himself, a part that had been brought iatrogenically to the forefront of his brain.

That part of him, at least, believed that he was vulnerable. And that part was profoundly afraid. Zattout did not know of the hidden sensors, nor the strength of the marine guard. To him, the thought of an intruder was far from inconceivable.

"Have you found the good feeling?" he asked in a murmur.

No reaction.

"Look into the feeling. Imagine that a child is feeling this. Children feel pure things, don't they? How wonderful and pure it must feel, to the child."

Zattout mumbled, vowels without consonants.

"Let the child come up inside you. Let the child know that you're there to help with the suffering—that it's all right to feel the good feeling."

"Aaa," Zattout said.

Finney paused.

"Aaa."

"The child is you, isn't it?"

Zattout's head tossed the other way, to the right.

"We can stop, if you like. But wouldn't you like to embrace the good feeling? If we can make the child feel better, you'll feel better. But to do this, you must accept the child. Hold it close."

For the next several heartbeats, Zattout fought. Then a change occurred. His face washed with acceptance; then with frightened shame.

"Good," Finney said.

He watched for a few seconds, to see if the regression would hold. During that time, he saw it take even firmer root. The effect was eerie: a full-grown man manifesting the expression of a miserable, anxious child.

For a few moments more, Finney studied the prisoner.

Then he stood, very quietly. He let himself out and switched off the light inside the cell, plunging Zattout into darkness.

16

OUTSIDE THE TEMPLE, black rock cut by veins of agate wandered down the mountainside. In the far distance a spume spray leaped from the lake, filling the air with mist.

The gods were restless tonight, the master would have said. But the assassin looked at the spume spray and saw only the work of a strong wind. Closer to the arched doorway were twin butterflies, hovering motionless despite the breeze. There was a balance between the wind and the water, between the butterflies and the temple—but the gods had nothing to do with it.

The master was seated before a marble shrine. For a few moments, the assassin watched from the temple's doorway. Then he marshaled his courage and stepped forward.

"I did not understand the lesson tonight," he told the master's back.

The wind lowed through dark mountains behind him. At length, the teacher indicated with one hand that his pupil should come and join him on the cold floor. He spoke without looking away from the shrine, his tone as aloof as his eyes.

"Little mouse," he said. "You question everything."

The assassin held his tongue.

"Half of your mind is not here," the master went on. "It is in the outside world. You cannot take the lessons when only half of you is listening."

He felt a flash of shame. The fault was Rana's, of course. Part of him had stayed with her. But one could not study beneath the master and have an expectation of returning to society. The ancient ways were not taught to be put to use in the outside world. They were used to settle ancient enmities—*private* ancient enmities.

"Do not pretend," the master told him. "Be honest with yourself. Always."

IT CAME FROM NOWHERE—a vision.

He tried to push it away. He needed to stay focused, to remain in a place of silence and solitude.

But the vision, if that was what it had been, pressed itself back upon him immediately. Because he had not been honest with himself, he thought. Because he had avoided confronting certain questions directly.

Why was he here—risking his life for a cause in which he did not believe?

Be honest with yourself. Always.

It was for Rana.

Imprudent. Infantile. She would not even remember him. He was behaving like a lovesick child . . .

. . . so be it, he thought.

He would do the opposite of what he had been taught

at the temple. He would use the master's lessons for material gain, then to win the love of a woman. So be it. He would apply the ancient techniques to the outside world, without respect. And what was to stop him? There were no gods, controlling the wind and the water. He had waited for the rain. He had controlled the weather, after a fashion.

But he felt wretched, lost. The compartment felt like a coffin. The gods were against him . . .

. . . the gods had nothing to do with it.

So much darkness, and cold, and wet. Any man would lose his focus, staring into such an abyss. But it almost was over. If he could keep his concentration for just another few hours, it would be over.

Someone was in the compartment with him.

The girl.

Her body had bloated; she smelled of rotten eggs. The insects inside her body had spawned, multiplying. Soon her parchment skin would no longer contain them. They would spill out through her every orifice and climb over him, invading his own nose and mouth. And he would be trapped here, helpless, unable to move, as they laid their eggs in soft yielding hollows. . . .

His concentration had broken.

He forgave himself.

He found the temple again. Past it, carved into the mountains, was the ice cave. He picked his way cautiously to it; and inside he knelt, and meditated.

A HAND FELL on Thomas Warren's shoulder.

He lifted his head. It was morning, but still dark outside; rain continued to fall. He had come into the kitchen for some breakfast, fixed himself a bowl of cereal and a cup of coffee, and then promptly laid his head on the table, closing his eyes. And now someone was touching his shoulder . . .

. . . he looked around, and saw the DCI.

The director would not have come in person unless he had bad news. The bad news, of course, would be that Warren's chance had passed. He would be removed from the operation, put out to pasture. If the director had not been friends with his father, the time would have come long before.

"Tommy," the DCI said. Beneath his thick glasses he had donned an avuncular expression, touched with regret. "Hanging in there?"

Warren rubbed at his face, and nodded. He picked up the cold coffee and set it down again.

"Looks like you could use some fresh air," the DCI said. "How about a walk?"

On the way out they passed Hoyle, Cass, and Moore, bent over desks with attitudes of extreme concentration. Without new results coming in, there was little work to be done—but judging from their body language, they were making stupendous progress. But of course they were, Warren thought. The principal had entered the classroom.

They took umbrellas from the ornate stand inside the door and then stepped out into a cold drizzle. For the first turn around the block, neither man spoke. Warren felt himself waking up, bit by bit. The approaching sunrise was frustrated by the rain; gray dark changed to gray light in subtle gradations, like hardening wax.

Halfway through the second circuit around the block,

Warren decided it was worth trying to stave off the inevitable. "What brings you down?" he asked.

The DCI looked at him knowingly.

"We're making progress," Warren declared. He took out his cigarettes, juggling the umbrella into his other hand. He shot out a Camel Light, lit it, and coughed. "I realize the results haven't been perfect. But you know what my father used to say: Problems are just opportunities in disguise . . ."

"Results, Tommy?"

"We've got a description. We've got a photo on every newspaper in the tristate area . . ."

"And nothing to show for it." A delivery truck was unloading on Sixth Avenue; men hustled cartons through the rain. "I'll tell you what we've got. Brace yourself."

Warren braced himself.

"We've got the media shining a bright light on the fact that we can't even catch one man."

Warren considered arguing. As far as the media knew, the search was a police effort. But it seemed the wrong time to point that out.

"We've got too many resources on this," the DCI went on. "We've got our pants down around our ankles. Anytime the Bureau decides to take a kick, we've got our ass hanging out. It'll make a hard target to miss."

Now would be the chance. Now Warren could broach a subject with the DCI—*let me throw something at you,* he'd begin, *just to see if anything sticks.*

On the surface, he would acknowledge, yes, it looked bad. If he'd been the DCI, he might well have put himself

out to pasture. But in fact, Warren had made advancements in the hunt. They were the kind of advancements
that one needed to be very careful about phrasing aloud,
however, because—frankly—they sounded absurd.

I know where to find the man we're seeking, he
would say. Ready for this? The reason we can't see him
is that he's too close for our eyes to focus. And the place
we'll find him is . . .

. . . the safe house itself.

Here the director would raise a derisive hand. But
Warren would rush on, convincing him. He would not
mention the half-dream, with the magician producing an
axe while kudzu flapped against the barn. He would
confine himself to hard facts. The fugitive had been
eliminating the members of his cell. Why did a man kill
every member of his own faction? To cover his tracks,
of course. And who was the only remaining al Qaeda
member even tangentially related to the cell? Zattout.

The DCI would be skeptical. No man would seek entrance to that compound, he might opine—at least, no
sane man. And if the man they were seeking was insane,
he would not have eluded them until now.

But Quinlan, Warren would answer, had provided the
cell with information about compound security. Sketches,
impressions, possibly even blueprints. If the intruder
were armed with blueprints . . .

But it wouldn't stick. The director would think he had
lost his mind, if he suggested such a thing. And Warren
wasn't completely sure he would be wrong. Better, perhaps, to bargain. Let the DCI remove him from the
search effort. As long as he was allowed to retain control
of KINGFISHER, he would accept the decision.

"It's finished, Tommy."

They were coming around the block's final corner, returning to the brownstone. The DCI carefully avoided his eyes as he continued: "You had your chance. Now I've got to take it away from you."

Warren smoked his cigarette. *Let me throw something at you,* he would start, *just to see if it sticks.*

But the DCI would not be convinced. "Let me keep KINGFISHER," he heard himself saying instead.

"I'm not sure the results we've gotten can justify that."

"Just a little more time. We're close to breaking through."

"When's the last time you looked in a mirror, Tom?"

In fact, it had been just before breakfast—if one could call falling asleep over a bowl of cereal *breakfast*. The dark bags beneath Warren's eyes had turned reddish purple, the color of bruises.

"You need a vacation," the DCI announced.

"One more week."

The director shook his head.

"Tommy," he said. "You're relieved. Get some sleep. Then get upstate and pack your things. Then go someplace warm for a while."

"And what happens when I get back?"

The director's pitying gaze contained all the answers Warren needed.

"We'll see," he said, and then waved a hand, allowing Warren to move up the brownstone's steps ahead of him.

ALI ZATTOUT stood on a spit of slippery rock, surrounded on every side by white-capped waves.

The rock underfoot was treacherous, slicked with algae. Just below the surface, he could see serrated reefs. These would be the reefs on which his head would split open if he tried to move. He might achieve one step, or even two. Then his feet would slip out from under him; his arms would pinwheel. The last thing he'd ever see would be the cliffs skewing sideways—

But he could not stay here. For the *aschishin* was coming for him.

He knew it in the most secret place of his heart. He had no conscious memory of the words spoken by Louis Finney; yet they had penetrated to his core. Why would his captors be asking about the *aschishin*? Because his own brothers had hired the ghost wind to silence him. He could not blame them. Had their positions been reversed, Zattout would have done the same.

And he would deserve his fate, when the ghost wind came for him. He had commiserated with the enemy. He had not given his full cooperation; he had given only a fraction. Yet it had been enough. And now he would pay for his weakness.

He moaned: a complicated sound, of fear and shame and confusion.

It was August and he was visiting the vacation home of a young man who conducted business with his family. The business was construction, and the young man owned a house on a tropical bay. A very rich house. This was where Zattout had walked across the slippery, algae-smeared rocks. One moment it had been all fun: high on champagne, paddling kayaks in a small bay, climbing onto the spit of stone. The next moment, the young man who owned the house had vanished along with the kayaks.

Zattout could not swim back to the house alone. He never had learned to swim; this was his very first trip to a tropical clime. He had grown up on the Arabian Peninsula, and at seventeen had not yet traveled farther abroad than Syria, Pakistan, and Sudan. Yet now he was here, stranded on the spit of rock. He could not stay put—for the assassin was coming. But nor could he walk across those treacherous stones . . .

The crescent-shaped scar on his right ear itched.

His brothers surrounded him, catcalling. He was fourteen, and a virgin. But not for long. The French called it *tournantes,* or take your turn. As the youngest, Zattout had been allowed to go first. In a matter of moments he would lose his virginity—

Then the girl's hand came up, clawing at his face and catching his ear, tearing the skin and sending a bolt of pain into his skull.

He wondered if he should take his own life. Then the itch might leave him in peace. But how would he do it? He could step off the rocks, into the water, and drown himself. Except he was afraid. He did not want to die. But he would die either way. Better, perhaps, to take the initiative . . .

. . . but already it was too late.

The *aschishin* had come for him.

He moaned again, thickly.

THE PRESENCE IN HIS CELL was like a puff of air from a crypt, ethereal and mephitic. It had come in through the vent, through the cracks in the walls. Zattout couldn't help himself. He began to murmur, prayers mixed in with pleas. *Mercy,* he said. *Mercy—*

In the darkness he caught a glimpse of the figure. The man wore black: a black cowl, a black tunic. He would punish Zattout for his crimes against Allah. At this man's hands, he would experience suffering unlike any he had feared at the hands of the Americans.

Or was it all a dream? He was in the cell, with the man in the black cowl; but he also was standing on the slippery rock spit, trying to summon the courage to cross back to land.

After the girl clawed at his ear, he backhanded her. Then his eldest brother stepped forward to take his turn, although Zattout had not completed the act. A dog was watching from a dusty courtyard. The dog was smiling, or so it seemed. Its tongue lolled out. A single bead of blood trickled down the side of Zattout's head. The girl had wounded him. He would have a scar to show for it. . . .

At one point, in his mid-twenties, he had built himself a spectacular screening room where he had watched movie after movie. The movies had come from Hollywood. He had enjoyed them all, sipping Moët or Cristal as he watched, with his arm around a beautiful woman, as often as not. But that had been a long time ago. Since then he had grown more religious. For a few years, before his capture, he had lived by a strict moral and social code. Yet inside, the part that liked Hollywood and fine champagne always had remained.

Of course he deserved his fate. He had lived a life of material wealth, a life of sin. He had cooperated with the enemy. And now the ghost wind was here.

The mongrel dog laughed at him.

The bead of blood rolled down Zattout's jawbone, onto his throat.

Some cruel part of his mind tried to offer hope. Perhaps he could convince the assassin that he had not given his full cooperation to the Americans. Perhaps he could make it understood that he was sorry for what he had done. And perhaps the man would spare his life. He had something to offer, after all. He had seen the enemy camp from the inside. He had not told them much. Not the most important secrets. If only he could make the assassin understand this—

Was he awake, or asleep? It didn't matter. He could speak, in this state, without taking responsibility for what he said. He could open his mouth and let it all go, begging for his life. He had been set free. By the . . .

. . . current, passing through his body . . .

. . . by the trance state into which they had put him, these men who interrogated him . . .

. . . that had been only a dream.

He found spit, and moistened his parched tongue.

"I told them nothing," he said in Arabic.

"You've betrayed us."

The words also were spoken in Arabic—a rough, pidgin version of the language.

So it was real. The stealer-in was not one of them. He came from farther east; an outsider. But now he was here. Zattout shook his head. "I told them lies. All lies."

Only quiet, from the *aschishin*.

Zattout sucked in a great breath. He found more spit, enough to form the words he needed. If he talked quickly enough—if he moved quickly enough—he could avoid falling off the rocks; he could avoid meeting his fate.

He told the man everything, in a torrential, half-sensible jumble, stumbling over himself in an effort to convince the assassin that he deserved mercy.

ON THE OTHER SIDE of the one-way mirror, Louis Finney watched.

He couldn't see clearly in the gloom; nor could he understand the words Zattout was speaking. But Hawthorne, in the cell with the man, wearing the black uniform and the hood, would understand. And the tape slowly unspooling on the table before him would catch the confused jumble, for future analysis.

He had judged Zattout correctly: his fear of the words Finney had spoken, the prominence of his child-identity.

The man talked ever faster. Desperate to tell everything, all of a sudden. As the effects of the shocks faded—as he began to regain his wits—he would come to realize that he had been tricked. But by then, at this rate, he would have told them everything he knew.

Finney kept watching. His mouth was doing something strange, something it had not done in longer than he could remember. The sensation was so alien that it took him a few seconds to identify it.

The strange twitching motion made by his mouth was the beginning of a smile.

17

ALI ZATTOUT SPOKE until his voice turned hoarse.

At times, during the four-hour recitation, he seemed almost rational; at other times he uttered nonsense. For one six-minute stretch, he did nothing but plead for his life. But when they pored over the results later that morning, sitting in the living room before the limestone fireplace, they found a considerable amount of hard information within the jumble. Tantalizing clues were scattered throughout—a blueprint for future interrogation.

By the time the initial analysis was finished, Finney felt on the verge of collapse. His sinuses were clogged; his head throbbed. He went upstairs and lay down on his bed without bothering to undress. He slept for four solid hours, until two on the afternoon of May 1.

WHEN FINNEY WOKE, it was still raining.

He had slept heavily. For five minutes he sat dead still on the side of the bed, listening to the rain. His nose tickled. The contents of his clogged sinuses had shaken loose. The cold was receding, he thought. Not gone yet—but going. There was a light at the end of the tunnel.

He showered, then dressed. As he added his old clothes to a drawer full of laundry, he wondered if he would be wearing them again at the safe house. The interrogation would continue; but he had done the heavy lifting. Whoever took over now would have plenty of ammunition at hand.

He went downstairs, feeling strangely boneless. The woman who handled cooking and housekeeping duties—Miriam Lane—served him soup and a sandwich. As he ate, she puttered about the kitchen, wiping counters and filling the dishwasher, chattering about the weather. Rain like this, she said, the road back to town would flood for sure; she'd be lucky to make it home tonight without floating clean away.

Finney listened, spooning chicken and noodles into his mouth. He had finished the soup and was halfway through the sandwich when James Hawthorne emerged from the pantry. The elderly housekeeper quickly removed herself.

Hawthorne looked weary. His glass eye drifted farther to the right than usual; a single sprig of hair stood on end. But there was relief in the way he sat, a looseness in the throw of his legs. "What do you suggest for the next few hours?" he asked.

Finney touched his mouth with a napkin. "Let him sleep. When he wakes up, let him eat."

Hawthorne nodded.

"Then leave him alone—long enough to let what's happened sink in. I'd say another night should do the trick. We'll confront him in the morning."

"He really believes someone's coming for him," Hawthorne said, wonderingly.

"Part of him believes it—the child part. It's an illogical fear. An emotional one."

"No basis in reality?"

Finney contained a smile. "If he hadn't been locked in a cell for weeks . . . and that, on the heels of years in hiding, and on the run . . . not to mention the initial stages of depatterning . . . in other words, if his mental defenses had not been completely decimated—he never would have believed it."

Hawthorne examined his cuticles. "Tom Warren called again," he remarked. "While you were sleeping."

Finney picked up the sandwich. From the living room, a vacuum switched on.

"Asking me to double the frequency of security patrols," Hawthorne said.

Finney paused.

HIS INTERNAL CLOCK struck twelve.

Twelve was a time of power. At this twelve—twelve noon—he would begin the transitory processes that would return him to the land of men. At the next—twelve midnight—he would undertake the final stages of his mission.

In his mind, his eye opened; but in reality, his eyes stayed shut.

He backed slowly out of the ice cave, planting his

feet carefully. He navigated a long, dark tunnel. Energy was shuttled from meditation to awareness, one pulse at a time.

Penetration of the enemy camp was hindered by two factors, boundaries and sentries. Thanks to the woman's trustfulness, he already had passed every boundary. Both walls, with their guard towers and searchlights, were behind his current position. Between him and them were trees and driving rain, providing cover.

But sentries remained—passing once every three hours, armed with modified Tec 9 machine guns set to full automatic, with thirty rounds in each clip.

The sentries led Dobermans on chain leashes: one dog for every two men.

And then there were the mechanical sentries—the cameras and sensors.

For now, he didn't concern himself with these things.

He stimulated the proper mental channels, accelerating his blood and dispatching it to his extremities. Soon his entire body was tingling. He inhaled, and checked each organ in turn. He exhaled, and rested.

At last he had made the transition. He opened his eyes. He was folded double into the space beneath the backseat of the Honda; the gloom was close, the air still tinged with a medicinal smell. Rain undulated against the car, rhythmically.

His right hand was touching the panel. He pressed out. It fell from its grooves onto the floor mat with a soft thud. Gray light trickled in, making him blink.

He rotated his wrist, checking his watch. Forty minutes past one.

He began to worm his way from the compartment.

Remotely, he felt hunger. More immediately, thirst. He set them aside.

By ten minutes past two, he was out of the compartment.

Lying on the floor, he traveled up and then down his spine, seeking tension and banishing it. He stretched. He examined his blood and his breath, then returned to his center.

He drew the hood over his face, then inched up onto the backseat and achieved a position from which he could see over the windowsill. He oriented himself by finding landmarks: the scarecrow, the wide oak on the far side of the parking lot, the farmhouse itself.

The three-o'clock patrol was five minutes late. The guards had their heads bowed against the storm; they moved through the gray swirl without looking up. They were not alert, the assassin thought. Immediately he corrected himself. Underestimating the enemy was an amateur's mistake.

He waited. Presently the patrol emerged again from the rain, the Doberman high-stepping primly through puddles.

When they had gone, he waited two minutes more. Then he drew a breath, and reached for the door.

ZATTOUT WAS AWAKE, sitting on the edge of his bed.

He appeared slightly recovered from his travails; his eyes were focused, if dazed. On his face Finney read a blend of confusion, relief, and fear. It was not the illogical child-fear Finney had seen before, but the near-rational fear of a man who knew he had been tricked—who was realizing that the game was up.

He watched for three minutes. Then he climbed two staircases, and found James Hawthorne in his bedroom. At Finney's knock, Hawthorne glanced up from his SIG P226. He gestured for Finney to enter.

The room was even more spartan than Finney's own. Personal effects were limited to a brown valise in one corner and a book turned facedown on the desk. From the window came the sound of water gurgling through a rooftop gutter. Finney took the desk chair, then indicated the components of the gun spread across the bed. "Expecting someone?"

"Routine maintenance," Hawthorne answered—but Finney wondered.

Hawthorne raised the gun's slide, looked down its length, and blew. Finney forced himself not to stare at the man's glass eye. "I thought we might discuss my departure," he said.

Hawthorne reached for a brass brush, coated it with solvent, and began to clean the gun's bore without comment.

"I'll stay for as long as you think necessary," Finney went on. "But if I had some idea of—"

"You'll have to talk with Warren. If you can wait a day or two, I'm sure he'll find the time."

"One day, or two?"

He had the sense that Hawthorne was on the verge of saying something blunt. But the agent kept his attention on the gun, and said mildly: "What's the hurry?"

Finney shifted on the chair, and didn't answer.

"There's always a demand for talented watchmen," Hawthorne continued. "You might want to take some time to—"

"I'd like to go home."

"—consider what would be the best way to—"

"I'd like to go home."

"—find some kind of balance, instead of—"

"I'm through," Finney said. "I was through twenty years ago."

"It's a goddamned waste."

Finney shrugged.

"It doesn't have to be all or nothing." Now a brisk edge in Hawthorne's voice betrayed suppressed anger. "You've done well with Zattout. But it's only a beginning. There's always more to be done."

"That's what I'm afraid of," Finney said, and left Hawthorne alone with his gun.

THE LEFT REAR DOOR of the Honda cracked open.

The movement was not registered by the passive infrared cameras; for the car door manifested no warmth. When a figure slipped stealthily from the car onto the wet gravel, over the next few moments, the cameras remained off. The dark tunic around the figure diminished its body heat from 11 microns to 8. The cold whipping rain did the rest. Thanks to the drop in temperature, even a camera located directly beside the figure would have measured only 7 microns of heat—below the threshold needed for activation.

Nor did the array of microwave sensors trained on the parking lot send a signal to the primary guardhouse. The sensors were tuned to the Doppler shift between 20 Hz and 120 Hz, the frequencies related to the movement of humans. A more sensitive tuning would have resulted in incessant nuisance alarms, triggered by falling rain or roving wildlife. Yet the current setting suffered an Achilles' heel: With knowledge of the sensors' placement, one could make maximum use of obscuring objects—cars and trees—to block or absorb the microwaves. If at the same time one moved at a rate slow and steady enough to avoid the alarm activation pattern, the sensors could be bypassed.

The figure that came from the Honda moved at a very slow and steady rate.

The hands remained palm down, the elbows close to the body, the legs spread. Only the black-cloaked head raised more than five inches off the gravel, as the man scanned the area before him.

The cant of his body resembled that of a stalking cat; and as he moved, he slinked with a similar supernatural grace. First came an extension of the arms. Then the left leg drew forward. The weight was borne on the forearms and the leg, from knee to ankle. After movement had been accomplished—a matter of centimeters—the body relaxed, and lowered. The movement was repeated with the right leg bearing the weight, giving the left a chance to recover. Yet it was a continuous process, a painstakingly smooth and fluid advance.

The rain fell in sheets, slapping against the house and the cars, drenching the man in black as he pulled himself meticulously across the gravel parking lot.

By 3:30 P.M., he had reached the lot's far edge. Beyond it was a thick oak—his target for the time being. Once behind the oak, he would be concealed from both security sensors and human eyesight. The rain and the tunic guaranteed that his scent would not linger. He would be safe there until midnight. Then he would retrace the path he just had followed, and gain entrance to the house itself.

He moved behind the tree, muscles quivering. He sighed, but carefully—shallowly. He put himself into a cross-legged position, leaving the hood covering his head, keeping his eyes trained down so they would not flash. The oak provided some measure of shelter from the rain, but not enough. The black material of the tunic clung to him like a second skin; the bag also had become weighted with water.

Then he thought no more. He closed his eyes, retreating.

At 4:35, another guard patrol passed. From behind the tree, he noted this almost subconsciously. So the schedule had changed. Having noted it, he dismissed it without exploring the thought further. Exploring the thought might have caused fear; and if he surrendered to fear, the dog would smell it.

The Doberman was tired and wet; it wanted to go back to its kennel. The four-thirty patrol made its rounds without incident.

The assassin was aware of the six-o'clock patrol, as he had been aware of the previous ones. Shortly after it passed he was aware of the modified Honda rolling back down the gravel road, heading for the gates. Miriam Lane was on her way home.

The seven-thirty rounds were cursory. The men hurried through the lashing storm, flashlights penetrating less than three feet into the miasma surrounding them. The dog held its head higher than the marines, proudly. But all gained speed when the patrol was ending and they could head out of the rain.

He was aware of all of it.

He remained cross-legged under the tree, head bowed, waiting for midnight.

THOMAS WARREN II was on the highway.

He had reached a stage of exhaustion in which it was impossible to keep his mind focused on a single idea. The windshield wipers were squeaking in a steady, merciless way that made his nerves sing; the cup holder near his right hand was empty, and he was considering pulling over soon to get a refill. He was on his way to the safe house in a rented Toyota Corolla, the only car he'd been able to get on such short notice. He wished that McDonald's had real milk for their coffee, instead of those little plastic containers of fake cream, and he wished he'd been able to find a car besides the clunky old Toyota. Lately it seemed you couldn't even find unflavored little plastic containers of fake cream at McDonald's—they all had hoity-toity additives, like hazelnut or mocha blend, and they all tasted sour and artificial and chemical.

Part of his mind was thinking about McDonald's coffee; part was falling asleep, and part was doing math. He had been on the road for nearly three hours, which meant he had about two hours left. His current ETA was around 12:30 A.M. He had come 143 miles, which meant he had about 112 to go. Every few minutes he went through the routine again, shaving the figures, shaping them. As he calculated, he smoked, puffing Camel Lights down to the filters, grinding them out in the ashtray, and lighting fresh cigarettes five minutes later.

Despite the rain, he had the air-conditioning turned up high, hoping the cold blast would keep him awake.

The radio was tuned to WXRK, a rock station out of Manhattan, but he was losing the signal as he drove farther north. He left the radio on anyway, even as it dissolved to static. The sky was umber mixed with silver, sheets of rain illuminated by reflecting headlights.

A sign came up on his right: REST AREA 2 MILES. NEXT REST AREA 73 MILES. The exit loomed in his headlights; he turned the wheel, touching the brake. The rest area was a big one, laid out in a sprawling circle. A pavilion featuring restrooms and vending machines sat in the center, with concrete paths leading to parking spaces.

He ran to the bathroom through pounding rain. When he came back into the night, the downpour had slackened a bit.

Mentally he rejigged his ETA. Part of him was worried that the road to the safe house might wash out if the rain picked up again. Another part insisted that when he did reach the house, he would find the dark magician there, increased security or no . . .

. . . but he would get there; he would see what there was to see. And that, for now, was that.

He got back on the highway, pushing the speedometer up to seventy on the slick roads.

FINNEY HAD JUST SET the kettle on the burner when he heard a sound from outside.

He pulled the curtain from the kitchen window, peering into the night. After half a minute, a flash of lightning illuminated the parking lot, the stand of trees, the guardhouse, the rain. But nothing else.

He let the curtain fall closed. He looked at the doorway, where faint light spilled in from the living room.

James Hawthorne had retired to sit before the limestone fireplace, bringing a book—and, Finney had noticed, his gun in its waist holster.

He looked back at the kettle.

The kitchen smelled of timber. The rain seemed to have brought out the nature in the house: the walls and floor aspiring their wood scent, a spider scuttling in one corner. He found the phenomenon strangely comforting. It reminded him of home.

Tomorrow, or the next day, he would speak to Thomas Warren. Zattout had given them more in four hours than during the four weeks preceding—enough to keep Warren and his analysts busy for months. Finney's presence no longer was required. His duties had been discharged.

The wind rose to a dark howl. Rain crossed the roof in tiny battalions. The kettle whistled. He prepared a cup of tea, and carried it to his bedroom.

The cold had fooled him—journeying from his head to his chest. He climbed into bed, pulling the blanket up to his chin. He balanced the cup of tea and stared at its placid surface. His exhaustion was luxurious, voluptuous. The congestion in his chest felt almost gratifying—a valid reason to stay in bed, as the wind played outside and Hawthorne stood guard downstairs.

For five minutes he stared at the tea. Then he set it on the night table without tasting it. He picked up the paperback, and set it down again. All he wanted was sleep. Escape. Oblivion.

He snapped off the light, and stared at the darkness.

*   *   *

THE STORM danced with the forest, bowing and dipping the trees, lashing the grass into trembling acquiescence.

As he took the exit, Thomas Warren experienced a vivid premonition: The road would have washed out. He would not reach the safe house tonight.

At the bottom of the ramp he paused, wiping a hand across his mouth and listening to the squeaky pound of the windshield wipers. The wipers no longer accomplished anything except the pretense of clearing away the glass. So of course the road would have washed out.

Indeed, it was closed off; a police barricade had been dragged across the mouth. He pulled the Toyota to the side of the road, cracked open the window, lit another cigarette, and looked dourly at this latest obstacle.

Beyond it, the road was a rushing brook. But this was the bottom of the hill—the runoff. If he could get through the first puddle without the Toyota's engine flooding, he would have a chance.

After a few puffs, the mist coming through the cracked-open window turned the cigarette limp. He pitched the butt, threw open his door, and crossed muddy ground that tried to suck off his shoes. He took hold of the barricade and dragged it a few feet to one side. Then back behind the wheel.

He put the car in gear, and hesitated for a last moment.

It was all too easy to picture the Toyota achieving a few feet, then flooding. The engine would die; and here he would remain until morning, bobbing up and down like a cork. Unless, of course, he wanted to walk the rest of the way. In which case he would have a fever by the time he reached the house, if he even could find it without headlights.

But as his father would have said: nothing ventured, nothing gained.

He stepped on the gas.

Hitting the puddle caused two hissing waves to arc away from the Toyota. He pressed harder, flooring it. The engine welled, struggling. Then the car was drifting to the left—not drifting, but floating. He struggled to hold the wheel straight.

The engine whined. The tires hit solid ground. With a thudding lurch, the Corolla was mounting the hill. His premonition had been wrong after all.

He defogged the windshield with tight, quick circles of one hand. The radio was still playing quiet static. He snapped it off. He considered lighting another cigarette—but now he was almost there; he wouldn't have time to finish it. The stale stench rising from the ashtray made him feel nauseous anyway. Too much smoke, too much bad coffee, not enough real food or rest.

But once he had seen with his own eyes that all was well, he would be able to relax. Then he would eat, and sleep. In the morning he would face the problem of what to do with the rest of his life, now that the DCI had let him go. "A vacation," he'd called it. It was not that. But it may have been an opportunity.

Coming up on his right: the gravel road, leading to the log gate.

He took the turn, sending another arc of water up from the Toyota's tires.

* * *

THE NINE-O'CLOCK PATROL was wrapping up.

Rain-soaked leaves had clogged the paths; each step taken by man or dog sloshed heavily. Soon enough, the wet and bedraggled team headed back toward barrack and kennel.

Still the rain continued to fall.

His body was wet, and cold, and stiff. His mind was far away, observing the discomfort from a remove.

The ten-thirty patrol lasted only twelve minutes. From the gait of the marines, he guessed that some amount of alcohol had been consumed.

He waited.

At midnight, the patrol's intoxication was even more clear. One man told a joke to the second; the second laughed too hard. The second man continued chuckling beneath his breath as they returned to the guardhouse.

Then a shadow detached itself from the other shadows around the parking lot.

It moved low to the ground, trickling through the wet and the leaves and the night, pouring itself slowly but steadily in the direction of the farmhouse.

Inside, a light was on. But he would avoid the light; he would avoid the hidden interior cameras. Just as long as he could keep his concentration, until he reached the porch. Just as long as he didn't give in to uncertainty and haste . . .

The wasplike sound of an engine reached him, tinny at first, deepening as the car approached.

He saw headlights heliographing through the rain. Who was this, driving up in the middle of the night? No time to wonder now. The splintered wood of the lowest porch step was just in front of him. He drew himself up the stairs. Then he was out of range of the sensors and cameras. He exhaled with a shudder, sagging.

He slinked away from the door, into the deep shadows at the porch's end. Then he flicked a blade into his hand, dropping to a crouch.

THIS TIME Finney knew he had heard something.

He left the bed to look out the window. In the murk he could make out a car, drawing to a stop. The taillights winked; the headlights died. It would be Tom Warren, he thought. Returning to duty. Perhaps Quinlan would be with him. And so perhaps Finney could arrange his own departure, even sooner than expected.

From the closet he withdrew his white bathrobe. He was stepping out of the bedroom when a flash on the nightstand caught his eye: the doubloon.

He stopped, returned to the room, slipped the coin into the robe's pocket, then stepped out into the wood-smelling hall.

The roof overhead pattered softly. He took the stairs to the first floor, where all was dark except for the glow of the reading lamp from the living room. He went there, expecting to find Warren and Hawthorne and possibly Quinlan.

But there was only Hawthorne. The agent looked up from his book, knitting his brow.

"Where's Warren?" Finney asked.

Hawthorne gave him a blank look.

"A car just pulled up," Finney said. "Out front."

The knot in Hawthorne's brow complicated itself. He set down the book. Then stood and moved toward the front door, resting one hand on the grip of the holstered gun as Finney followed.

THOMAS WARREN II reached the parking lot before the farmhouse at 12:27 A.M.—within three minutes of his ETA.

The engine died with a murmur. He rolled the window up the last inch, sealing out the storm, and opened the door.

Puddles splashed underfoot; his hair, already slicked to his skin from the adventure with the police blockade, promptly became plastered to his forehead. He clambered onto the porch, pushing the wet hair back. His hand touched the knob. On the other side of the door, James Hawthorne was reaching forward as Louis Finney—one step behind—flicked on the porch light.

The bulb blazed to life, silvering the rain that drifted beneath the overhang.

The shadows on the porch shriveled. Thomas Warren II experienced a dawning awareness of a presence to his left. He turned his head, even as his hand fell from the knob.

Someone was on the porch with him.

A small man, wearing black.

The dark magician.

18

JOSH WAYNE ABBOTT, PFC, Marine Corps, turned away from the row of monitors to reach for the bottle of Jim Beam.

He dashed two slugs of whiskey into his coffee. Outside, thunder echoed across the valley. The rain showed no sign of letting up. It was going to be a long night, he thought. He added another finger before capping the bottle, then raised the Irish coffee and took a bracing sip.

Over the rim of the mug, his eyes returned to the monitors. The microwave sensors were dormant. The motion-activated cameras remained inactive. He looked to the bank on his right: the house's internal surveillance system. James Hawthorne, who had been sitting in the living room reading a book, had disappeared.

He found the agent on another monitor—approaching the front door, with the doctor trailing behind. Going to meet Thomas Warren II, Abbott thought. Ninety seconds before, Warren had passed through the gate outside this very guardhouse.

He drank more whiskey-laced coffee. On the other side of the room, Toby Grant was bent over a crossword puzzle.

" 'Carpet type,' " Grant said. "Four letters."

Something about it struck Abbott as funny. He guffawed. Then he turned in his chair, unsteadily. "Have a drink," he told Grant, and held forth the bottle.

THE LIGHTS CAME ON; the man at the door saw him.

The assassin's arm whipsawed. The blade left his hand, arcing through the silver raindrops, and buried itself in Thomas Warren II's right eye.

Warren bared his teeth. He let out a gasp—almost a bleat. Then he was folding forward, collapsing onto the porch. He landed facedown; the haft of the knife hit unyielding plankboard, driving the blade squarely into his brain.

The front door was opening.

The assassin straightened, putting his back to the wall. He slipped another blade into his hand with a flick of his wrist. Only two remained in the sleeve.

They would suffice. Whoever stepped out would join the man lying facedown on the porch. As long as the guards did not realize he was here within the next ninety seconds—that was all he needed. Into the house, into the pantry, down to the cell. Do what he had come here to do. Then back up again, and out.

The door was open. But nobody stepped out. Because the corpse was lying there in plain view, of course.

They would not come to him.

So he would go to them.

He took his back from the wall.

JAMES HAWTHORNE saw the body lying facedown on the porch.

It was Thomas Warren; he recognized the wet hair on the back of the head. Dark blood spread below the man in an expanding puddle. The puddle was expanding even as he looked at it. Because Warren had just died, Hawthorne thought. And so the cause of his death would be—

—coming into view, raising his arm.

Hawthorne withdrew his gun from its holster. But he was too slow, and he knew it. Already a weapon was leaving the intruder's hand. It arced forward and kissed James Hawthorne in the throat, stealing his breath. Suddenly he was halfway to death . . . watching himself go, waving a melancholy goodbye.

Behind him was the doctor. Past him, in the bowels of the house, the prisoner. The intruder was here to kill Zattout, Hawthorne understood. But he would never make it. There were too many guards, too many cameras. These thoughts crossed his mind in a millisecond, as blood began to trickle from the knife stuck quivering in his throat.

He saw a pink glow in the night sky, behind the clouds. The northern lights?

One hand continued to raise the gun, tugging it up through cold molasses. The other reached for the doorjamb, to steady him. But now his legs were turning hollow. He was sinking down, deflating.

The man who had killed him was pushing past.

Trying to enter the house, Hawthorne felt the flesh pressing against his, surprisingly cold through wet cloth. *You killed me,* he thought dreamily.

His throat burned. That vicious kiss. It would leave a mark.

Then he was on his knees. He was falling backward as his killer rudely shoved his body out of the way. His head touched the floor; his eyes rolled up. He saw the doctor, upside-down, backing away into the gloom. And the killer, stepping forward.

He had raised the gun over his head. But he didn't have the strength to aim. His finger tightened on the trigger. A wild shot—

—*Huzzah,* he thought.

Then the clouds parted. Beyond them was space, and a million brilliant stars.

"'SHAG,'" Grant said. "Gotta be—right?"

Josh Wayne Abbott didn't answer. He lowered the bottle, looking back over his shoulder.

Something was happening inside the house.

The cameras did not cover the porch. But the doctor was backing away from the front door, reacting to something there. Then a shadow melted through the doorway. It bucked violently, spinning halfway around.

He blinked.

The shadow disappeared. Slipping exactly out of range of the cameras. As if the shadow had known just where the cameras were located. The doctor was moving—turning to barrel through the foyer, ramming into a piece of furniture, then continuing into the kitchen.

"Or is it 'pile'?" Grant asked.

Abbott flicked the cover off the alarm by his right hand. He slapped down; a klaxon shattered the night.

FINNEY SAW A FLASH of light touch Hawthorne's throat.

Beyond Hawthorne, on the porch, was an object. He caught a sense of clumsy lifelessness, of dead weight. And a sense of the opposite—something fleet and fast, moving like quicksilver.

Then the second thing, the fast one, was coming at him. It was trying to push past Hawthorne, who stood blocking the doorway, the light still touching his throat like a jeweled necklace.

By then Finney was stepping away.

He backpedaled through the foyer, bumping solidly against the Pennsylvania cupboard without feeling it, passing the antique sideboard and the shadowed oil paintings. The pantry. The pantry was secure; the dead bolt would buy him time.

When death had come for Lila, it had not been fleet, not like this. It had come leisurely, treading softly. In her eyes had been fear and pain and anger. Those eyes had pushed him away, even as he'd tried to get closer. But Lila's death belonged only to Lila. Despite their years together, he could not share her burden now. Did that explain the anger in her eyes? Had she expected more of him, at her moment of extremis? He had done his best to be with her. But his best had not been good enough. He had been sitting by the bed. But she had died alone.

Everybody died alone.

Something exploded: the gun in Hawthorne's hand.

The intruder spun around, buying Finney the seconds he needed to reach the kitchen—*shot,* he understood remotely.

Then he was in the kitchen. A second later, in the pantry. He scrabbled for the hidden door. Canned food rained from the shelves, clattering.

He opened the door and went through it, and by the grace of God found the dead bolt on his first try.

THE ASSASSIN felt no pain.

Instead he felt a terrific pressure. A locomotive had slammed into his shoulder. The force of the collision spun him around. He lost his footing and tumbled down

(no)

but retained enough of his wits to immediately withdraw from the range of the cameras mounted in the foyer.

Back onto his feet. The pressure in his shoulder welled. The man he'd killed had shot him. Already the man was dead; it had been only reflex. But bad luck

(no, not luck)

bad luck

(fate)

bad luck, beyond any doubt.

The other man was turning, slamming into a piece of furniture and then slipping away.

The secondary exit route, he thought. He still could escape.

But he was so close. Too close to give up now.

The gunshot would attract attention. But how long

would it take guards to reach the house? Thirty seconds? Forty-five? It would be enough.

He sucked in a breath, and followed the man who had run into the kitchen.

THE ALARM broke open the world.

Finney's eyes moved to the row of video screens that pictured the countryside surrounding the house. All were flooded with light: night turned to day, rain frozen in glittering still life.

Then to the reverse landscapes. The study, the living room, the dining room, the foyer. All dark, except for the marginally lit living room. But the thing was not there. The thing was just outside the pantry—

—trying the knob.

Finney spun to face the low table lined with syringes and vials and microphones. He tore through the equipment, ripped a fresh syringe from its paper packaging, then found 75 milligrams of morphine and filled the hypo with hands that shook violently.

The doorknob stopped rattling.

The dead bolt would keep the intruder out. The alarm was whining; help was on the way.

His tongue crossed dusty lips. He held the syringe in his right hand as his left clawed at the bathrobe's pocket, finding the doubloon and bringing it out. For Hawthorne, it was too late. But for him and Zattout . . .

He heard a small, metallic sound, even over the keening alarm.

Then another.

The dead bolt.

He backed into a corner. His heart was trying to climb up through his throat, to burst out of his chest. He thought of the knife growing from Hawthorne's neck like an aberrant tumor. Then, crazily, he thought of his father: showing him the library book, poring over images that played tricks with the eye.

The door was opening.

AT THE SOUND of the klaxon, the assassin's arms burst into gooseflesh.

Then light was flooding the kitchen, burning into the pantry through the open door.

So close. Too close to turn away.

Calm, he thought desperately.

He got the lock casing off. He pushed the retaining pin into the housing. He turned the plug nut counterclockwise until it came free. All within two seconds. He released the pressure on the retaining pin—too fast; it shot from the lock, along with its spring, over his wounded shoulder. No matter. He concentrated. He finished picking the lock.

He returned the slim tool to his sleeve, then palmed one of the two remaining blades. He needed to reach the target and then proceed to the secondary escape route—which emphasized speed—immediately.

He moved to one side and pushed open the door. The remaining man was in there, stinking of fear, trembling, holding something. A weapon.

The assassin angled the blade, using it as a mirror. The narrow reflection revealed an older man, bearded, wearing a white robe. As the spot of light crossed his face, he flinched. The weapon in his hands was not a gun—only a syringe.

The assassin moved into the space, disarming the man with a swipe, driving the knife into his ribs.

The blade penetrated skin, penetrated flesh, and then stuck. The assassin tried to withdraw it, giving the haft two sharp tugs, without success. He let go, slipping down the stairs even as the man slumped to the floor behind him.

It had not been a clean strike. Because he was rattled, by the alarm and the floodlights and the bullet in his shoulder. The man had managed to block the thrust with one hand. But he could not afford the delay of back-tracking to finish the job.

The alarm howled, up and down. They would be closing on the house now. All those lights . . .

. . . he never would make it out of here alive.

Sonya Jacobs was laughing.

He reached the bottom of the stairs with three loping strides.

The door to the cell was reinforced. He was forced to pause, to fumble again with the lock pick. *Calm,* he thought, but it was only a word, meaningless.

Through the window was Zattout—roused to his feet by the alarm, facing the glass under the merciless glare of the bare bulb.

The lock clicked.

The door opened.

Zattout froze.

Then cried out; but already the assassin was inside the cell.

He shot the last blade into his palm. Zattout was reacting to his presence, but with a delay, almost in slow motion. What had they done to their captive? Something diabolical. It was not a man he faced, but half a man. Death would be a mercy.

He cupped Zattout's chin with his left hand, lifting it. The half-man made a show of resistance—but he was working on some other clock, running slow.

The assassin drew the blade across the trachea. Zattout made a gurgling sound, like a man blowing bubbles on the surface of a bath.

The assassin flung the body backward, onto the cot.

From somewhere beyond death, Sonya Jacobs continued to laugh.

He moved out of the cell, and up the stairs.

A PEREGRINE FALCON wheeled through a clean blue sky.

Louis Finney watched. Then he raised his arms. He was going to fly himself, now. He would soar up beside the falcon and then past it, and perhaps Lila would be there, arms open, eyes smiling.

But he wasn't lifting off the ground. He was holding out his arms for no reason. He could not fly; he was not going to join the falcon, nor Lila, in that clean blue sky. Not yet.

His right hand moved across his ribs, finding the wound. The wound was below his left hand. His left hand was pinned to his chest; his chest felt like a very wet mouth. The vision of the falcon was fading, and he was back here, in the pantry, surrounded by broken glass and the stench of his own fear and the sharp odor of

fruit, with his left hand pinned to his chest like a butter-
fly pinned to a mounting board.

Another image came to him, with startling clarity:
Hawthorne's gun.

He could see the components spread across the man's
bed, Hawthorne methodically polishing them one at a
time. He could smell the gun oil. Then he saw the gun as
it was now: lying inside the front door beside Hawthorne's body, in a puddle of blood.

He tried to stand; but the hungry mouth in his side
was sucking air. He fell to one knee. He entered the
pantry at a crawl, then pulled himself into the kitchen,
using his right hand to drag his body forward.

Blinding lights shone through the windows. The
alarm wheeled like the falcon, looping around and
around.

The gun seemed very far away.

He vomited. Then rolled over on the cold stone floor,
landing on the hand pinned to his chest, hissing air. There
was something else there, he realized—something between the knife and his heart. A small, hard metal object.

The doubloon.

He had forgotten he was holding it.

He thought of the gun again; but then a figure was
emerging from the pantry. The dark killer.

He closed his eyes, and played dead.

BEFORE LEAVING THE PANTRY, the assassin angled the blade into a mirror.

The blade was slicked with blood. He wiped it clean
on his sleeve, then looked again. The pantry was empty.
So the strike had been even sloppier than he had realized.

The man not only had lived but had been able to drag himself away.

The one that mattered, however, was dead—Zattout.

The alarm climbed, hovered, fell, and climbed again.

He moved through the pantry, into the kitchen. Light glared through the windows, picking out fine details. A dead man on the floor. He had pulled himself from the pantry, only to expire here. From outside: shouting men and barking dogs.

He headed for the living room, staying low and keeping as much as possible out of view of the cameras. The French doors opened into the backyard—his secondary escape route.

Through the doors he saw soldiers. A half dozen, fanning out around the house. They would establish positions around the perimeter. Then what? Tear gas? He would not be here to see it.

Before making his dash, he took a hasty inventory. The blade in his hand. The lock pick in his sleeve. Inside the bag strapped to his chest, a grappling hook on a length of chain.

He breathed. Speed, but not haste.

It was almost over.

He would make it.

But the gooseflesh on his arms remained. Beneath the determination was fear. Beneath the determination he was only a frightened little mouse, after all.

Now the soldiers outside the house had stopped moving. They had taken positions, raising their weapons beneath the floodlit rain. Past them was forest; dogs; guard towers; high walls . . .

A dull pop. Shattering glass. A tear gas grenade tumbled into the room, spitting.

He went.

HE WAS THROUGH the perimeter before they could react.

A round whizzed past his ear. Another pounded into the earth, sending up a spray of mud. He charged forward, making for the trees while keeping his head down. A dog was giving chase. But it was not on him—not yet.

In the next heartbeat he was in the woods, in darkness. But a floodlight was following, trying to track him. And the dog was nearly upon him.

He turned, raising his forearm, bringing up the blade behind it.

The dog died with a whimper—but not before sinking its teeth through his sleeve, just above the slim metal bar that might have offered protection.

Another round thudded into a tree, splattering bark. By then the floodlight had found him. But by then he was moving again, trying to withdraw the blade from the dog's body and failing, leaving it behind.

His arm was bleeding. He shut off the pain.

He slipped in the wet mud, and regained his feet.

Across a shallow brook. Two more dogs; he could sense their haunches tensing as they prepared to leap. Without slowing, he reached for the bag and tore it open. He found the grappling hook on the length of chain and pulled it free, turning at the same time. One dog was in the air, descending. He caught it on the side of the jaw with the hook. The barbed tongs sank into flesh, and the hook was torn from his grasp. Then the other dog was coming. He gave it the same arm he had given the first dog—already bleeding, already pulped. He jammed a gloved thumb in the dog's left eye as its jaws clamped around his forearm.

They rolled across the ground. The dog howled, blind but alive. He ripped his arm free. He found the grappling hook, withdrew it from the meat. Then spent a fraction of a second pulling the bag off his chest. He moved again, leaving the bag behind, holding the hook on the length of chain with both hands.

To his right, beyond the fringe of forest: a group of men assuming firing stances. The floodlight found him again; a volley of bullets followed. He threw himself down, onto the wounded arm, crying out.

Up again, and onward.

The first wall rose before him. A guard tower fifty yards to the right, with an M63 A1 inside, capable of firing seven hundred rounds per minute. But only if they could find him. And he was too quick for that, wounded or not.

He used an underhand toss to put the hook atop the wall. Then he scrambled up, feet barely touching the stone, shoulder pulsing. For an instant he was poised atop the wall in the darkness between floodlights, with barbed wire curling around his feet. He was aware of the M63 swinging around to bear; but by then he was down, on the other side.

He hadn't been able to bring the hook along with him.

The second wall therefore would present a problem.

As he charged through the trees, his forearm and shoulder bleeding, his lungs burning, a story came to him.

A man crossing a field encountered a tiger. He ran to a precipice and there he saw a vine. He took hold of the vine, swinging out over the abyss. Trembling, he looked down, and saw another tiger waiting at the bottom of the ravine. Worse, the vine could not sustain his weight. It was beginning to unravel.

Then he saw a strawberry growing on the cliff face before him. Holding the vine with one hand, he reached out and plucked the berry free. How sweet it tasted!

That was the story.

Again he slipped, spilling down in the mud.

Again he gained his feet, and advanced.

They could not get over the first wall, even with the hook showing them the way. They were too slow, too weak. And now the second wall was looming . . .

He flung himself at it, grabbing for the top, and— somewhat to his surprise—found purchase on the first try.

Pulled himself up, his arm radiating agony where the dogs had chewed it, his shoulder screaming distress.

But he was going to make it, after all.

Past this wall, into the countryside. Then he would run as never before. He would avoid the roads. Their machines would not help them. He would use brooks to erase his scent, throwing off the dogs. There would be roadblocks. But he would get farther away than they thought possible, before acquiring a vehicle; he would avoid the roadblocks. And then what? The nearest border was Canada. Before crossing he would need to come into some money, and some identification. The bag had been left behind. But this was the land of plenty. Opportunities would present themselves.

Then over the border, into Canada. Or would that be a mistake? It would be just what they expected: going for the nearest border. Perhaps it would be wiser to head south. The Mexican frontier was infamous for its lax patrols. Once he was out of this country, he would disappear. Not Europe—too close, too connected. South America, he thought. For a time. Then east again—to find Rana. Or had she gone west? *In the West,* she had said, *children play all day. They do nothing* but *play.*

He wasn't concentrating.

Men on the far side of the wall—taking aim.

He dove forward, tucking and rolling, as gunfire sounded. Something scraped his temple. The world seesawed and he landed on his left side, missing his feet. The wind was knocked out of him. So it was over.

Except the men were not firing again.

Instead they were coming forward—meaning to take him alive.

Fools.

He breathed. Regained his wind somewhat. One man was closing on him. The second held back, weapon leveled. Still the alarm shrieked; still the wind whipped bitterly, turning the rain into projectiles. Dogs were howling. But they could not get over the wall. They needed to go around, through the gate.

He pulled himself onto his knees, then into a standing position. He staggered, playing up his dizziness. He showed them his back, putting his hands on his head.

As the man reached forward, he stepped to the right with his left foot. He pivoted sharply, seizing the enemy's hand—the cuffs there jangled—and lifting it. He spun the soldier around, pulling the arm down in a hammerlock, and used the enemy's own shackles to secure his hands in the small of his back.

He kept the human shield between himself and the other sentry. Now men were racing in their direction from the front gate. Tigers below; tigers above. And no strawberry to be seen. Only the rain, whipping across his hood, pummeling him.

He bent, retrieved the pistol his prisoner had dropped, and shot the man standing before him.

Then placed the barrel against his prisoner's temple, and fired again.

Voices, echoing through the rain. Floodlights wheeling, finding him. The dogs, hoarse and close. He dropped the body in his arms and took a single step. Machine gun fire tore up the earth in a furrow; he reversed direction.

A rifle cracked. An adamant hand pushed at his leg; he lost his grip on the gun. The light stayed on him as his knee buckled.

Then he was surrounded. A dozen men fanned out around him, with dogs straining at leashes.

The circle closed with an odd, grand languor, as if he were a land mine that might still explode.

He decided to goad the men into shooting him. Better death than capture.

At the last instant, as hands were reaching for him, he pushed up. He went for the fallen gun, presenting his body as a target.

The balance between him and this world was changing, even as gunfire spun him around. Something shifted dramatically; he was set adrift.

Then dragged back to earth by grasping hands.

Shackles closed around his wrists with a double click. They pawed at him with his lifeblood slicking their fingers, seeking to hold him down.

He slipped out from between them, lithesome and sleek as mist.

Then turned to look back at himself. His body was surrounded by soldiers and dogs, on ground soaked red. There seemed to be snow on the ground, beneath the blood. Then he realized: the red was not blood but pulsing light. And the snow was not in the place he was leaving. It was in the place he was going—the cold, icy place high in the mountains.

They did not yet know he had escaped, one last time. They bent over him, applying pressure to wounds, calling for medics.

But he had been too quick for them.

He smiled. The mission had been a success. Zattout was dead. And once again, he had escaped.

A vehicle was approaching. His body was being lifted onto a stretcher. Still they had not given up. The doors closed and the vehicle pulled away, siren blaring.

But the assassin was not inside the ambulance. He watched it go and then turned to look again into the cool, icy place.

He moved forward, into the chill.

19

THE SEASON FOR BIRDING was drawing to a close.

Over the past week Finney had twice glimpsed a Great Gray Owl during daylight hours: yellow eyes circled by finely detailed feathers, black chin bordered by patches of bright white. After breakfast he made his way into the fields behind the house, binoculars in one hand and cane in the other.

He spent several fruitless hours pounding through the underbrush, searching for the owl. In early afternoon, a squall blew in and the prospect of bird watching no longer stood. He limped back to the farmhouse—limping more than he needed to, the doctor would have said—and went to his study. Then he sat in his chair, trying to come up with some other reason not to visit the cemetery today, now that walking in the fields was no longer an option.

When he'd been a boy, his family had owned a golden retriever named Wendy.

The name had been chosen by his mother, a devoted fan of Peter Pan. Some of Finney's earliest memories centered around the dog—a sunny-dispositioned animal, with a tail that wagged so hard it could whip a red welt onto an incautious little boy's skin. As Finney had become a teenager, Wendy had entered old age. Thunder had started to scare her. Each time a thunderstorm came she would retreat into a closet, to huddle alone in the dark. Finney had spent hours trying to coax her out. One day his father took him aside, put his huge hands on Finney's shoulders—by then, as a teenager, Finney hadn't appreciated the physical contact—and explained that maybe it would be better to leave Wendy alone. If the closet made her feel safe, why not let her hide in there? Think of it, he said, as her den.

Finney didn't know why he thought of that story now.

Or perhaps he did.

Since the day of Noble's funeral, he had ventured from this farmhouse only infrequently, and never farther than town. After stocking up on supplies he'd come straight back to his study or his fields, tail between his legs.

A frightened, cowering dog—making the sad transition from midlife to old age.

THE FUNERAL had taken place on a gray, punishing morning; the heavy April rainfall had not yet paid off in May flowers.

To the south of the cemetery was a miniature town, looking like a child's replica accompanying a train set. After considering it for a moment, Finney turned to look at the cantor. The cantor was blowing his nose. He offered a slight, apologetic smile. *Spring colds,* that smile said ruefully. Then he pocketed his handkerchief and faced the two men standing by the graveside. "As we go through life," he declared, "we give many kindnesses."

The man beside Finney listened with hands folded and head bowed. He was perhaps fifty-five, wearing a dark tailored suit and a glittering Rolex watch. To the best of Finney's knowledge, he never had seen the man before. Might this be Noble's brother? An uncle, or a cousin? Or some long-lost friend, come out of the woodwork to pay his last respects?

"For many of these kindnesses, we claim to expect no recompense. When a neighbor asks if he may borrow a cup of sugar, we provide one for no reason except charity. Yet deep inside, we know that someday our situations may be reversed. Someday we may be the ones who require charity—who require a cup of sugar. Does this make our act less kind? No. But the purest form of kindness—the most selfless form of kindness—is one for which we know we have no reason to expect future reciprocation."

Finney felt brutalized by the words. Partly, the feeling came from the number of funerals he'd been attending in such a short space of time. The week before they had laid Thomas Warren to rest. The following week would be James Hawthorne, although Finney had yet to decide if he would attend the services. The cumulative demands of the dead on the living were making him resentful, querulous.

"The kindness we now give to Arthur Noble is the purest form of kindness. In applying earth to his coffin, we are giving of ourselves. Yet since he has left this world, we know the kindness will not be returned to us. When you lift the soil, you will use the back of the shovel. This is because the shovel is not a tool when used for this purpose. Through its inversion, the shovel becomes a sacred object."

The man Finney couldn't place wiped at his eye. A friend, a classmate, a teacher, a fellow spy? Or none of these things—something Finney couldn't even imagine. Amazing, he thought, how little he truly knew of Arthur Noble, who had affected his life so dramatically.

"We do not wish to make the task easy for ourselves. Instead, we wish to make it difficult. Hence, the back of the shovel. In undertaking this difficult task, with no possibility of Arthur Noble returning the favor in the future, we are giving him the ultimate kindness—the ultimate blessing."

As the cantor turned to the shovel, Finney looked past the waiting hole in the earth, at the next row of graves. He saw three headstones: Margaret, Emily, and Elizabeth Hastings. Beside them, Judd Hastings and Marianne—"She served faithfully."

Beyond that row of headstones was another. Then another, and another. The graves did not quite stretch as far as the eye could see—the cemetery was a small, private affair—but they were far too numerous to easily count. And the names were far too plentiful to be remembered.

Then the cantor was moving to the pile of earth beside the open grave. He turned over the shovel and scooped some soil onto the back. He tossed the soil onto Noble's coffin, where it sprinkled softly. He looked up, found the eye of the man with the Rolex, and nodded.

The man accepted the shovel, dipped it upside down into the mound of earth, and tossed dirt into the grave. He looked at Finney and offered the handle.

Finney paused.

He swallowed.

He shook his head.

Disapproval emanated from the cantor and the man. But neither said anything aloud. The cantor wiped at his nose with the handkerchief; the man with the Rolex jammed the shovel back into the pile of dirt.

"'The Lord is my shepherd; I shall not want. He maketh me to lie down in green pastures: He leadeth me beside the still waters. He restoreth my soul: He leadeth me in the paths of righteousness. . . .'"

WHEN IT WAS OVER, Finney and the man with the ostentatious Rolex walked to their cars.

The man introduced himself as Roger Ford, a classmate of Noble's. He asked if Finney would care to have a drink in Noble's honor. Finney agreed, grateful for the chance to offer some kind of acknowledgment of his mentor's passing—an acknowledgment that stopped short of what the cantor had called "ultimate blessing."

Two miles from the cemetery was a strip mall, with eateries and hardware stores and multiplexes and gas stations. They found an open bar in an upmarket barbeque restaurant serving lunch. Both ordered Noble's brand: Cutty Sark. The toast was wordless.

In school, Roger Ford announced then, everybody had known Noble would go far; but nobody had realized how famous he would become. Ford wouldn't be surprised if something was named after him, a library or a foundation. He raised his glass, tinkling around the ice cubes. The world was worse off, today, than it had been when Noble still had graced them with his presence. . . .

Finney managed a few mumbled blandishments of his own. Noble had been intelligent, and ambitious. Then they sat in a paradoxical silence, both uncomfortable and hazily comforting.

Roger Ford looked at the bottles lined up behind the bar. "Well," he said. "That one was for Arthur. Now how about one for us?"

He chose a better brand of scotch and ordered two more drinks, water back. Again they toasted wordlessly.

Ford stirred through a bowl of cocktail peanuts. He popped one in his mouth and chewed. A change occurred in his body language: a tightening of the neck and shoulders, a rising tension. Finney noticed it, and prepared himself for whatever the tension presaged.

"Listen," Ford said.

Finney listened.

"I did meet Arthur at school. But there's more to it than just that. We've worked together, on and off, in the years since."

A spy after all, Finney thought. The most surprising thing was how unsurprised he felt.

"I've done a lot of scrambling, over the past few weeks, trying to wrap up some of the loose ends left by his passing. He truly was an amazing man. He stayed so busy, right up until the end. . . ."

Ford left the hook dangling. " 'Busy,' " Finney echoed at last.

"KINGFISHER wasn't the only operation he was involved with. He served as watchman on two other high-priority interrogations. But the hardest roles to fill will be the administrative ones." He raised another peanut, looked at it, and set it on the bar. "One in particular," he said. "Called LONGSHOT."

Finney said nothing. He drank deep.

"I'm aware of your . . . mixed feelings . . . about government work. And after the experience you've just had, one could hardly blame you for any reservations. But as I said, some of the roles that need to be filled are purely administrative. No hands-on testing whatsoever. Yet they're sensitive. We can't bring in just anybody to take over. We'd prefer a candidate who's already been proven . . . like yourself, Doctor."

"Arthur told me he hadn't accepted a contract in years," Finney said thickly.

"Because otherwise you wouldn't have spoken to him. A little white lie."

Finney drank again.

"Take my card," Ford said. "And if you find yourself thinking you may want to give a little something back . . ."

A card came out of his wallet. He set it on the bar beside the peanut, and pushed it in Finney's direction. Finney looked at it. He took it, only to avoid conflict. A little white lie of his own.

". . . he'll be missed," Ford said. He wiped at his eye again, although as far as Finney could tell, he wasn't crying.

HE HAD MISPLACED the card.

Now he wondered how serious the misplacement had been. Was it in the bottom of a desk drawer, beneath birding magazines and knickknacks? Or had he left it in a pile of trash, and thrown it away?

And why was he wondering at all?

Because staying locked in his study, huddled in his den like an aging dog, did not suit him. Because he could sense Lila's frustration, even from beyond the grave, at what he had become.

He was alive—wasn't he?

Why don't you act like it? Lila demanded.

Outside, the autumn rain gained force.

He wanted to feel the rain.

He walked into the downpour without bringing an umbrella. After thirty seconds, he was soaked through. He kept walking anyway, alongside trees whipped color- less by the weather. The cold had hounded him through much of the summer, turning into bronchitis before he'd finally beaten it. Now it would return as pneumonia, he thought.

Let it.

He sneezed, wiped at his nose, sneezed again, and kept walking.

Noble had been lying, when he'd claimed not to have accepted a government contract in fifteen years. Was it any surprise that Finney found himself unable to pay his respects to a man who never had given him anything but lies?

But that wasn't quite fair.

At the beginning, there had been no need for lies. The top secret international jaunts, the generous funding, the cloak-and-dagger élan; all had conspired to over- come any misgivings Finney felt about taking part in MKULTRA. He had been nestled under the wing of a brilliant young doctor, and some of Noble's glow had been passed to him through osmosis. He had seen the envy in other students' eyes when they looked at him. Even Lila, he thought, had been attracted to his new success. No, there had been no misgivings worth mentioning—not at the start.

But reality soon had set in. The clinical results they obtained were nebulous, difficult to quantify; yet Noble put a polished gloss on the reports he sent off, which always happened to coincide with a need for more funding. The fast-and-loose interpretation of the results had been disillusioning. But they had been only the tip of the iceberg. Far more troubling had been the nature of the enemy—*the other side,* as they'd called it then. In practice, the other side had seemed to be composed of mental patients, prisoners, and soldiers drawn from their own ranks. It was a dirty game; and when one played it, one's hands did not remain clean for long.

Yet the game needed to be played. Noble had liked to illustrate this point with a quote from George Orwell: *Men sleep peacefully in their beds at night because rough men stand ready to do violence on their behalf.*

Finney had seen the wisdom in the quotation. The desire to protect men who slept peacefully in their beds—in addition to the flattery and the money—had been a prime motivation for continuing with MKULTRA. But when faced with the consequences of his choices . . . when faced with the Susan Franklins . . . he had transferred the responsibility for his decisions onto Noble.

Cowardly, he thought.

Weak, cowardly, proud, and vain.

He remembered a dream: Lila standing with him

before Noble's grave, urging him to place a stone on the headstone. *Forgiveness isn't a gift you give someone else,* she said.

Then he thought, *It's a gift you give yourself.*

He came to a halt.

For almost two minutes, he stood motionless in the driving rain.

At last, he sneezed again. Then he turned and moved back to the farmhouse at a faster clip, past thickets and stables. Only a glutton for punishment—or a fool—stayed out in the rain.

THE BUSINESS CARD was in the bottom of his drawer, between a roll of masking tape and his checkbook.

He put it beside the telephone and looked at it for five minutes. Then he dabbed at his nose with a Kleenex, shook his head at some unarticulated thought, and picked up the receiver. He dialed.

"Roger Ford's office," a young woman said.

Ford played it as if he were pleasantly surprised. "Doctor!" he crowed. "Do you know, I'd just about given up on you? What's it been, six months? But do you know, we still haven't been able to fill that position I mentioned. There's been—"

"You said no hands-on testing," Finney interrupted.

"Absolutely. Whatever makes you comfortable. We'd be honored to have you aboard in whatever—"

"Just because you don't do the tests yourself," Finney said tautly, "doesn't remove the burden of responsibility."

A few moments of silence.

"No," Ford agreed cautiously. "But if the undertaking is worthwhile, taking the responsibility can be a pleasure. And the nature of these tests is benign, Doctor. There's no suffering. In fact, I'm told the subjects find it quite pleasurable."

Finney squeezed the pockmarked doubloon in his hand, and didn't answer.

"I'll tell you what. Why don't you take a look and judge for yourself? I could send a car, if you like. Just tell me when."

"I won't compromise myself."

"I wouldn't ask you to."

"I won't," Finney said again.

"Come take a look," Ford said, "and you can make up your own mind."

HE MADE AN APPOINTMENT for the following Monday.

Then he poured himself a stiff drink. After that, another.

The doorbell woke him up.

He'd managed to fall asleep in the chair behind his desk: not a bad trick, with the window open and a sharp snap of cold air blowing in. Finney tottered to his feet as the doorbell rang again. He found his walking stick leaning against the Queensleg desk, then humped out into the foyer. Considering the amount of time he'd spent prowling the fields behind the farmhouse, over the summer and fall, his continuing lack of strength came as something of a surprise. According to the doctor, the physical damage had healed. Yet Finney was not the man he once had been. He doubted that he ever would be that man again.

On his way to the door he paused to pick up the wicker basket he'd left on the hall table. Inside the basket were two dozen bite-size Milky Way bars. Most of the candy would be wasted; only eight children managed to reach the remote farmhouse for trick-or-treating, and that was on a good year. By now, the Tyler children probably were in high school. Without them, only four could be counted on: the three Travaglioni sisters and little William Finneran, who dressed every year in the same castaway blue sheet with jagged holes cut out for eyes.

It was the Travaglioni sisters. Finney opened the door and then recoiled in mock horror at the princess, the mermaid, and the witch standing on his doorstep. Mrs. Travaglioni was behind them, costumeless, holding the keys to her station wagon in one hand and displaying a forced smile.

"Trick or treat!" the girls called, more-or-less in unison.

Finney put a hand on his chest. After recovering, he offered the basket. "Take two," he urged. "Take three. They'll only go to waste."

The girls obeyed, with the mermaid taking four. Then they turned to flee; their mother stopped them, spreading her arms into a barricade. "Mr. Finney," she said. "How are you feeling?"

"Well, thank you. And yourself?"

"Fine, fine," she said. "Fine. Girls, don't you have something to say to Mr. Finney?"

Thank yous were muttered without eye contact. Finney could only imagine how he seemed to these children: the mysterious old man with the cane, living in the rambling decrepit farmhouse, making appearances in town to stock up on supplies only about once a month.

Creepy, no doubt, was how he struck them. Particularly on Halloween night.

And they didn't know the half of it.

Mrs. Travaglioni's forced smile broadened into a grimace. "You look well," she told him.

"Thank you," he said.

"I'm afraid we've got to run along. Lots of trick-or-treating to squeeze in tonight!" As if the circuit of candy-givers was not limited to five houses, and then only if she was willing to shuttle her children up and down this road fifteen miles in either direction. "Happy Halloween, Mr. Finney! Say goodbye, girls."

When they had gone, he returned to the study. He'd been halfway through a drink when he'd fallen asleep. He pushed the glass away, looking out the window at the lowering twilight.

Tomorrow, perhaps, he would pay a visit to the cemetery.

He would place a stone on Noble's grave. It would not symbolize forgiveness, he thought. He would not go through the motions of something he did not feel.

Yet it would symbolize something. A letting go . . . or was it the opposite? A bringing to . . . a taking of responsibility.

For Noble wasn't the one who needed forgiving, after all.

On Monday he would meet with Ford, and see what LONGSHOT was about. Then would come a decision. The decision would be made by Finney, and by nobody else. This time, he would go into it with eyes wide open—

The doorbell rang again.

He heaved himself out of the chair, found the stick, and clopped into the foyer. He carried the wicker basket to the door and opened it.

Nobody was there.

For ninety seconds he scanned the front yard, the black skeleton trees and the final smear of daylight on the horizon. A trick, he thought. Perhaps the Tyler children had grown too old for the treat part of Halloween and had graduated to mischief.

That was all it was. Local teenagers, playing a trick.

By his feet was a jack-o'-lantern he had carved the previous afternoon. After going to the trouble of carving it, he hadn't bothered to place a candle inside. He had lost his will to proceed. Suddenly this rankled him profoundly. Why, he had left too many things unfinished, hadn't he? He had started down too many roads, then given up before reaching their conclusions.

Like Susan Franklin, he thought. What was stopping him from checking on her again, from seeing if the damage they had inflicted truly had healed?

Perhaps Roger Ford would be able to provide an address. Perhaps Finney could find the strength within himself to put many unfinished things to rest. Susan Franklin; a visit to Noble; even his service to his country . . .

He wasn't taking anything for granted. There was no guarantee that these things would reach a satisfying end.

But if he didn't try, he would never know.

He went to the kitchen and found a candle and a knife. He brought them back to the porch, crouched with a grunt, then dug a crater in the bottom of the jack-o'-lantern. He placed the candle inside and lit it. Light capered to life inside the pumpkin's eyes.

For a few seconds he stayed where he was, watching it.

Then he turned. Night was falling in earnest. He went inside and washed the pumpkin seeds from the blade of the knife. Instead of rinsing them down the drain, he gathered them together—a handful of small, slippery pods—and set them in a glass.

Throughout the evening, the doorbell stayed quiet. But at a few minutes past midnight he sat up in bed with his heart catching in his chest. There had been a sound outside the house. More mischief. More tricks.

He went to the window and looked out. He saw nothing except the jack-o'-lantern—darkened now, but still standing vigilant guard on the porch.

Beyond it, in the yard, shifting dark shadows. Only the trees, and the wind.

He went back to bed, listening to the wind.

He did not sleep again that night.

ACKNOWLEDGMENTS

Thanks to Robert and Jane Altman, Dr. Mark Branon, Kevin Connell, Richard Curtis, Brendan Duffy, Jed Freeman, Richard Galganski, Ned Higgins, Pierre Honegger, Evan Metcalf, Neil Nyren, and Sarah Silbert.

By 1943, the U.S. had rounded up every
Nazi spy on American soil—except one...

A GATHERING
OF SPIES

JOHN ALTMAN

0-515-13110-5

"An irresistible page-turner."
—Publishers Weekly

"Sizzling...A classic spy story."
—*Stephen Coonts*

"Faster-than-lightning."
—Boston Herald

*"This book has the feel of one of those great
old movies about World War II. If you were to
compare it to another novel, it would be
Ken Follett's* Eye of the Needle.*"*
—Arizona Republic

Available wherever books are sold or at
www.penguin.com

B058

"A MAJOR NEW TALENT." —Jack Higgins

A GAME OF SPIES

"Ranks with the best espionage thrillers."
—The Orlando Sentinel

"Impressive."
—Chicago Tribune

JOHN ALTMAN

Author of *A Gathering of Spies*

0-515-13463-5